With Honour in Battle

With Honour in Battle

J.T. McDaniel

Riverdale Electronic Books
Riverdale, Georgia USA

With Honour in Battle

Cover Painting by Chris Lee

For information, please contact:

Permissions Department
Riverdale Electronic Books
PO Box 962085
Riverdale, Georgia 30296

ISBN: 0-9712207-3-5

Revised Edition

Originally published by: Writer's Club Press, an imprint of iUniverse.com, Inc.

Printed in the United States of America

For Richard, Elizabeth, and William

Contents

Chapter One
New Command

A cold shadow fell across the open bridge as *U-702* left the late afternoon Baltic sunlight and glided slowly beneath the monolithic concrete roof of the pen. It was only then, with his command at last safe from the constant danger of enemy bombs, hidden away beneath seven metres of heavily reinforced concrete, that *Korvettenkapitän* Hans Kruger finally began to relax.

Even with the newly-fitted *Schnorchel*, which had allowed him to run submerged on his powerful diesels while keeping the batteries fully charged at all times, the journey back to Kiel from the killing ground in the North Atlantic had been the worst he could remember in almost five years of war.

It would be Christmas in a few days, Kruger thought. Perhaps the last he would ever see, and certainly the final Christmas for the Third Reich. For it was 15th December, 1944, and the Allies had achieved almost total control of the convoy routes even as their victorious armies fought their way through Europe, inexorably closer to the borders of the Fatherland.

It was not always so. There had been a time, earlier in the war, when U-boat duty had been an almost ideal existence, once you got used to the cramped quarters, the almost complete lack of privacy, and the stink of sweat and bilge water. The 'Happy Time,' when the U-boats had the whole of the central Atlantic as their killing ground. The 'Gap,' the enemy

1

had called it. That broad stretch of waters beyond the range of any land-based aircraft except the huge, lumbering blimps the Americans sometimes used for anti-submarine patrols.

But the blimps had never been much of a problem. Their considerable size and slow speed meant that a U-boat's look-outs would normally sight them first, giving plenty of warning to dive and creep away.

When Kruger had first been posted to a U-boat in 1940, they had spent many days in the 'Gap' lazing on deck in the sunlight, only submerging when a warship was sighted, or to close in for an attack. But now there were miniature aircraft carriers sailing in most convoys, so that surfacing in daylight had become foolishness bordering on the suicidal. Nor was it much safer after dark. Most enemy patrol bombers were now equipped with highly efficient radar, giving them the terrifying ability to sweep down out of the inky-black night with guns blazing, dropping depth charges all about their unwary prey.

There were radar detectors, but they didn't always work, or else gave the warning too late. And, too often in such cases, the sudden emergency dive would be the last, with the boat driving out of control to join her sisters littering the ocean floor.

There were times when you *had* to surface, but now you did it as infrequently as possible, and with the utmost wariness. Even as the sinkings of enemy ships grew fewer and fewer, the number of U-boats that failed to answer a signal, or to return, had assumed gross proportions.

Of all the men who had begun the war in U-boats, only a handful still survived on sea duty. The old 'Aces,' men like Prien, who had manoeuvred his tiny *U-47* right into the Royal Navy's main fleet anchorage at Scapa Flow and sunk the bat-tleship *Royal Oak* at her buoy, who had been hunted down and killed in a depth charge attack. Or Schepke and

Kretschmer, exceptional commanders with long strings of kills, both lost in a single night. Kretschmer had been captured, but Schepke was killed, crushed between the outer part of the bridge and the periscope when his boat was rammed by a British escort as the crew was trying to abandon.

Kruger was also an 'Ace,' a winner of the Knight's Cross with Oak Leaves and Swords, the Iron Cross First Class, and the German Cross, along with a wartime record of nearly half a million tons of enemy shipping destroyed. He had served continuously at sea since 1940, and considered the fact that he was still alive as proof that it *was* sometimes possible to beat the odds and survive.

He was equally certain that, if he were sent out again, he would not come back alive. No one could rely on luck forever.

"All secured, sir," the Boatswain called, from the forecasing.

Kruger nodded wearily, looking at the man as if he had never seen him before. The Boatswain had been a leading hand in *U-105*, Kruger's first boat, when Kruger himself had still been a brand-new *Oberfänrich*, just out of the Naval Academy and still learning the ropes. In those days the man had been fat, constantly joking; now he was lean, almost haggard, with a nervous, hunted look.

And am I that different? Kruger wondered. I am 27-years-old and I look about 50. Already there is too much grey hair, and the lines are growing deeper each day. The visible evidence of the dangers we face daily, the heavy responsibility for the safety of 44 officers and men, the need to seek out the enemy despite his deadly advances in detection and killing ability, and which a captain must pretend to ignore for the sake of the men.

The iron-nerved captain, holding the crew together in the face of danger while he slowly consumes himself from the inside.

He looked down as the IWO*, Richter, emerged through the tiny hatch at his feet.

"Shall I fall out the crew, sir?" Richter asked.

Kruger peered down onto the forecasing at the twin lines of sailors, still standing stiffly in their neat formation. As usual, they had all dressed in their best uniforms for entering harbour, but the neat clothes did little to cover the bone-weariness and strain. Nor would they cover the stink for anyone not inured to it by constant exposure.

Kruger nodded. "Yes. Give them a rest, Number One. God knows they've earned it."

"Aye, aye, sir." Richter walked to the front of the bridge, leaning across the screen. "Fall out!" he bellowed.

Below, the crew broke ranks and vanished down the main hatch. They would be thinking of leave, and the comforts of the shore billets with hot showers, and fresh uniforms that had not been three months in a stinking hull.

Richter turned back to his captain, hesitating. "It *was* a good patrol, sir? Wasn't it?"

Kruger rested his arms on the target-bearing-transmitter, his head nodding wearily. "We *survived*, Number One. That in itself makes it a good patrol. And we *did* sink that tanker. Only 6,000 tons, but at least we have *something* to show for ourselves." He paused, his eyes moving across the bridge, down onto the casing. The men were gone now, but the sea slime, and the ragged scar, livid with rust, where a British depth charge had torn a wide gash in the casing, yet somehow miraculously spared the pressure hull just beneath, still remained as reminders of their incredible luck.

---

*IWO. *Erster Wachoffizier*: First Watch Officer. the Executive Officer.

"A year or two back," Kruger continued, "I would never have been satisfied with that. A 6,000-ton tanker the only thing to show for almost 8,000 miles of steaming and 14 torpedoes expended. But now—well, survival *is* the whole thing, isn't it?"

Richter looked doubtful. "We may manage to save it all yet, sir. To win in spite of the odds. We've all heard reports on the radio, the secret weapons that will drive the damned Allies back into the sea. *Herr* Goebbels says it is only a matter of time now."

Kruger sighed. Richter was a good officer, but after two years in U-boats still somehow strangely naïve. "You don't speak English, do you, Number One?"

"No, sir. Spanish, but no English beyond the simplest phrases."

"So the only broadcasts you can understand are our own, correct?"

Richter nodded. "That's right, sir."

"*Herr* Goebbels is right on one thing," Kruger said. "It *is* only a matter of time. But time favours the wrong side just now." He smiled suddenly. "Still, the promised miracle *may* be just around the corner, eh? Even the enemy commentators admit that General Galland's new squadron of jet fighters is raising holy hell among their bomber formations. And if the bombers can be held back, perhaps the new U-boats will make it into service."

Richter touched the salt-encrusted screen. "*U-702* is good enough for me, sir," he said. "Though you'd not hear me object if she were a bit faster under water."

"The new ones are, Number One. Many more cells in the batteries, and more powerful E-motors. Also, the hulls have been designed for efficiency *beneath* the surface, not on it. They've even got rid of the deck gun to reduce drag."

Richter shrugged. "No one is likely to miss the gun," he said. "I can't even remember the last time I saw a U-boat's deck gun fired, except as part of a drill."

"I can," Kruger said. "It was in July, 1941, and we were shelling a British freighter because our captain didn't want to waste another torpedo. She was a straggler from some convoy, evidently damaged earlier by another boat. I think we'd fired a half-dozen shells when a damned destroyer came charging in at 30 knots, blasting away with her main armament." He grimaced. "It was a damned close thing, Number One. But what was *most* annoying was that the destroyer was *American*! And this was six bloody months before they were even in the war!"

"Before, sir?"

"Before. Some bloody lunatic had sunk one of their destroyers by mistake, and Roosevelt decided that the best way to protect their so-called neutrality was to sink any U-boats that came within range. Not *any* submarine, mind you. They didn't attack British boats. Just ours."

"Well, sir," Richter shrugged, "old times, eh?" He looked along the length of scarred hull. The dockyard workers would be along soon, swarming over and through her, putting right the damage to make her ready for one more patrol.

"Will there be leave for the crew, sir?" he asked.

"I expect so, Number One. Local leave for the entire crew, once the boat is safely handed over to the dockyard people. After that, we'll see what headquarters will allow in the way of home leave."

"I'd like to get back to Frankfurt," Richter admitted. "See if there's anything still left of my family."

Kruger turned away, cursing inwardly. Why did it still bother him? He should be hardened to it by now, but every little reminder still brought back the pain. So far as he knew, only his Uncle Fritz remained alive. His brother, Otto, had been missing since the fall of Stalingrad. The rest had been killed in a British raid.

"*Kapitän* Kruger?"

Kruger looked down onto the walkway along the starboard side, oddly surprised to see someone standing there. A full captain, in dress uniform and greatcoat. With the infernal racket inside the pen, where a crew was hard at work on another boat, the sound of a single man walking could easily pass unnoticed, but it was still startling to have him suddenly appear.

"I am Kruger, sir."

The captain, a pudgy man of about 40, nodded. "I have new orders for you, *Herr Korvettenkapitän*," he said. "Permission to come aboard?"

"Granted, sir. Welcome aboard."

The captain came up the brow and stopped on the fore-casing for a moment, looking around. What does he see? Kruger wondered. From his insignia, he was a U-boat sailor, but how long had he been out of it? Years, probably, since promotion took him off the bridge and safely ashore.

After what seemed an eternity, the captain came around the base of the tower and climbed the ladder to join them on the bridge.

"I am *Kapitän* Siegfried von Saltzmann," he said, producing an envelope from inside his greatcoat. He looked from Kruger to Richter. "You are *Oberleutnant* Richter?"

"Yes, sir."

"These are for you. You'll find three sets of orders in there. The first is your promotion, for which I congratulate you, *Herr Kapitänleutnant*."

Richter looked embarrassed. "Thank you, sir. I really don't know what to say."

"Then say nothing, lad. If you don't open your mouth, you'll find it much harder to get your foot into it, eh?"

Kruger was grinning. "Congratulations, Konrad. You deserve it."

Von Saltzmann went on. "The second set of orders appoint you as commanding officer of *U-702*, to take effect upon receipt. You won't actually *have* her for the first month of so, of course. The dockyard people will be too busy performing major surgery. That's where the third set come in. While your boat is being refitted, you'll be on your commanding officer's course."

"You should enjoy it in Gotenhafen," Kruger commented. "I know I did."

"He'll not be going there," von Saltzmann said. "The course will be right here in Kiel. Things are getting too hot in the east lately." He grinned. "Now, if I were you, *Herr Kaleun*, I'd say the proper words to *Korvettenkapitän* Kruger, and then I can take him with me, eh?"

Richter turned to face his leader of the last two years. Very slowly he came to attention, and a moment later Kruger did the same. His hand rose in the salute, the old Naval salute, which Kruger stubbornly continued to use despite orders mandating the ostentatious out-thrust arm of the Party salute. "Sir," Richter said, formally, "I relieve you."

Kruger returned the salute and they both relaxed. It was over. Now *U-702* had a new master, and Kruger was merely a guest, soon to depart forever.

They shook hands. "Take good care of her, Konrad. She's a good boat, and she'll treat you well if you give her the chance."

"We will be one of the best, sir."

"Just be one of the survivors, Konrad. When this war ends, Germany will need her leaders. You could be one of them, but you'll have to survive first." He smiled. "Now I'm off to God knows what, so you take care of yourself—and the men.

He turned to face von Saltzmann. "What *am* I off to, by the way, sir?"

"New construction. That's all I can tell you just now, I'm afraid." He moved toward the ladder at the rear of the bridge. "The Admiral will fill you in directly."

•   •   •

There were constant security checks as they moved through the great naval base, with Naval Police seemingly at every turning with a new demand for identity cards or passes. And once they had reached what was left of the headquarters building and started down several long flights of concrete stairs into the bomb-proof world below, the checks became even more thorough. It was as if the High Command was expecting an enemy agent or saboteur to attempt to slip in at any moment.

Or a madman? It had not been all that long since the outrage at Rastenburg, when a traitor had somehow managed to carry a powerful bomb into a meeting and nearly succeeded in killing the *Führer* himself. If such a thing could happen in so closely-guarded a spot as Hitler's East Prussian headquarters, how much more likely would it be elsewhere?

Finally, they came to the last door, and once again their papers were scrutinised by a pair of unsmiling Naval Policemen. Then the door was opened, and the two men walked through into a small, Spartanly furnished reception room. The only furnishings were four old straight-backed chairs against the bare concrete wall, and a cluttered desk, where a leading writer of the Navy Women's Corps was hammering away at an ancient typewriter.

She looked up as they entered, smiling as she recognised von Saltzmann. The 'errand boy,' as he was called behind his back. A full captain, yet most of the time he seemed to be running about engaged in some minor task which could as easily have been entrusted to a raw recruit. Because of her job, the girl knew better, but kept it to herself, knowing the image was a carefully cultivated one. The innocuous, know-nothing captain, not worth an enemy agent's time.

In fact, von Saltzmann was a brilliant staff officer, responsible for more of the Admiral's strokes of genius than the Old Man himself. He just made sure it never showed on the outside.

"Good afternoon, gentlemen," she said.

Von Saltzmann smiled. The girl was stunning, and always made him feel younger than his years. "Good afternoon, Hannah," he replied. "This is *Korvettenkapitän* Kruger. I believe the Admiral is expecting us?"

The girl nodded, looking at her book. "Of course, sir. We didn't know just when *Korvettenkapitän* Kruger's boat would get in," she said, sounding somehow as if she meant not 'when' but 'if.' "However, the Admiral has kept this afternoon clear, so I'm sure he will be able to see you soon." She smiled. "Why don't you both sit down and I'll tell him you're here."

As they took their seats, Kruger could feel her watching him as she dialed. He was wearing his best uniform, but beneath it his body was still filthy and stinking. Von Saltzmann had given him no time at all—not even to check into the officers' billets for a quick shower and shave. With his hair and beard uncut in three months, and his face no cleaner than could be managed with a brief salt-water wash while waiting for their escort to guide them into Kiel, he looked like the old prospector in a Western movie.

What is she thinking? he wondered. That this is really some hobo masquerading as a U-boat commander? Or wondering why *Kapitän* von Saltzmann would bring this tramp into her clean office? He shook his head. *God, I hate to think what I must smell like by now! A clean uniform stuffed full of stinking refuse in the shape of a man!*

The girl replaced the telephone handset on its cradle. "You may go in now, gentlemen."

Von Saltzmann hopped to his feet, while Kruger rose more slowly, his body still conditioned to expect his head to make violent contact with the deckhead at almost any moment. Kruger stood 193 centimetres, and U-boats were always hazardous places for tall men.

The girl sat quietly for a moment after they had gone in, looking at the door. *If he was with von Saltzmann they must have something interesting planned for this commander. It could be nothing easy,* she was sure of that. Dönitz had made it a habit to meet with every returning commander when they were still in France, but he had other things to worry about now, and *her* admiral was not the same type. If he wanted to see a commander it was either to light a fire under his tail, or to give him some out-of-the-ordinary assignment.

She wondered if this one would be up to it. *He didn't look it. What he needs more than a tough new job is a long rest. He looks ancient, and he is probably little older than myself.*

Then, with a quick shake of her head, she returned to her typewriter, wondering how long it was going to take to finish this letter when the damned "E" kept sticking. It was better to worry about that, and forget some submarine commander, no matter how attractive he seemed beneath the dirt of a long patrol.

These days, they didn't live long enough for anything to come of it.

•   •   •

The man behind the desk was slim and grey-haired, with a considerable area of pink scalp working its way forward at the top of his head. His uniform, with the one broad and three narrow rings of a General-Admiral at each sleeve, was perfectly tailored and immaculate, looking as if it had just come from the tailor.

In comparison, Kruger felt even dirtier.

The Admiral motioned for them to sit down, but he remained standing behind his broad desk. This office, unlike the reception room, was paneled in carved oak, and made to look as much as possible like one of the larger offices in the old headquarters building above. There was even a false window, with a view of Kiel harbour beyond so cunningly painted that you could almost swear you could see the ships moving at their buoys.

A disheartening view now, Kruger thought, for it depicted most of the aborted Plan Z fleet, showing the harbour filled with dozens of giant battleships, cruisers, and aircraft carriers, most of them in reality either never built, or already destroyed.

After a few moments, the Admiral also took his seat. "Did you have a good patrol, *Herr Korvettenkapitän*?" he asked.

Kruger sighed. What was a good patrol now? One you lived through? "We sank a single British tanker, sir," he replied. "Six thousand tons. And we made it back in one piece."

The Admiral nodded. "So survival has become the mark of a good patrol now, eh? *Ach!* But the good days are over for us now, it seems."

"But not for *Korvettenkapitän* Kruger, sir," von Saltzmann offered.

The Admiral shrugged. "We will discuss all that later, Siegfried," he said. He looked at Kruger, studying him, remembering the days when he had also returned from patrols, looking every bit as filthy and nearly as haggard, though he had never been charged with the ultimate responsibility in the boat. And that had been in the last war, when U-boat service had been a pleasure cruise compared to now. In those days the enemy had not yet learned the way to hunt U-boats, so that most of the danger was from mines, or from gunfire while the boat was surfaced. But now there were aeroplanes, Asdic, and depth charges that worked properly.

I'm damned glad I don't have to go out any more, he thought. Though at times it might seem easier than sending these good men to die in my place!

"We were almost sunk coming through the Skagerrak," Kruger added. "The Tommies have a killer group patrolling there now."

"I know," the Admiral said. "Four frigates and a small carrier. They have accounted for several of our outward bound boats in recent weeks."

"The *Schnorchel* helps," Kruger continued, "but it's not enough. Particularly if there is any sort of sea running. If there is, the damned valve keeps closing on you and the diesels suck all the air out of the boat. There is no adequate description of just how horrible it feels to be suddenly trying to breath in a vacuum."

"Were you badly damaged?"

"One was close. There is a fair amount of damage to the casing, but we held it together. Considering how close the damage is to the port saddle tank we were lucky to make it back at all."

The Admiral shuddered, as if suddenly very cold. "I was second watch officer in a boat that had her ballast tanks destroyed, back in the Mediterranean, in 1918. Most of us made it out and finished the war in a British prison camp, but the Chief and six others went down with the boat." He smiled. "At least the captain survived. Things might be very different if he had not. And even *more* different if some had paid more attention to his ideas early on."

"Sir?"

"He's been promoted since then, of course," the Admiral explained. "I expect you've heard of him—a very sharp fellow, name of Dönitz."

"The *Grossadmiral?*"

"The same. Well, a lot can happen in 26 years, eh, Siegfried?"

The pudgy captain nodded. "A great deal, sir."

"Now, Kruger—I suppose you're curious about your new command?"

"*Kapitän* von Saltzmann told me it was new construction. Beyond that he said nothing, so, yes, sir, I am curious."

"The captain will be working very closely with you on this project," the Admiral said. "Actually, he probably knows more about it than I do. But I wanted to give you the basics myself."

Kruger nodded, wrinkling his nose. It smelled as if something had died in the Admiral's office. It took him a moment to realise that he was noticing his own stench for the first time after being removed from the rancid atmosphere of his old command. How can these two stand it? he wondered.

"I'm giving you *U-2317*, Kruger," the Admiral said. "She is brand new, just finishing her trials, and will probably be the first of her type to become operational."

"Probably, sir?"

"Her trials are not quite complete," von Saltzmann explained. "You will see to it that they are, and once you've determined her ready for operations you will take her to sea."

"If her trials have begun, I presume there was a previous captain?"

"Yes. *Kapitänleutnant* Scheutte. He was killed in a raid last week. With your record, you were an obvious choice as his replacement."

"Frankly," the Admiral said, "you are just about the only operational commander left who has won the swords. The others have either been promoted out of their commands, captured, or killed."

"What sort of boat is she, sir?" Kruger asked. "One of the new *Typ* XXIs I've been hearing about?"

The Admiral shook his head. "No, Kruger. She is a *Typ* XXVI. To be perfectly frank, compared to her, a *Typ* XXI is about as advanced as one of the old *Typ* II 'dugouts' that *Kapitän* von Saltzmann commanded back in 1937."

"She is the closest thing yet to being a *true* submarine," von Saltzmann said. "Your main propulsion will be diesel and *Schnorchel*. You will also have an advanced E-motor and an enlarged battery capacity. But the main advances are in hull design and high-speed engines. She's designed to spend most of her time submerged, and the hull is most efficient under water. For high-speed propulsion she is fitted with the new Walter hydrogen-peroxide turbine, which will give you an extremely high underwater speed, either to escape your enemy, or to pursue him."

"How fast, sir?"

"On her trials," the Admiral said, "*U-2317* recorded a top speed of 25.7 knots at full power running at a depth of 100 metres. Moreover, you should be able to maintain that speed for about 160 nautical miles."

"And then?"

"And then you run out of fuel," von Saltzmann said. "The turbine is not for ordinary use. The majority of the time you'll use your *Schnorchel* and run submerged on your diesel." He smiled. "Even on batteries you should be able to manage a top speed of about 11 knots, and maintain it for about four hours. At five knots you'll be so quiet you may wonder if the motor is even turning, and unless an enemy escort actually gets you locked in his Asdic beam you should be able to steam right under him without his ever realising you were there."

Kruger sat back in his chair, wondering if it could all be true. It sounded *too* good. There must be some shortcomings as well. "How is she armed?" he asked.

"Ten tubes, but no reloads," von Saltzmann said. "You'll have four tubes in the usual position in the bow, and the other six are located amidships, three on each side, firing astern, all accessible from the single bow torpedo space."

"But no reloads?"

"You'll be able to pull the torpedoes for maintenance," von Saltzmann said, "but there simply isn't enough room for spares."

"She is little bigger than your last command," the Admiral said. "She grosses 850 tons. There will be more room, though. The crew is smaller, for now seven officers and 28 men. Two of your officers are *Oberfänriche*, both of them qualified for promotion to *Leutnant* when you see fit. You'll also carry a doctor. At least for a while. He will function as medical officer if need be, but his primary duty will be to observe the crew. The boat is a radical design, and you'll spend very little time on the surface. No one really knows just how men will react under those conditions, and we need to find out."

"Is this to be a war patrol?" Kruger asked. "Or an experiment?"

"A little of both," the Admiral admitted. "With a boat as new as yours that's inevitable. But your main job will be to seek out the enemy and destroy him. Psychological experiments come a long way second."

"There is *one* thing that may seem a little odd to you, Kruger," von Saltzmann said.

"It *all* sounds a bit odd to me, sir. But what do you mean, particularly?"

"Your L.I.* is a *Fregattenkapitän*. The Walter turbine is really still experimental, and we thought it best to assign an engineer with some experience on them. *Fregattenkapitän* Eisenberg worked on the prototypes with Professor Walter, so we hope he can keep everything working for you. In any event, rank aside, he's engineering branch, not a line officer, and *you* are the captain, so he'll do as you say, just as he would if your ranks were reversed."

"What you are going to be doing is probably an example of too little and too late," the Admiral said. "Enemy bombers have taken their toll. By now, there should have been 100 *Typ* XXVI boats ready for operations. As it is, there is only one. The *Typ* XXIs are nearly ready to begin working up, but again only a few of them. Had production proceeded as scheduled, we could send 200 advanced boats into the Atlantic now, completely reverse the situation there, and drive the damned Allies from the sea. As it is, all we can do is delay things long enough to either get the rest of the boats ready, or make the enemy accept some sort of terms."

The Admiral rose and began to pace behind his desk. "That's the problem, Kruger. The war would have been over months ago if the Allies weren't insisting on this 'Unconditional Surrender' doctrine of theirs. Who's going to surrender if the enemy is going to be able to write all the terms including, probably, stringing up the losers? Without that bloody doctrine we should have been able to draw up terms that would at least permit Germany to exist more or less as always. So now delay is our only hope. That's your job, Kruger, to provide that delay. At *any* cost."

●　　　●　　　●

---

*L.I., *Leitender Ingenieur*, or Leading Engineer. The senior engineering officer in a U-boat.

"I don't see that any single U-boat is going to make that much difference in the outcome of this war," Kruger said, stepping carefully over a grotesquely twisted length of railroad track. "If the boat is all that you say, then certainly we can raise bloody hell with enemy shipping, but just how much can that really delay anything?"

Von Saltzmann shrugged. "That will depend upon just what you sink, I should imagine." He led the way around a corner, away from the pen where Kruger's old command would by now have been emptied of her crew as the dockyard people set to work putting right the damage inflicted during her last patrol.

"Seeing you come in today brought back memories," the pudgy captain said.

"You were there?"

"In the shadows. Once we got word from the trawler that you'd managed to make it back in one piece I came down." He frowned. "It's not like it was, I can tell you that! I was promoted out of a sea command in early 1940, but I can remember what it was like. My little 'dugout' had such a limited range we could only operate in the North Sea, but when we came back in from patrol there would be a brass band blaring away on the pier, and all the nurses from the base hospital, and any other personnel who could get free, would come down to watch."

He shook his head. "And now? Now all you get are a few line handlers and an over-worked staff officer."

Kruger looked around. "Aren't we going the wrong way, sir? The pens are back that way."

"Your new boat is in a different pen, well concealed from the air, and nearly as well from the regular dockyard workers and any sailors without good reason for being there. She's still on the secret list, you understand."

Kruger nodded, and they continued on their way. Security would be vital with a new type of boat. If the enemy once discovered its location they would drop every bomb they had on the pen, just to keep it from coming into service.

"What do you know of my crew?" Kruger asked suddenly. "Competent, I presume?"

"The best we could find. Hand-picked, in the best sense of the word. Your Number One, for instance, *Kapitänleutnant* Rolf Wiegand, is a regular, born in Berlin. Twenty-two years old. He's had a command of his own, but agreed to accept the IWO's job in this boat after we told him he would probably get the next one commissioned for himself."

"Will he?"

"I imagine so, if there *is* a next one. Between the Allied bombers, and the slow-moving idiots in the yards, I sometimes think the war will end first!"

Kruger grimaced. He had often felt that way himself, wondering when the promised new generation of U-boats would arrive to replace the superannuated relics they were forced to fight with. And now *he* would have the first of them.

He would also, consequently, have the first chance to die in one, if the boat failed to prove herself in battle.

"You said he had a command?" Kruger asked. "What happened?"

"He had an old *Typ* VIIc, without a *Schnorchel*. They were on the surface at night, charging batteries, when an enemy patrol bomber got them off Ferrol. Wiegand and most of the crew made it to shore and we smuggled them back across the border into France and got them home. They were bloody lucky, actually. The boat was ready for the breakers. No *Schnorchel*, an old Metox that couldn't detect micro-wave radar frequencies—I'm damned if I know how he made it as far as he did!"

Kruger nodded. They had all served in boats of that sort at one time or another. Not everyone had survived. But it told him something about Wiegand. He had to have been competent to make it as far as Ferrol, no matter where his home port had been at the time. Biscay was one of the most heavily patrolled areas. You just didn't survive without being damned good.

A siren began shrieking and von Saltzmann grabbed his arm. "This way!" he shouted, hurrying down a narrow alley between two bombed-out shops. "There's a shelter just down here."

Kruger needed little prodding. The enemy had shown himself entirely too proficient at hitting even moving targets with his bombs. How much better would he be, then, with an unmoving dockyard?

Then they were in the shelter, a makeshift bunker excavated beneath a ruined office block that must have been ancient even during the Kaiser's war.

"The staff used to meet directly above us," von Saltzmann said, after they'd found seats on one of the crude benches set along the walls. "Of course, that was back about 1915, when they didn't have to worry about some bloody lunatic dropping things on their heads."

"Are the raids that bad now, sir?"

"Worse every day. You've seen what it looks like up there. Most of the dockyard bombed to fragments. Some cranes are still standing, of course."

Naturally, Kruger thought. A dockyard crane was one of the most difficult targets to destroy, for the open girders making up the base provided little for the shock wave of an exploding bomb to work against. Most of the blast just passed harmlessly through the openwork. It took a direct hit to knock one down, or enough near misses to undermine the base.

Von Saltzmann pointed at the low ceiling. "There was a building up there until about three months ago."

"It's not much better at sea, sir," Kruger commented.

"No, I don't suppose it is. Right now it will be the British up there. They come after dark. The Americans come in the daytime. I think the civilians prefer to be bombed by the Yanks. They can at least see what they're doing most of the time, so their bombs are generally confined to the base. The bloody British just drop them anywhere. I'm not really sure how they divided it up. Possibly it simply indicates that the Americans are braver than the British when it comes to facing our fighters and flak."

"Or stupider?"

"Also possible. In any event, *Herr* Göring has at least stopped his boasting about his 'invincible' Luftwaffe. Not that I care much for the price of his silence."

"I just wish I had more time," Kruger said. "It wasn't an easy patrol, and I'm not really sure I'm even up to a new command yet, no matter how fascinating it may sound."

"You will be. It should be almost a pleasure cruise with your new boat." Von Saltzmann sat back, folding his arms across his chest, as if expecting a long wait. "Besides, no patrol is easy now, my friend. It's not like when I was still an operational commander. That was when our boats had the middle of the ocean to themselves, and the enemy had still forgotten all the lessons they'd learned in the last war. Just single ships, sailing whenever they liked." He sighed. "It was so easy in those days. So bloody easy."

The shelter was filling up with dockyard workers and sailors now, and the two men fell into silence. They would not speak of the new command when there was any chance the wrong person might hear.

Kruger felt almost at home. Many of the workers had the same hunted look so common in U-boats. Probably the relentless bombing, he thought. It would have that effect on anyone after enough time.

They could feel the regular pounding as the bombs exploded throughout the yard, like depth charges detonating at a safe distance. Here and there was the heavier crash of one of the huge bombs the British had developed for use against the U-boat pens. A direct hit from one of those monsters was more than capable of doing the job, as Kruger had seen in France. Seven metres of reinforced concrete shattered, dropped onto a pair of brand-new boats, by the detonation of a single bomb.

Blockbusters, the Tommies called them. So big that a single bomb would make up the entire payload of a heavy bomber, which would have had to have been specially modified to carry the monster.

Von Saltzmann was snoring softly, his head lolling on his chest. How can he do that? Kruger wondered.

Then it was over, and the all-clear was being sounded. Kruger looked at his watch. The raid had lasted a full hour and a half! How many planes did the enemy have now? Millions?

It seemed that way.

He nudged von Saltzmann, who came awake sputtering like an old outboard motor.

"They're gone now," Kruger said.

The pudgy captain yawned, easing himself to his feet. "Then let's get to your boat before they decide to come back," he said, starting for the entrance.

"How long do we have?"

"Not as long as we need, Kruger. Neither between raids, nor to get your boat ready and to sea."

The pair came up out of the shelter and once again began to pick their way through the blacked-out dockyard, toward the secret pen where *U-2317* lay waiting for her new commander.

"This is all too bloody soon," Kruger said, after they had passed yet another inspection by a pair of Naval Policemen, who had emerged out of the darkness like Max Schreck in *Nosferatu*. "I don't need more sea time. What I need is a good, long rest." He sniffed. "And a shower."

"You can shower on your boat." Von Saltzmann laughed suddenly. "And you're right—you bloody well need one!"

"Mostly I need the rest."

"I agree. So does the Admiral, if you want my opinion. But you'll just have to rest while you're at sea." He smiled. "I know it sounds absurd, but in your new boat it should be easy enough. Just stay deep during the day, running at silent speed. With your battery capacity you can creep along at five knots for a few hours over three days. The boat's equipped with carbon dioxide scrubbers to keep the air breathable, and if you need, you can release a little oxygen as well."

"Identity cards please, gentlemen?"

Kruger sighed and pulled out his wallet. How many Naval Policemen were stationed at Kiel now? Or had they been pulled out of every other base and dumped here with orders to be as big a nuisance as possible?

"Escorts should give you very little trouble," von Saltzmann said, when they were able to continue. "The older ones, corvettes and Asdic trawlers, you can simply run away from. Even if you just use batteries you should be able to get away. Use your turbine and you'll leave anything but a destroyer behind, and the destroyer should be unable to use her detection gear at those speeds. Also, your boat is equipped with the latest type detection gear—*Nibelung* active sonar, and the latest version of the *Balkon Gerät* passive array hydrophones. Your operator will be able to key the *Nibelung*, which sends out super-sonic pulses and shows the echoes on a screen, with your boat always at the centre. About three pings should be sufficient to establish what's around you with sufficient accuracy for working up a targeting solution."

"Sounds like some sort of radar."

"Except that it works under water. Hydrophone range is about 50 miles at 100 metres, *Nibelung* about half that. A surface ship's Asdic is good for perhaps three kilometres under ideal conditions. So if there are any ships about, you should know about them long before they discover you."

Kruger grinned. "Maybe I *will* get some rest at that! And you say there's a shower aboard, too?"

"Two of them—one for officers, one for other ranks. It's a benefit of your turbines. They operate on high-pressure steam, some of which is condensed back into fresh water. Most will probably go overboard, but the rest you can use as you see fit. You can't drink it, though."

"Showers seem a fine use," Kruger said. "But she sounds like a very different sort of U-boat."

"Very. A slightly larger boat, but sophisticated enough to get by with a much smaller crew. Showers, air-conditioning, even a bit of privacy. You have a cabin, you know."

"With a door?" Kruger sounded as if the very idea was impossible. In his old *Typ* VIIc, the captain's 'cabin' consisted of a bunk just forward of the control room, with a narrow board attached to the bulkhead at one end to serve as a desk, and a curtain that could be pulled closed for privacy. A wide space on the central passageway and nothing more.

"With a door," von Saltzmann assured him. "Here we are. You'll see in a minute."

Two more Naval Policemen were waiting at the bunker door, with a young *Oberfänrich* standing beside them, shivering in an ill-fitting greatcoat.

"Identity cards, please," the petty officer said.

When he had the cards, he consulted a clipboard, with a typed list attached. "You're on the list, *Kapitän* von Saltzmann," he said. "Your companion is not."

"Give him your orders," von Saltzmann suggested.

Kruger pulled the folded sheets from his greatcoat pocket and handed them over. The *Oberfänrich*, watching over the petty officer's shoulder, seemed suitably impressed.

"Good enough, sir," the petty officer decided. "Go on inside."

"Welcome aboard, sir," the young officer said. "I'm Ostler, senior *Oberfänrich*."

Kruger extended his hand. "Good to meet you, Ostler. Have you been to sea before?"

"No, sir." He hesitated. "At least, not in U-boats. I spent six months in an S-boat, stationed in Den Helder, before coming to *U-2317*."

"See any action?"

"Some. Running fights, mostly with British motor torpedo boats. No great battles."

Kruger shrugged. "The last great sea battle was the Skagerrak, which was fought before I was born."

"There was *Bismarck*, sir," Ostler offered.

"One battleship against the entire Home Fleet? It was a battle, but more than a little one-sided."

More than that, it had been a stupid waste, he thought. If Lutjens had simply had the common sense to keep radio silence *Bismarck* might have made it safely to France, where her damage could have been repaired.

"Why don't we go aboard?" von Saltzmann suggested.

Kruger nodded. "Yes. Good idea."

The two men entered the bunker, leaving Ostler with the Naval Policemen.

"You want to watch what you say around that one, Kruger," von Saltzmann warned. "He's a bloody little Nazi who'd probably turn you in for undermining morale if he thought he could get away with it. He's political right through. One of the shower we've been cursed with since Rastenburg. As if the Navy needs reminding of its duty!"

Kruger hardly heard him. He had come to a shuddering halt, his mouth hanging half open.

She was like no vessel he had ever seen. Long and sleek, her casing gently rounded, flowing in a smooth line from her blunt bow all the way to her tapered stern. There was no deck gun, no guns of any kind, and the low tower was shaped like an upended aeroplane wing, rounded at the front, and tapering to a wedge at the rear, where the *Schnorchel* head was nestled on its retracted tube.

The two periscopes were fully extended, but behind them was a more remarkable appendage. A retractable radar scanner of the most recent design, which together with a pair of long radio antennae made up the visible part of *U-2317*'s electronic gear.

"Radar, too?" Kruger asked.

"Yes. The best available." He smiled. "We stole the design from the British, to be honest. There's a detector in the *Schnorchel* head, of course, but if you're surfaced your own radar will be a lot more useful. That set should pick up a fighter at 80 miles. Farther, if he's high enough. It's not as useful as your sound gear for surface search, though. The antenna is too low, so you've got no more than about a 15 miles range. Aircraft detection is the most useful feature. If you're searching for targets, you'll find them easier at about 50 metres."

"Can't they home in on our signal?"

Von Saltzmann shrugged. "Probably. But by the time they reach you I'd think you'd have pulled the plug and got away, right?"

Kruger grinned. "Right!" He looked her over more carefully. Everything was streamlined. Even the mooring bitts were obviously retractable. "She's like something out of Jules Verne," he said.

"An apt description," von Saltzmann replied. "I went along on one of her trials, and I must say I was very impressed. Once submerged she is like a dream." He chuckled softly. "Or a nightmare, if your name happens to be Churchill! Fast, very manoeuvrable, and extremely deep diving when required. We haven't tested her to design depth yet. The engineers say she should be able to operate at 350 metres. We've had her as deep as 250 and hardly a groan from the pressure hull. You've four centimetres of tempered steel surrounding you. Thicker than anything ever built before. Personally, I have a suspicion the engineers may have been a bit conservative in their estimates. The main thing is that, in the unlikely event that you can't escape a depth charge attack by running away, you can dive deeper than any escort commander is ever likely to set his charges. Possibly deeper than he *can* set them."

Kruger nodded. "There are still the hedgehog mortars, of course. Those only explode on contact. *U-702* now has a deck gun with two metres of its barrel blown off to prove it."

"You should be able to out-manoeuvre those, I should think." The captain moved toward the brow. "Well, *Herr Korvettenkapitän*, come aboard. Your new command awaits."

•　　•　　•

Kapitänleutnant Rolf Wiegand lifted his half-filled glass, winking at the paunchy torpedo officer, *Oberleutnant* Karl Himmler, who was poring over a long letter written on pink stationery and absolutely reeking of some cheap fragrance.

"Hear anything from the Gestapo lately, old pal?" Wiegand asked.

Himmler smiled weakly. The only thing that might have made things worse would have been if his mother had named him Heinrich, which, thank God, was a fate with which she had already unknowingly cursed his elder brother. It didn't help that he vaguely resembled the SS *Reichsführer*. So the jokes were only natural, and entirely good-natured. It was just that one could tire of anything after a time.

"Not a thing, Number One," Himmler replied, looking over his letter. His wife was a dedicated correspondent, but her habit of spraying everything with perfume was becoming annoying. Especially lately, when the choice of scents had become both limited and revolting. "However," he went on, "I *did* mention to my Uncle Heinie that I had it on good authority that you were secretly Jewish."

Wiegand, whose father was a Lutheran bishop, laughed and sipped his brandy. It was the good stuff, French, brought in before the recent reverses on that front. Now it was to be savoured, as it seemed unlikely that they would be able to replenish their supply in the near future.

"Are you *really* related, Karl?" he asked.

"In a vague sort of way. Seventh cousins, fourteen times removed, or some such. Not close enough that he'd worry about me if one of his henchmen ever got hold of me."

Fregattenkapitän (Ing) Parsifal Eisenberg, the *Leitender Ingenieur*, looked up from a technical manual. "I understand the new captain will be joining us today, Number One?"

"So I've heard, L.I.. At least, his boat was due in today."
He shrugged. "Whether they actually made it, however, I have
no idea."

"The odds are just slightly in favour of *not* making it, I
should think," Eisenberg said.

Seaman Schwartz, who served as wardroom steward, stuck
his head in the door. "Air raid on up topside, gentlemen," he
announced.

Wiegand groaned, sinking deeper into his chair. "Thank
you, Schwartz. Be sure the rest of the crew are informed."

"Zu Befehl, Herr Kapitänleutnant!"

"If the bloody Tommies are dropping things on us again,"
Himmler commented, "I'm glad I'm down here out of the
way."

"Aren't we all?" Wiegand agreed.

Himmler glanced over at the Exec. He seemed in a fairly
good mood today. They all did. It was the boat, he thought.
For the first time in many months, everyone seemed to feel
that not only did they stand an excellent chance of surviving,
but it seemed likely they could inflict some major damage as
well. The new torpedoes, the 'eels,' as they were called, were
going to raise all kinds of hell if they could slip under a convoy. The enemy was so far unaware of their development, and
thus had no good countermeasures ready.

Oberleutnant Reuter, the navigator, stepped into the wardroom and flopped into a waiting chair. More than for any of
the others, *U-2317* represented a chance to him. After his last
cruise, in an ancient 250-tonner that had never left the Baltic,
nor done any damage to the enemy, this boat was like heaven.

Even the omnipresent *Typ* VIIs, by far the most common
type, did not have the luxury of a real wardroom. There was
only a central corridor, running the length of the boat, and
everything and everyone was squeezed in at one side or the

other. Here the officers had this compartment to themselves, and the captain had a private cabin. The wardroom was small—particularly when you considered that *U-2317* was carrying four extra officers for the present—but with the berths folded up it was adequate for their needs. The other ranks, as usual, had to share their bunks with their counterparts on the opposite watch.

"Any news?" Wiegand asked.

"There's still a war on," Reuter commented. "Otherwise, what, exactly, were you interested in, Number One?"

"Did the new captain's boat make it in?"

"No idea. I *was* going up to the Edelweiss, but it's raining British bombs out there just now." He grinned. "Besides, a grieving *Leutnant* just informed me that the bloody Yanks dropped a rather large bomb on the place a few hours back."

"Pity," Eisenberg commented. He was a *very* married man, and had never understood the younger officers' need to drink themselves half blind and bed every female in sight.

"They say," Reuter announced, rather dramatically, "that it killed Lotte."

"*Ach!*" Wiegand sighed, even more dramatically. "The horrors of war! Struck down in the bloom of youth! My God, I'll wager there must be at least a quarter of the officer corps she hadn't got around to yet!"

"A fine tribute, sir," Reuter said. "Fine."

"Actually," Wiegand remarked, "she *was* a rather nice girl, leaving out being a bit fat in the behind."

"Oh, decidedly," Reuter put in. "Why, as whores go, she was one of the very best. Never caught a bloody thing off her, either."

"Crabs," Himmler said.

"What?"

"Ostler got crabs from her."

Eisenberg looked up from his manual. "Serves him right, the little prick."

"God!" Wiegand moaned. "You mean *he's* been there, too?"

"I don't know anyone who hasn't," Himmler said, ignoring Eisenberg's scowl, "with the possible exception the *Grossadmiral.*"

"And Beethoven," Reuter offered.

Beethoven was *U-2317*'s mascot, a grey ceramic cat secured to a shelf in the wardroom.

Their laughter was cut short as Schwartz stuck his head in the door again. "*Kapitän* von Saltzmann is on the catwalk," he announced. "Looks as if the new captain is with him."

"What does he look like?" Wiegand asked.

"Filthy. Like someone who's just come off a long patrol. But he's wearing a white cap and has three rings around his sleeves, so..."

"That's probably him, then," Wiegand said, nodding decisively and getting to his feet. "The rest of you stay here for now. He may wish to get cleaned up before general introductions. If not, we'll know where to find you."

•   •   •

Korvettenkapitän Hans Kruger looked around the neat little cabin with a lingering feeling of disbelief. Since leaving the Naval Academy in 1940, he had spent the entire war in U-boats, but this was the first time he had ever seen such luxury afforded a captain. There was a bunk, with drawers beneath it for his clothing, along with a tiny desk and chair, and several shelves fixed to the bulkheads. There was also a telephone and an intercom station, both within easy reach of either bunk or desk, and a gyro repeater and depth gauge at the foot of his bunk.

When he had come aboard he had found his kit had
already been sent over from the storage facility ashore. In this
boat, the captain wasn't limited to what he could carry in a
tiny ditty bag, but would keep his full issue with him at all
times.

Within five minutes of coming aboard, he had been standing beneath a hot shower, scrubbing away the accumulated
filth and stink. Then a good shave, painful, as was common
after three months without touching razor to face, but doing
wonders for his appearance. At one time he had thought of
simply growing a beard, but when he had tried he found that
the sides never filled in properly, and a mustache and goatee
tended to give him a unwanted Satanic look. So now he just let
his whiskers grow as they might while on patrol, and removed
them as soon as possible after returning.

Then, clean again, he had dressed in fresh fatigues and
gone right through the boat, with Wiegand and Eisenberg taking turns as guide. The boat was magnificent, and the crew
every bit as good. 'Hand picked,' von Saltzmann had called
them. For once, the term actually seemed to fit.

His questioning had brought out that all of the seamen
were fully qualified in their specialities, most of them with
examinations passed, ready for promotion at the first available
vacancy. The petty officers, always the backbone of any boat,
were equally well qualified. One of them, Chief Coxswain
Heinrich Stauber, had won both the first and second-class ver-
sions of the Iron Cross, as well as the 'fried egg,' the German
Cross, Germany's only award for individual acts of bravery.

There was even a cook, Petty Officer Willi Dorfmann, who
had been second chef in a fine restaurant in Potsdam before
the war. Kruger had sampled his handiwork that evening.
Using the same basic rations as were found in every other U-

boat, Dorfmann had turned out a genuine treat. It was not the food that was usually bad, Kruger thought, but the cooks.

The Admiral, and those under him, had drawn them all together in this boat for a special purpose—to delay the end of the war as long as possible. It was probably too late for that now, Kruger thought, but the gesture was still necessary. And, in a boat like this, they might even accomplish something. Make the enemy stop and think, reconsider the odds.

It was worth a try.

Von Saltzmann had given him an outline of the plan. The details would come later. *U-2317* was to slip out into the Atlantic and disrupt the convoy routes as much as possible.

Once out of the Baltic, through the gantlet of the Skagerrak, she would be based in Bergen, whence she could sortie with equal effectiveness against the British Isles or the northern convoy routes to Russia.

"You'll be buying us time," von Saltzmann had explained. "The new boats are almost ready for active service. *Typ* XXIs, mostly, but they'll soon be followed by more like your own. The only thing needed to get them into the war is time, and *that* is the one thing we are desperately short of just now!"

It was quite true, Kruger thought. The new boats had the potential to completely reverse the Battle of the Atlantic. But, as yet, there were not enough of them, and none had ever sailed on a war patrol. The war was still being carried on by the older boats, like *U-702*.

Only one out of four ever came back.

"Bloody depressing," he muttered, picking up the leather-bound Captain's Log from the desk. He had glanced through it earlier, but put off a detailed study until after he had been through the boat and had a good supper. Now there would be time, and the late *Kapitänleutnant* Scheutte's observations would give him some extra insight into both the boat and her crew.

He glanced up at the neat reefer jacket hanging from a hook by the door. That was one thing that was very different in this boat. Everyone tended to wear dress uniform when not engaged in some task where fatigues would be more appropriate. There was none of the usual mixture of uniform and old civilian clothing that was standard in other boats.

It was like being in a battleship.

Even Kruger had put aside his old leather watchcoat, exchanging it for a clean shirt and tie, and his best reefer jacket. He smiled suddenly. A few months ago he would never have considered wearing his best uniform except for special occasions. Now, no matter what they accomplished with this particular boat, the war would not last much longer.

When it was over he doubted if the condition of his best uniform would be of much concern.

He opened the log, and had just started reading, when there was a soft rap at the door.

"Enter."

Oberfänrich Gerhard Ostler stepped over the coaming and stood uneasily just inside the door. "I should like to speak with you for a moment, sir," he said. "If I may?"

Kruger nodded, putting down the log. "What is it, *Oberfänrich?*"

"It is—well, sir—*Kapitänleutnant* Wiegand seems to have an inexhaustible supply of minor jobs, and he assigns *all* of them to me."

"Are you suggesting that the Executive Officer of this boat is being purposely unfair to you, Ostler?"

"No. No, sir. It's not that, although I *am* senior, and *Oberfänrich* Schultz never seems to have as much to do."

"Don't complain, Ostler. Perhaps *Kapitänleutnant* Wiegand simply thinks that a more experienced officer can get the job done faster?"

Ostler nodded, hesitantly. "Perhaps, sir. But, you see, sir, when I was assigned to this boat I was told in Berlin that along with my regular duties, my most important job would be to inform the crew of their correct attitude toward *Führer* and Fatherland." He shook his head. "Did you know, sir, that there are only *three* party members in the entire crew? And *I* am the only officer!" He flinched, biting his lip. "Except for yourself, of course, sir."

Kruger laughed, shaking his head. "Sorry, Ostler, but you are *still* the only one. When I joined the Navy it was illegal for a German officer to join *any* political party, so politics were not something we ever concerned ourselves with. I have not got out of that habit." He smiled as benevolently as he could. "However, I will speak with the IWO about your duties, eh?"

"Thank you, sir. Right now I have no time, but..."

"Yes. Exactly. Go tell *Kapitänleutnant* Wiegand I wish to speak to him, will you, Ostler?"

"Zu Befehl, Herr Korvettenkapitän!"

Wiegand arrived a few minutes later, looking puzzled. "Young Ostler told me you wished to see me, sir?"

"Yes. Sit down, Number One."

"He was grinning like he'd just been promised a direct promotion to *Grossadmiral*."

"He was just in here, complaining about being too overworked to make his little speeches and inspire the crew."

"I do my best to keep him that way, sir," Wiegand replied. *"Kapitänleutnant* Scheutte preferred it."

Kruger grinned. "I trust you'll be able to keep it up?"

"There will always be more than enough work for an *Oberfänrich* in any boat," Wiegand said. "Particularly a bloody little commissar like Ostler."

"Exactly," Kruger grunted. "I'm damned if I know why the high command has suddenly seen fit to allow the Party to meddle in Navy business. It was the bloody *Army* that tried to blow up the *Führer*, not us!"

Wiegand nodded. "I've certainly never had any doubts about my own loyalty, sir."

"Nor I about mine. So keep the little bugger busy, eh?"

"I will, sir."

"Oh, and what about our other young gentleman? What's his name?"

"Schultz, sir. Jurgen Schultz. No problem with him. He comes from an old Navy family, father commanded a destroyer at the Skagerrak, grandfather was an admiral. He's been set on a naval career since infancy, and I don't think he gives a damn *who* runs the country so long as he can have it."

Kruger nodded. "Good. That's the sort of officer I like." He held up the log. "I've been reading through this," he continued. "Sounds as if there have been some problems with the turbine?"

"Some, sir. It's still a new system."

"I'll want to speak to the L.I. about it, in any case."

Wiegand stood. "I'll see to it, sir."

Kruger held up his hand. "Not just now, Number One. I want to finish reading this log first, and I could use a bit of rest. Have *Fregattenkapitän* Eisenberg report to me at 0800 tomorrow, right?"

"Yes, sir. Will there be anything else?"

"Not for now. I'll finish my reading and go to sleep. Anything less than a British invasion of Kiel, or the arrival of *Grossadmiral* Dönitz aboard, *you* handle."

"Aye, aye, sir."

Wiegand stepped out into the passageway and walked the few steps to the wardroom. He was glad to find out that the new captain agreed with him on keeping politics out of things. There was more than enough to worry about as it was.

More than enough.

Chapter Two

Happy Christmas

Kapitän zur See Siegfried von Saltzmann walked slowly to
the window of his hotel room and peered through the thick
curtains at the crowds, which, even in this ghastly winter of
defeats, were streaming along Unter den Linten as if they had
not a care in the world. Most of the men were in uniform, the
field grey of the Army predominating, and the pale blue of the
Luftwaffe. Here and there, standing out against the snow, was
the deep blue of the Navy.

At least, he thought, you no longer saw many of the cursed
black uniforms. The political branch of the SS. The Armed SS
were nuisance enough—at least their officers were—the rank-
ers were much the same as any other conscript, the so-called
exclusive standards for that 'elite' force long since having been
abandoned in the face of mounting losses. But he had never
been able to understand the power of the politicals. Or how the
Generals had ever permitted Hitler to raise up what amounted
to a second army, to compete with them for the best personnel.

They looked like a pack of damned fools, he thought, pos-
turing in their fancy uniforms. And if half the stories were
true, well, it was a wonder anyone could stomach their company, much less give them any authority. Germany needed a
strong leader, but a jumped-up lance corporal, no matter how

great his personal bravery in the last war, was just not the same as a man trained in the art of leadership from birth.

He grinned suddenly. I sound like a bloody monarchist! he thought. *Long live the Kaiser!*

With a sigh, he let the curtains fall back over the window and sat down on the edge of the bed. His meeting with the Admiral would not be until the afternoon, but there was still a great deal to be done before then. He had Kruger's reports in his locked briefcase. Barring unexpected problems, which were not uncommon, the man himself would be arriving in Berlin by train in a few hours.

So far it all sounded good.

Von Saltzmann removed the tiny key from his watch-chain and unlocked the old leather case. His mother had given it to him when he was commissioned, all those years ago. Unlike almost everything else he owned the case had somehow stayed with him through the years. At the moment it contained the papers that would either set the project in motion, or kill it before it really started.

He wondered what some of the jokesters in Kiel would think if they knew the real extent of his power? The 'errand boy.' He was aware of the name, and quite willing to let it pass unnoticed. It made him sound like a bumpkin. Good camouflage for one of the most important planners on the Naval Staff.

Both the *Grossadmiral*, and *Konteradmiral* Godt, who had taken over the submarine branch after Dönitz had succeeded Raeder as Commander-in-Chief, were more than willing to listen attentively to almost any suggestions von Saltzmann put to them.

Then there was the Admiral, not actually a part of the submarine branch chain of command, but in charge of the section of the *Kriegsmarine* closely corresponding to the British Special Operations Division. When von Saltzmann had suggested diverting *U-2317* from use as a training boat, valuable only for preparing crews for the trickle of *Typ* XXVIs anticipated in mid-1945, the Admiral had seized on the idea and pushed it through. Von Saltzmann had reasoned that the boat would be of more value on operations than in training, particularly since, if nothing was done to stem the Allied advances on all fronts, trained crews for *Typ* XXVI boats would be superfluous, as their boats would not reach service before the war ended.

He pulled the red-bordered folder from the case and opened it on the bed. There would be considerable risk involved in the plan—almost all of it borne by Kruger and his crew. They were the best men available, but the boat was still relatively untried, the power plant inclined toward unexpected problems. Given time, the Walter turbines could be made as reliable as diesels, or else the engineers and physicists, finally freed from the idiotic notion that physics was 'Jewish' science and therefore suspect, would actually develop their proposed uranium steam generator. He had seen the plans, but the engineers were hampered by the fact that the Nazis had shortsightedly driven the best physicists from the country during the 1930s, and because of sabotage at a plant in Norway where they were producing something called 'heavy water.'

The boat they were planning would make even *U-2317* seem primitive, but it would probably not be built before 1950. Much too late to do the Reich any real good.

So it was up to Kruger. His boat was the most advanced available, and he had an excellent engineer. On patrol in his old boat, his chances of survival would be no better than one in four. In *U-2317*, they would be tremendously increased, provided nothing broke down at a critical moment.

And that risk, he thought, was one every U-boat sailor had to live with.

• • •

The formal luncheon struck Kruger as being somehow obscene in the face of Germany's imminent defeat. Mess-jacketed staff officers at either side of the long table, politely discussing almost anything but the war, while they dined on perfectly cooked food and drank the most expensive wines. What little talk there was of the war was encouraging, stressing the recent German gains in the Ardennes campaign. But that ignored the obvious: Germany's industrial strength was badly damaged by enemy bombing, stretched to its limits and beyond by the demands of a war as devastating to Kruger's generation as the Great War had been to his father's. America's industrial might was untouched, her manpower pool still enormous even after three years of war on two widely separated fronts.

The Ardennes offensive might cause some delay, he thought, but in the end the outcome would still be the same.

Kruger sliced off a thin piece of beef, feeling distinctly out of place. It was more than the fact that he was wearing his standard dress uniform, and not mess dress. He had never bothered buying that particular uniform, having spent his entire career at sea, where the need did not exist. On the other hand, he did have the Knight's Cross with Swords at his throat, and the Iron Cross, First Class and the German Cross pinned to his jacket. There was only one more highly decorated officer at the table, and that was a *Vizeadmiral* whose decorations had been earned in the Imperial Navy.

It was, he decided, a matter of attitude. The others were all staff officers, the majority of them from the surface fleet. Of the few who had served in U-boats, none had done so recently. Even von Saltzmann, for whom he had formed a certain

attachment, had been quite candid in admitting that he had
last taken a U-boat to sea in early 1940, a period when the
war at sea was still strongly favouring the Fatherland.

For most of these officers, the greatest fear they had known
would be what they experienced while sitting out a raid in a
shelter, listening to the enemy's bombs exploding throughout
the city. It was frightening enough, Kruger supposed, but not
at all like the fear that could grip you as you crept along at a
bare two knots a hundred metres beneath the surface, while
half a dozen relentless escorts rumbled overhead, the infernal
pinging of their Asdic against the hull the prelude to the jolt-
ing blast of depth charges. Sometimes it seemed to go on endlessly, hour after hour, one day merging with the next, the air
turning foul, the crew lying in their bunks, moving as little as
possible, so that they would not breathe any more than absolutely necessary, until the nausea began, and the constant
yawning as your lungs tried to suck in oxygen that was no
longer in the depleted air. And through it all the pinging and
the depth charges, and never knowing when they would finally
go away, or when one charge would explode just that fraction
too close, starting a tiny crack in the toughened steel of the
pressure hull that would grow with alarming suddenness until
the whole boat was torn apart by the tremendous pressure of
the sea, the black water pouring in to crush and drown.

Eiserne Särge, they called the old boats. *Iron Coffins*.

It was an apt name, when you considered the thousands of
U-boat sailors now resting on the bottom of the Atlantic in
their shattered hulls.

"We're really showing those damned Americans what it
means to tackle a superior force in Belgium, eh, Kruger?" the
man next to him said. He was a *Fregattenkapitän*, but not a
U-boat man.

"So it would seem," Kruger replied, holding up his glass for a white-jacketed steward to refill.

Then von Saltzmann was beside him, smiling benignly. "It's time," he said. "Had enough?"

"More than enough." Kruger was glad of the interruption. Another moment and he probably would have told the other officer exactly what he really thought of their chances in Belgium. About equal to those of a pretty Jewish girl in a room full of SS men—unlikely to emerge with either her honour or her life.

"Down here," von Saltzmann said, starting down a long flight of stairs into the inevitable bunker. It seemed that very little of the war was still conducted from above ground. It was said to be much the same in England, so that only the Americans, safe from bombing behind 3,000 miles of ocean, could work with windows and fresh air.

Eventually they came to a steel door, set neatly at the end of a concrete corridor.

A pair of guards, SS men this time, checked their papers and then passed them through.

It was the same girl behind the desk, Kruger noticed. The Admiral's personal secretary, presumably.

"Good afternoon, gentlemen," she said. "And happy Christmas."

Kruger shook his head. "You know, I'd forgot."

Von Saltzmann laughed. "Well you won't forget after this evening, I can assure you. There is to be a party at *Vizeadmiral* Wünche's house in Potsdam. You'll be going, naturally, as my personal guest."

What the hell? Kruger thought. "I'd like that," he said.

Von Saltzmann looked at the girl. She was smiling again, still making him feel younger. Like Uta used to do, before… "You'll be coming as well, won't you, Hannah?" he asked.

"I've been invited." She shrugged. "I'm really not sure that I'll go. It's a long drive, and there's always the danger of a raid."

Kruger grinned. "You really *must* come," he said. "If you don't I'll have no one to talk to but *Kapitän* von Saltzmann, who no doubt will have better things to do than to entertain me all evening."

She looked at him curiously. He seemed to have grown younger in the last few days. He was still not really young. Youth had been ground out of him in almost five years of constant battle, so that he probably would never again be as young as his years. But he *did* look more relaxed. So whatever the Admiral and this chunky little captain had him doing, it obviously agreed with him.

"All right," she said. "I'll be there." She laughed. "But just to rescue you from the Captain, eh? I've been with him at parties before. The more he has to drink, the more boring he becomes."

They all laughed, von Saltzmann most of all.

The telephone buzzed politely and the girl picked it up, listened for a moment, and replaced the handset. "He will see you now," she said.

Hannah Meisenhelder sat very still behind her desk, her chin resting on her fist, watching the thick door close behind the two men. He really does look so much better, she thought. Not handsome, exactly, but attractive enough, tall and slim, with brown hair, just a bit wavy, and dark eyes. He'd do me, she thought.

She frowned. What the hell is the matter with me? The man is a bloody U-boat captain! A walking dead man!

She turned back to her typewriter, a slight smile on her face. It's the damned war, she thought. It's driving me stark, raving mad!

•   •   •

"What do you think of your new boat, Kruger?" the Admiral asked. "Now that you've had time to get the feel of her?"

Kruger smiled. "She's everything that you and *Kapitän* von Saltzmann told me, sir. All that, and a great deal more."

The Admiral nodded, frowning slightly. "I'm sorry to have to inform you that you will not have as much time as we would like to give you for working up. The war is in a critical phase just now, and even with our recent gains in Belgium, I am just not sure we can pull our pot from the fire before it's hopelessly burnt. You will have until the first of the year. By then you must either be operational, or the boat will be returned to training duties, and you and the crew distributed through the fleet where most needed."

Kruger could think of nothing to say for a moment. *U-2317* represented a chance to him. A way to survive. And now it was to be taken away if they could not certify her as completely ready within the next week!

"You can't mean that, sir!" Kruger said. "The boat is a marvel—more than anyone could have hoped. We can't allow a few minor technical problems to stand in her way! Not when her success can mean so much to the Fatherland!"

"I agree, sir," von Saltzmann added. "*U-2317* is an historic boat no matter how you look at it. First of her type—perhaps the first true submarine. Better that her history be written with honour in battle, not training crews for boats that may never be finished!"

The Admiral held up his hands. "Gentlemen," he said, "this is *not* my decision. This deadline comes directly from the *Grossadmiral*, though I suspect it originated with Godt. He wants his boat back." He leaned forward across the desk. "*This* is how he intends to get her."

"I *think* she can be ready, sir," Kruger said. "Her diesel and E-motor are both perfect. Our two master mechanics, Petty Officer Braun and Leading Seamen Mertens, have seen to that. The only potential problem is with the Walter turbine, and *Fregattenkapitän* Eisenberg probably knows more about that system than anyone other than Professor Walter himself."

The Admiral nodded. "I can promise nothing, Kruger. But I still think this project has merit, and I think that if anyone can bring it off, you are the man. I am going to see the *Grossadmiral* myself this afternoon. With any luck I can persuade him that a few more days will hurt nothing, and may result in a great deal of good. Try to persuade him as an old shipmate."

"I will try to have her ready by New Year's Day, sir," Kruger asserted.

"Good. Now, wait outside for a few minutes, will you, Kruger? I have a few points I wish to discuss with *Kapitän* von Saltzmann."

"As you wish, sir."

"Now, Siegfried," the Admiral said, as the door clicked shut, "just what do you *really* think of this project? It was your idea, after all. Will it come off?"

Von Saltzmann shrugged. The Reports are all favourable, sir. Except for the Walter turbine, and if need be the boat can sail without that on line and bring it up to par under way."

"So it will succeed?"

"Who can ever really say, sir? I think it will, but only the battle will give us the proof."

•   •   •

Korvettenkapitän Hans Kruger swore angrily, tugging viciously at the ends of his tie. It was the fourth attempt, and still he had not mastered the rebellious bit of black cloth. The Japanese had the right idea, he thought. Their dress uniforms had a standing collar; no tie was ever worn.

Particularly not a damned bow tie.

He glanced at his watch, which was laying on the top of the old, heavily carved dresser. Von Saltzmann would probably be there at almost any moment, he realised, and he still wasn't completely dressed. Still, Kruger thought, dress uniform wasn't that common for officers on sea duty. And even when he wore it, it was normally with a regulation necktie, not a damned bow tie, so it was, at least, understandable that he might have lost the knack.

Eventually he got it right, then pulled on his jacket and stood in front of the mirror for a moment to survey the result. Much better, he thought, than a few days before. The beard was gone now, as was the constantly hunted look. In his new command he did not expect to see either return. The new boat, and a full night's sleep each night since returning to Kiel, had done wonders.

Perhaps the party would do him good as well, though he would have preferred to catch the next train back to Kiel. It was always possible that the Admiral's interview with Dönitz would have won a reprieve, but that was not something Kruger intended to count on. There might be a little more time, but only God could grant them as much as they really needed.

Kruger frowned. If even a small part of what Otto had told him of seeing the SS do in the Ukraine was true, it was unlikely God would look too kindly on the country that had spawned them.

Kruger knew that he had killed many men since 1940. He didn't know how many, and he didn't want to know. They had died in the searing blasts of an exploding torpedo, or more slowly, drowning if they were lucky, or being roasted alive in the inferno of a blazing tanker and the burning oil that always surrounded such ships. Others had succumbed to the quick, relatively painless death of the Arctic convoys, where a man could die of exposure in minutes. His torpedoes had killed men in all of those ways, but at least their deaths, perhaps brutal, even horrible, were the result of combat action, and no different from what British submarines were inflicting on German seamen. It was a consequence of a conscious choice by his victims to serve at sea; a risk they all assumed, as did his own men, when they left port. But it was not deliberate murder.

Kruger had heard all the stories on enemy propaganda broadcasts. The old tales, resurrected from the Great War, of U-boats surfacing amongst their torpedoed victims to machine-gun any survivors, or racing full throttle through the lifeboats, smashing them to matchwood. Yet Kruger had heard of only a single incident of a deliberate machine-gun attack on survivors, by a desperate commander seeking to cover up the sinking of the wrong ship. But he was a prisoner of war now, and Kruger doubted he would escape punishment for his crime. And while there had undoubtedly been lifeboats rammed by surfaced U-boats, he thought it more likely to have been the result of darkness and the chaos of a convoy battle than deliberate malice.

As far as Kruger was concerned, once a ship was sunk, what happened to her crew was their own problem. A few times, when it had been safe to do so, he had surfaced long enough to give the survivors a bit of extra food, or sailing directions to the nearest land. Twice he had removed someone from a lifeboat and brought him back to base, in both instances a senior officer.

But there had been no attempts at wholesale rescue of survivors. It was too dangerous, and U-boats were simply not equipped to carry passengers. Hartenstein had proved that after sinking the *Laconia* and, when he attempted to rescue as many survivors as possible, having his boat bombed while running on the surface, with her deck crammed with those he had rescued and a red cross flag prominently draped over the deck gun. He had made it back to base, but after that Dönitz had forbidden rescue attempts.

Ironically, of the *Laconia* survivors, most of whom were Italian prisoners of war being transported to camps in England, most had survived the sinking and bombing, while the American bombs had killed most of the British survivors.

For that matter, he thought, the enemy frequently made no attempt to pick up their own torpedoed crews. So just who were the barbarians?

He frowned. The damned SS were. The Navy kills in battle, he thought. They seemed to do it just for pleasure.

There was a rap at the door. Kruger sighed and went to open it, almost tripping when his heel caught in a worn spot on the rug. Before the war it would have been replaced long ago. Now there was nothing to replace it with.

Von Saltzmann was at the door, looking splendid in full dress and medals.

"Ready, Kruger?"

"Just let me get my cap."

"Bloody early," von Saltzmann commented, "but with the blackout and the danger of raids it sometimes takes forever to drive out to Potsdam." He grinned. "Not like before the war, eh?"

Kruger shrugged. "I wouldn't know, sir. I grew up in Emden. The first time I was in Berlin was 1943, when the *Führer* gave me the swords."

Von Saltzmann stood in the open door, his heavy greatcoat folded over his arm. "It used to be something, my friend," he said. "Something very special. There used to be a little cabaret, not very far from here, in fact. One of the girls was called Uta. She could sing, dance—other things." He grinned. "*Ach!* The legs on that woman!"

"What happened to her?"

"I don't know." He frowned. He didn't really *want* to know. The girl had been Jewish, and when he went to her flat on the day after *Kristallnacht* she was no longer there. If she was lucky, she was dead by now.

"Even the cabaret is gone now," he added. "When the war started it was turned into a club for non-commissioned officers. A few months ago a British bomb destroyed it."

Kruger settled his cap on his head. Away from his command, the standard blue cover was in place. Aboard *U-2317*, that would be replaced by a white cover, the mark of a U-boat commander. The cap was new, the brass and bullion still gleaming. His other cap, the verdigris-coated one he wore at sea, remained in the boat.

"Ready, sir," he said.

Von Saltzmann didn't reply for a moment. He was still thinking about the girl. It didn't take much imagination to guess what would have happened to her once the SS got their hands on her. She had been a beautiful, delicate-appearing girl. She wouldn't have lasted long in a concentration camp.

"Are you ready, sir?"

"What? Oh, yes—of course." With some difficulty, von Saltzmann collected his thoughts. It was wrong to even think about the girl. Even after six years, the memory was still too painful.

He started to pull on his coat. "The car is waiting for us downstairs," he said.

•　　•　　•

Kruger sipped reflectively at a tall whisky, watching the festive couples waltzing to a small string orchestra. The whisky was Scotch, and he wondered how their host had managed to get his hands on it after five years of war. Smuggled in through Sweden, probably.

Everyone seemed cheerful enough, as was only to be expected after the recent successes in Belgium. Certainly the Army types were enjoying themselves.

"They *look* happy, don't they?" von Saltzmann said.

"Happy enough." Kruger watched one couple, who had been dancing as though glued together at the hips, slip off down a darkened hallway. The man, who wore the uniform of a Luftwaffe captain, with the Knight's Cross, had the look of a cornered stag on his face, and Kruger wondered if he was just back from the front, or if the girl was the reason?

Perhaps, he thought, the man had a wife nearby.

"Fools, most of them," von Saltzmann went on, speaking very softly. "We are doing quite well in Belgium now, eh?"

"That's the report, sir."

The older man laughed bitterly. "I suppose it's true enough. For now. I have a number of friends on the Army Staff, and they say that what we are doing now is at best a desperate gamble. That we must either prevail very quickly, or give it all back up for want of supplies." He frowned. "The whole bloody war has been fought that way!"

"Considering the odds, sir," Kruger said, "we've done better than anyone could have expected."

"Sure. *Considering the odds.* No, Kruger, the war began much too soon. It was inevitable that we go to war, of course. No one could deny that. But it was *not* inevitable that it begin in 1939. The plan was for war about 1946 or '47, when we would have had a powerful fleet, complete with modern aircraft carriers, and battleships no other power could match. As it was—well, you know the result. *Bismarck* sunk, *Graf Spee* scuttled, *Tirpitz* put out of action by British midget submarines. And the only carrier even begun nowhere near completion, nor ever likely to be." He took a long swallow of his drink. "We were to have had 300 submarines in commission when war began," he went on. "Enough to impose a total blockade on Britain, force her to come to terms. Do you know how many we actually had, Kruger? Fifty-six! And we were lucky if we could put two or three into the Atlantic at any one time. My God, man, you couldn't effectively blockade the Isle of Man with that force!"

"There *is* my boat now, sir."

"And with a hundred more like her right now we could probably make a difference. But she is only one. Probably will *be* the only one…"

There was a sudden flutter of attention near the door, as if an important guest had just arrived. From where he stood, Kruger could see only a pair of SS officers, resplendent in full dress, towering over the other guests. Kruger recognised neither of them, so it appeared they were with someone, rather than being important themselves.

Von Saltzmann snatched a fresh drink from a passing waiter. "I see an old friend across the room," he said. "You go and mingle, eh? God knows, you're probably the only real fighting officer here! I'll go and have a chat."

"Right, sir."

Kruger smiled as he saw von Saltzmann walk, a trifle unsteady, across the packed room, coming to a halt before an attractive, middle-aged woman in a very *décolleté* gown. Old friend, indeed.

Kruger began to move through the crowd, recognising no one except their host, a retired *Vizeadmiral* who had served in the old Imperial Navy. He had retired even before the Munich *Putsch*, but he had also been an early supporter of the Nazis, and was said to still exercise a considerable amount of influence.

Wünche was speaking to a short man, dressed in a neat field-grey uniform. The man nodded, then turned suddenly, looking directly at Kruger from no more than eight feet away.

The U-boat commander snapped automatically to attention, then, when the man laughed and smiled, forced himself to relax. The man beckoned.

My God, he looks old! Kruger thought. He seems to have aged ten years since I last saw him!

"It is good to see you again, *Kapitän* Kruger," he said. If he seemed to have aged, his eyes were still hypnotic, his voice as compelling as it had been in the old days, when he held thousands spellbound at the great Nürnberg rallies. "Are you still at sea?" he asked.

"I am, my *Führer*," Kruger replied. "I have been given *U-2317*, presently working up at Kiel."

The little dictator smiled, nodding. "I have heard of her," he said. "A very extraordinary boat, if what your admiral tells me is true. He was, in fact, in my office this afternoon, asking me to overrule Dönitz and Godt. He can be very persuasive when he wishes to be, as I'm sure you are aware. So, tell me, are *you* satisfied with her?"

"Very much, sir. She is a remarkable boat."

"Well, Kruger—use her well. She could be vital to our war effort." He smiled. "And, who knows? Perhaps the next time we meet I can add diamonds to that cross at your throat, eh?"

"I will do my best, sir. As will my crew."

Hitler nodded. The man was a monster, Kruger thought, but a genial one. But even Genghis Khan had reputedly been kind to his horses and children.

The *Führer* turned back to his host, who was eying Kruger curiously. Being retired, Wünche would have no idea of why a particular U-boat should be so important. When von Saltzmann had introduced him to their host there had been no special significance attached to his command.

That had been intentional. *U-2317* was still a secret, but if too many were to become aware of her the enemy might make a special effort to destroy her before she could slip out into the convoy routes. They had done so with *Tirpitz*, sending in midget submarines to heavily damage her where she hid in her fjord. The bombers had finished the job a bit more than a month later. And for all her great firepower, *Tirpitz* had never been as much of a threat as *U-2317*.

If a battleship threatened a convoy, the logical response was simply to provide another battleship as escort. Or a carrier, with sufficient aircraft to overwhelm even the most powerful ship. A battleship was a threat, but a known one, and therefore capable of being countered with relative ease.

Particularly since the high command had evidently interpreted the *Führer's* orders not to take any unnecessary risks as orders to avoid battle with anything larger than a corvette.

But a U-boat, which could slip beneath a convoy's escorts in absolute silence, all the while maintaining a good five knots, then use her sound gear to locate her targets, and fire her torpedoes from a depth of 50 metres—there was a *real* threat. A weapon against which the enemy had no adequate defense.

With an underwater speed slightly in excess of 25-knots, there wasn't even an adequate means of retaliation.

We will do a great deal of damage, Kruger thought. *If the turbine doesn't blow us all to hell first!*

Someone touched his sleeve, bringing him back.

"Hullo," he said.

"You looked as if you were a million miles away," Hannah said.

"Just off winning the war single-handed," he replied. She looked very different now, Kruger thought. Back in the Admi-

ral's office she had looked coolly efficient in her neat Women's
Corps uniform and wire-framed spectacles, her long hair
pulled right back from her face in a severe bun, her face
devoid of makeup beyond lipstick.

Now, dressed for the party, the change was astonishing.

She had left her glasses at home, so that he got the full
benefit of her dazzling blue eyes. Her blond hair was piled
atop her head in a style that exactly suited her, crowned with a
little tiara that appeared to contain a small fortune in gems.
Her gown, which left her shoulders bare and offered up for the
inspection the smooth upper curves of her breasts, was of deep
blue velvet. Between her breasts, on a thick gold chain, was
suspended an enormous emerald, brilliantly framed in diamonds.

"You look wonderful," he said.

She smiled, with a slight curtsy. "Thank you, sir," she
replied.

He grinned. "Are your guards with you? I didn't realise
you were so wealthy!"

She touched his arm. The ring on her finger contained a
single, square-cut diamond of considerable size. "We *used* to
be wealthy," she said. "But that was a long time ago. Most of
the money is gone, the land sold to pay old debts." She smiled.
"As our estate—well, farm, really—was once in what is now
central Berlin, the land sold for a good price and now there are
no more debts. Nor is there any more land. These jewels, and
one or two good dresses, are all that remain to remind me us
of what used to be." She seemed to be looking off into the distance. "These, and a gutted building on land we sold off a
long, long time ago, when the Kaiser needed it to build the
Reichstag."

"That was your family's land?"

"Once, long ago. In any case, I have my job and my jewels, so I think I will manage."

"I suspect you will at that."

Hannah shrugged. "I have to. There are some distant relatives somewhere in America, but I am all that's left here."

"So am I. My parents were killed in an air raid, and my brother was either killed or captured at Stalingrad. I don't suppose it makes a great deal of difference now which it was. I know him well enough to know that he'd never cooperate with the Russians, so even if he *was* captured he's probably dead by now. Which leaves only myself—and Bruno."

"Another brother?"

He laughed. "My dog. An old Alsatian. When our house in Emden was destroyed, he somehow survived the blast. My Uncle Fritz is taking care of him now."

"So," she said, "here we are, a pair of orphans, eh?" She took a glass of champagne from a passing waiter and sipped at it reflectively. "Well," she mused, "it's Christmas Eve, which seems like a good time to forget all our problems and be cheerful and, well, even frolicsome!"

Kruger sipped at his whisky. "An excellent idea."

"Then put down that damned drink and dance with me, sailor!"

Kruger laughed and handed their glasses to a waiter, then took her in his arms as the music started up again. Something from *Die Lüstige Witwe*, he thought. Old fashioned, and very romantic.

"Did I see you talking with the *Führer*?" she asked, as they moved amongst the whirling couples.

"Briefly. He knew my name. Remembered me, I guess."

"You've met him before?"

"In 1943, when I got my swords. I don't know if he remembered me from then, or if your boss refreshed his memory this afternoon."

She nodded. The Admiral had come back from his appointment with Dönitz in a foul mood, then gone out again a few minutes later, after informing her that he would be at the Chancellery. An hour later he had returned, looking much happier, and wished her a happy Christmas before sending her home early.

"What did he have to say?" she asked.

"The usual. Sink a convoy for the Fatherland. Win your diamonds. Be a hero."

"He looks so different now. Older."

"I expect he has a lot on his mind just now," Kruger said. He grinned. "You are an excellent dancer."

"So are you." She moved closer to him. "You look younger than I've ever seen you tonight, *Herr Korvettenkapitän*. And rather handsome."

Kruger laughed. "Since I've not had surgery on my face, I must presume you've had a drink or two?"

"Absolutely sober. Just that one glass of champagne, which has hardly had time to do anything yet! Though I *feel* a bit intoxicated for some reason. All this twirling about, I suppose. And the heat."

"We could go outside for a moment, if you like?"

They had stopped dancing, so that she was standing in his arms, looking up at him, her eyes very blue in the shimmering light of the ornate crystal chandelier suspended above them.

"I would like that very much," she said.

He led the way through the crowded room and out onto a balcony, the heavy blackout curtains shutting off the light behind them, so that the only illumination came from the stars filling the clear, cold sky, and a quarter moon.

"We mustn't stay long," he said. "You're not dressed for this cold."

She turned to look up at him, her face and shoulders like old ivory in the faint light, while the rest of her, encased in the dark velvet gown, seemed to vanish.

"I can tolerate a little cold," she asserted. "And you're not dressed for it, either!"

He laughed. "I'm a U-boat sailor. I'm used to being cold."

She gasped. "My God! They're coming again!"

"Who?"

"There!" She pointed toward the northwest, where the searchlights were again stabbing at the sky, while sporadic flashes came from the ground, and the sky seemed filled with a million pinpoint bursts.

Suddenly a pair of searchlights came together, staying locked, the apex a narrow triangle moving slowly toward the north until, very suddenly, the spot where they joined erupted in a tremendous flash of flame and light. The flak gunners must have put a round right into his bomb bay, Kruger thought.

Then he realised that the girl was clutching him, shivering, her face pressed against his chest.

"Are you cold?"

"No. It's not that…" She seemed very near tears. Not mourning some nameless British bomber crew, surely? So why?

"What's wrong?"

"That plane that just blew up. My brother, Karl—he was a bomber pilot. They told me that his plane was blown up just like that, over London."

"I'm sorry, Hannah. I didn't know."

She looked up at him. "You couldn't have, could you? You never knew him. Nor my other brother, Wilhelm." She frowned. "Or perhaps you did?"

"Was he in the Navy?"

"Yes. *Kapitänleutnant* Wilhelm Meisenhelder. He was commanding officer of *U-309*, in the spring of 1943."

Kruger nodded. "I *did* know him. Not very well, mind you, but his boat was in our flotilla. He seemed a fine young man."

"He was."

Kruger held her close, feeling her tremble as she thought about the past. He had not known her brother well, but he could remember him. A tall, blond officer, the image of the perfect Aryan type. The last time he had seen him had been early in the morning of 5th April, 1943, at a farewell party for his boat, which was scheduled to leave the next day. He could not tell her the whole truth—that the last time he had seen her brother the man had been unconscious, reeking of schnapps and vomit, on the floor of the salon of a whorehouse just outside Sainte Nazaire.

The next day both boats had gone on patrol. For Kruger it had been more or less routine. Meisenhelder's boat reported all normal on the third day, then signed off the radio and was never heard from again. A drifting mine, collision with another submarine, a fault in the pressure hull, a broken fitting—God alone knew what had actually happened to them. They were simply gone, like so many before and since.

"My God," she muttered, "what is the matter with me?"

"Hannah?"

She pushed herself away from him, walking to the balcony rail and peering down into the darkness of the snow-covered garden below.

"Is there something wrong?" Kruger asked, concerned.

"Yes. You're too damned attractive."

Absurd, he thought. "Is that bad?"

"Yes. It's terrible! Because you are going to die soon, and I don't want to be attracted to you." She shook her head. "But I am."

"I have no intention of dying soon," he asserted, for the first time in many months actually believing it. "When the war is over, I will stay in the Navy, if there is one, or else go back to Emden and help my Uncle Fritz build houses. There will be a need then."

She was facing him again. "I wish I could believe that, Hans. But a U-boat captain thinking of the future? I know too much of the truth. In my job I see the casualty lists every day."

"Believe me, Hannah," he said, gripping her arms. "If there is any boat that will survive this war it will be mine. I wish I could tell you exactly how I know this, but…"

She nodded. "I know. Secrecy." She smiled suddenly. "And maybe you *will* survive."

He pulled her close and kissed her, her body melting against him after only a momentary resistance. "I will," he said. "You can count on it!"

She rested her head on his chest and sighed. "I hope so," she said. "I really do hope so."

He kissed her again, feeling her respond, sensing the urgency as she returned his kisses.

"I know a place," she whispered. "It's near here, and we can be alone. A girl friend suggested it when she thought I was having an affair with the Hungarian Naval Attaché. I wasn't—but I remember the place."

"What are you suggesting?"

"I must be insane, but I want you, Hans. I want you so very much!"

He kissed her again. "Then we will go. But I'll have to find *Kapitän* von Saltzmann first. Can't have him thinking I've been abducted by enemy agents, can we?"

She kissed him lightly on the mouth. "Then go tell him, Hans. I will meet you out front. My car will be there—an old, green Mercedes saloon. You see? With me, there is no need to worry about transportation!"

•   •   •

When he signed them into the tiny hotel, the aged landlord seemed not to care that the tall Naval officer's wife had lost all of her identity papers. Kruger had the feeling he was quite used to that sort of thing, and couldn't care less. He didn't even ask if they had luggage.

The room was small, high up at the back of the building, and almost completely filled by an enormous feather bed. The landlord stayed just long enough to light the gas fire and remind them to be out by 10:00 the next morning if they didn't wish to pay for a second night, then closed the door and left them to their desires.

For a moment they stood beside the bed, awkwardly, and then he pulled her close and kissed her.

She pulled away, sat on the edge of the bed. "This is not like me," she said. "I'm—I'm not a virgin, but there was only one other man. We were to be married, but he was killed at Normandy. And now there is you."

"Now there is me." He shrugged. "If you've changed your mind?"

"No." Her hands moved behind her back, and when she stood a moment later the velvet gown slipped from her body and collapsed into a dark blue pool at her feet. Beneath it she was naked, but for suspender belt and stockings.

"No," she said. "I've not changed my mind."

She came into his arms, giggling suddenly and wriggling free. "What's wrong?" he asked.

"Your damned medals are like ice!" she laughed. "Take off your clothes and get into bed where it's warm, eh?"

And then they were beneath the thick down quilt, their bodies moving in the ancient rhythms, while in the distance were the sirens and the muffled crash of bombs as they smashed some unknown part of the great city to rubble.

When it was over, they lay together for a long time, her head resting on his chest.

"Happy Christmas," she said, after a long time. "Happy Christmas, my love."

He smiled and stroked her long, fine hair, which now hung loose, falling across her shoulders. "Happy Christmas," he said.

She frowned. "And now I shall be constantly worried about you, Hans," she sighed. "Never knowing when the report of your death may come in."

"It won't. I intend to live at least until the next century." He grinned. "With you beside me, I suspect I'll accomplish that goal."

She almost purred, snuggling close to him. "I'll be there. Whenever you need me, I'll be there."

He sat up, scratching his head. "And now *I* am going to be constantly worried about *you*. I'll be safe out at sea, while you'll be here, in perpetual danger from the bombers."

She studied him, curious. How could he be so confident? Casualties in the U-boat service were astronomical now. No one could ever be certain of survival, much less of a future. Yet this man seemed so sure of himself.

Perhaps, she thought, that was what had attracted her to him. The first time she had seen him he had been filthy, haggard, just in from a dangerous patrol, and looking as if the very thought of another would be more than his mind could tolerate.

Now he was positive he would survive the war to go into the building business with his uncle.

And what of yourself, Hannah Meisenhelder? she wondered. After Wilhelm's death she had ordered herself never to even consider seeing any man in such a hazardous profession. Now here she was in bed with Kruger, very possibly on the verge of some permanent commitment. It was too idiotic for words, yet she felt powerless to prevent it. Something inside her had given way, and now she was bound to this man as surely as if a minister had stood before them and conducted the rites.

"I will survive," she said. "For you."

"You do that." His hand closed over her breast, the nipple hard against his palm as he bent and kissed her. Outside, the great bomber formations droned purposefully overhead, their bomb bays empty as they hurried for home. Back in Berlin, people were dead or dying, or wandering the shattered streets, their homes in ruins, their lives destroyed. Here, in this tiny room, two people who had been strangers only days before made slow, intense love, neither of them sure of when next they would meet. Only sure that they would.

At last, as the building shook to the crash of a Lancaster several blocks away, she gave a sharp cry of pleasure as she moved beneath him.

Then they slept.

Chapter Three
Breakout

Korvettenkapitän Hans Kruger stood tensely on the cockpit gratings, the boat pulsing eagerly beneath his feet to the powerful throb of the diesel. The sound echoed back from the concrete walls and ceiling of the pen, a reminder that the moment of departure was almost there.

Kruger rested his elbows on the screen, looking down at the small deck party on the forecasing. Rausche, the boatswain, was pacing up and down, keeping an eye on his line handlers.

Overhead, the radar antenna was already turning on its mounting, as if in anticipation of the danger that would come the moment *U-2317* backed from beneath the protection of the massive concrete roof. Kruger considered that the most dangerous part of the journey would be right in Kiel Bay, where he would have to remain on the surface for nearly an hour. Unlike every other boat he had ever commanded, *U-2317* had no anti-aircraft weapons of any sort. She would have to depend on her escort in that respect.

Von Saltzmann had also promised to lay on some sort of fighter cover, if he could get the Luftwaffe to cooperate for a change. A few hours earlier, at their last meeting before sailing, the captain had complained bitterly about the lack of a proper Naval air arm, laying most of the blame squarely at Göring's feet.

"The fool is so jealous of his control over everything that flies," von Saltzmann had complained, "that the Navy is forced to go begging to him for even the tiniest bit of co-operation! We have *him* to blame, more than any lack of critical materials or time, for *Graf Zeppelin* never having been completed. The Luftwaffe has *exclusive* rights to any military aeroplanes produced, so why build a carrier?"

Kruger had merely listened. Few in the Navy had any particular love of the fat *Reichsmarschall*. He was at best a braggart, hopelessly overestimating the capabilities of his beloved Luftwaffe. The British would never have made it off the beaches at Dunkirk if Hitler had listened to his generals instead of an over-promoted Great War fighter ace.

"So do we get our air cover?" Kruger asked, when von Saltzmann had at last wound down.

"Maybe. That's all the local commander can tell me. Maybe."

Maybe, Kruger thought. It could be an epitaph.

There was the click of boots on the ladder and a moment later Wiegand emerged from the hatch into the tiny cockpit. Unlike her more conventional sisters, *U-2317* lacked the usual open bridge, her fin-like fairwater smoothly plated over at the top except for a small cockpit at the front. It provided just about enough room for the commander and one other officer. The bridge lookouts had to squeeze themselves into the corners as best they could.

As the boat would operate submerged most of the time, the inconvenience was not too great. And, so long as the radar was working properly, lookouts could almost be dispensed with.

Almost. Radar was not as effective as the human eye when it came to spotting objects in the water.

"All departments ready, sir," Wiegand reported. "Escort is waiting to lead us out."

"Thank you, Number One." Kruger looked aft, around the edge of the tower. "Seems damned odd not to have anti-aircraft guns manned at this point."

Wiegand nodded. "Very."

After a moment Kruger shrugged, snapping open the cover of a voice pipe. "Lookouts to the bridge!" he called. "Stand by to get under way!"

The lookouts scrambled up through the hatch, each with his powerful Zeiss glasses suspended on a strap around his neck.

"E-motor astern," Kruger ordered, "dead slow."

The diesel had no reversing gear, so any manoeuvring that required going astern was done using the E-motor. Now, as Kruger looked aft along the streamlined hull, he could see the white foam as the great screw began to go astern.

"Cast off all lines!"

The greasy wires splashed into the oily water, to be snatched out again by the line handlers on the walkway alongside. All it would need to get *U-2317*'s first war patrol off to a perfect start would be to wrap a wire around the screw. Even with the *Führer*'s intercession, the deadline had been extended only two days, and they were making that by only a few hours. An accident at this point would be fatal.

On the casing, the deck party was retracting the mooring bitts, swinging them around on their thick pivots, so that they would hang down inside the casing, presenting only smooth deck to the sea. Rausche was right behind them, bellowing at the top of his lungs, urging the men on. By the time the stern began to emerge from the pen, the casing was deserted, the main hatch sealed tight.

Now the cockpit had emerged from beneath the roof of the pen, the boat gliding smoothly astern.

"Starboard twenty," Kruger ordered. "Slow astern."

Now clear of the pen, *U-2317* began to swing awkwardly around, her blunt bow turning toward the open harbour. The engineers believed that her single screw would be more efficient when she was submerged, but it made for poor handling if she had to go astern. Anything more complex than a gentle turn would have required the assistance of a tug.

"Port fifteen. Stop E-motor. Engage engine clutch, ahead one-half. Commence charging."

"Escort signaling, sir," a lookout snapped. "Red four-five."

"He says, *Follow me*, sir" Wiegand reported.

"Midships," Kruger called. "Steer zero-one-eight."

It was not yet completely dark as they followed the battered trawler through the almost deserted anchorage. Kruger kept his glasses raised most of the time, only relaxing his vigilance to pass course changes down to the control room. Even here, in Kiel Bay, the historic heart of the German Navy, the danger of enemy attack was a constant that had to be guarded against.

Something white was moving at the end of the great Tirpitz Pier, which jutted out into the bay like a giant's finger. Kruger lifted his glasses and spun the focusing knob. He smiled. There was just enough light to make out the bulky figure of *Kapitän* von Saltzmann, looking heavier than ever in his greatcoat, at the end of the pier. The white object was a handkerchief, and it was not von Saltzmann, but the slim, well-muffled figure beside him, who was waving it.

Hannah.

Von Saltzmann would have known, of course. Kruger was fairly sure that part of the captain's job, even at the Christmas party, had been to keep an eye on his young charge. Hannah would have been one of the few he would have trusted.

Kruger took off his white cap and waved it slowly over his head, watching the handkerchief flutter more furiously in response.

Then the moment was past, and he was once again scanning sea and sky for any hint of danger. It was only the previous day that a departing U-boat had been sunk within a mile of the dock by an unsuspected mine. The RAF always seemed to drop a few whenever they came over, and the mine-sweeping forces at the base were hard pressed to keep up.

Behind and above him, the radar antenna whirled on its mount, further insurance against surprise from the air. Like everything else in the boat, it was the latest design, its operator the most skilled man available. So far he had reported nothing, so if the enemy was not out yet, neither was their air cover.

"I wish we could move faster," Wiegand muttered, after what seemed like hours of creeping along at six knots behind the battered trawler. "This place is making me nervous!"

Kruger looked at his watch. "We should be able to dive soon, Number One," he replied.

"Position for diving in five minutes, sir," a voice reported. After a moment, Kruger recognised it as Reuter's.

"There," he said, "only another five minutes."

Wiegand looked skeptical. "A lot can happen in that time," he said, remembering when things had fallen apart in Biscay in no more than 30 seconds.

"Bridge—Radar. Ten aircraft, bearing Red one-two-five, range 60 miles."

Kruger bent over the voice pipe. "Good work, von Sänger. Keep me advised."

Wiegand looked nervously over the port quarter, as if he expected to see the aircraft streaking down at him. Yet they were still 60 miles away, beyond the vision of even the best lookout, and probably not even aware of his existence.

"I think I'm going to like having radar," Kruger said.

Wiegand nodded dubiously. "I'm not sure, sir. It seems to me that at times like this all it does is give you more time to be nervous."

Reuter shouted up. "Position for diving, sir. Depth is 45 metres."

"Local conditions?"

"Bottom drops gradually from this point, sir."

"That's it, then," Kruger snapped. "Signal the trawler, *Am diving. Thanks for your help.*"

"He says, *Good hunting,* sir."

"Right. Clear the bridge." His hand pressed the red button just under the screen. "Alarm!!"

For a moment he was alone on the bridge, and then he was dropping down the ladder into the red-lit control room, sealing the hatches behind him.

"Secure radar," he ordered. "Take her down to 30 metres."

"Diesel stopped, sir! Main induction and exhaust sealed!"

"E-motor, ahead one half," Eisenberg snapped. "Bow planes down five, stern planes down five. Open main vents."

No more than 30 seconds after Kruger had ordered the dive, *U-2317* was leveling off at 30 metres. It wasn't deep enough for comfort, but in the darkness they should be invisible from the air, and it was not safe to go deeper in the shallow water.

"Trawler is going about, sir," von Sänger reported. Having secured his radar, the young leading hand was now seated at the S-gear screen, his earphones clapped securely to his head.

Kruger walked to the plot table and studied the chart for a moment. The dead reckoning plotter was ticking slowly, moving the lighted 'bug' under the tempered glass tabletop to correspond with *U-2317*'s movements.

"Steer zero-five-one for five minutes," Kruger ordered. "Those planes probably don't even know we're about, but there's no sense taking chances." They might, he thought, even be the promised air cover, arriving too late. But it was safer this way. 'Friendly' pilots had already sunk more than one boat.

"Trawler is taking evasive action," von Sänger reported.

Moments later the hull throbbed to the distant detonation of a string of bombs. So the planes *had* been the enemy, it seemed. Though no longer a threat to the boat, the blast seemed to go on for a long time, until at last there was a harder, more powerful detonation.

Von Sänger looked up from this screen. "Trawler has been destroyed, sir," he reported.

Kruger nodded slowly. "Resume former course," he said. "Revolutions for ten knots."

There was nothing more to say. A trawler had been blown up, men killed. Once it might have incited comment. Now it was just another loss, insignificant when compared to the others which had gone before.

An hour later, *U-2317* swam up to periscope depth and put up her *Schnorchel*, turning north-east to begin her passage up the Great Belt and out through the Kattegat and Skagerrak, into the killing ground of the North Atlantic.

●   ●   ●

Fregattenkapitän (Ing) Parsifal Eisenberg put down his engineering log with a feeling of extreme satisfaction. During two brief test runs that afternoon the cantankerous Walter turbine had behaved beautifully, and as yet there was no sign of any problems with the fuel system. That was always the biggest risk. The Perhydrol fuel, which was a 95% pure hydrogen-peroxide solution, was extremely corrosive, and in tests during development it had been discovered that the piping system was usually where any trouble would first be seen.

The whole project had been a gamble. Eisenberg suspected that he was probably more aware of that fact than any other man aboard. Even the captain would likely not know the full extent of the risks he was taking.

But Eisenberg had worked with Professor Walter on the development of the system, and there were still too many bugs in it for him to whole-heartedly recommend its adoption. More time was needed to perfect the system, and, but for the desperate nature of the strategic situation, more time might have been provided. As it was, even the riskiest proposals were being adopted.

So far, he had to admit, it seemed to be paying off.

He thought back to the second full-speed run that afternoon. The first had confirmed *U-2317*'s trial speed of 25.7 knots. But it was the second that seemed most revealing. The first run had been conducted at a depth of 100 metres, but for the second they had dived to 300 metres.

On that run their top speed had increased almost a full knot. Twenty-six point five knots, the fastest underwater speed ever recorded by a combat submarine. Surprisingly, this occurred as they were passing through 115 metres, when they were making revolutions for 20 knots, the boat suddenly leaping forward, while the revolutions unaccountably increased at the same time. No one had touched the throttle, so it obviously had something to do with the depth. He would have to see if he could come up with a reason for that.

It did give him reason to hope. That speed was considerably faster than most of the older escorts. Faster, for that matter, than most of the ships in the enemy's merchant fleet. A destroyer could keep up with them, but not harm them—at full speed her Asdic would be useless.

Seaman Ritter passed by, carrying a tool kit.

"Where are you going?" Eisenberg asked.

"Mister Himmler wanted a bit of help repairing one of the reload trolleys in the torpedo room, sir," Ritter replied. "Okay?"

"Know how they work?"

Ritter shrugged. "No, sir. But I've never actually looked at one of them up close, either. Shouldn't be too tricky."

"Right. Carry on, then." Eisenberg watched him go. *Shouldn't be too tricky.* That one was going to do just fine in the Navy, he thought. If there *is* a Navy when this is all over.

●   ●   ●

Marinestabsarzt[*] Wilhelm Zimmerman closed his book and smiled. May was so reliable. The hero always bested the villains in the end. It made for a good story, and even if it was true that May's version of the American West was totally inaccurate, as one of Zimmerman's colleagues, who had lived for a time in El Paso before the war, had asserted, it didn't really matter. *U-2317*'s Medical Officer had never been nearer the United States than *Deutschland*'s sickbay during her 1939 cruise, and wouldn't have known a cowboy from a red Indian in any case.

What he did know was that he enjoyed a rousing good adventure.

He grinned. He was certainly in the middle of one now. A U-boat with a surgeon aboard was not unique, but it was something that hadn't been done in a long time. Not since it was realised that most injuries in a U-boat would either be suf-

---

Marinestabsarzt. literally "Naval Staff Surgeon," the Medical Corps rank equivalent to *Kapitänleutnant.*

ficiently minor for a sick-berth attendant to handle, or would involve the entire crew being killed, and their doctor with them. There were still serious injuries, and men *had* died for want of proper medical care, but the casualty rate among the boats had been such that the high command had decided the Navy's limited number of physicians could be better utilised where they had a greater chance of survival.

Zimmerman had been practising surgery at the base hospital in Kiel when he was drafted into *U-2317*. He had almost deserted then and there.

Almost.

But service in a U-boat had also represented an escape of sorts. A retreat back into the Navy's historic mission—to seek out the enemy and destroy him. A few ships, and any number of U-boats, were still doing just that, but for the rest of the fleet the primary job seemed to be ferrying refugees from the eastern provinces.

The stories of what the Russians were doing to their own people, who were only *suspected* of having been friendly to the Germans, were bad enough. No one was anxious to experience what they would do once they actually reached German territory.

Too many of the refugees had wound up in the hospital. More were certain to follow. A few soldiers and sailors, but mostly women and children, many in desperate shape after their ordeal.

As dangerous as U-boat duty might be, it now seemed preferable to the suffering he had seen in the hospital.

• • •

"Captain in the control room!"

Kruger came through the door at a run, leaving a half-finished letter on his desk. "What is it?"

"Sound contact, sir," Wiegand reported. "Five vessels, moving in formation."

"Range and bearing?"

"Green zero-three, sir. Range four-five-two."

Kruger smiled. "Plenty of warning this time, eh, Number One?"

"Seems like it sir. A bit over 45 kilometres. Plenty of time to size up the situation, do as we see fit."

Kruger walked slowly to the after end of the control room, past the polished steel cylinders of the lowered periscopes, to the Engineering Officer's panel. "Shut down the diesel and lower the *Schnorchel*, Chief," he ordered. "Go to E-motor. Revolutions for 10 knots."

"Aye, aye, sir!" Eisenberg turned to his panel. "Out main engine clutch," he snapped. "Main E-motor, ahead one-half, revolutions for 10 knots. Kill main engine."

With its usual clattering grumble of protest the diesel rattled into silence as its fuel supply was cut off.

"Close main induction and exhaust."

"Main induction and exhaust sealed, sir," Ritter announced. "Boat secured for diving."

"Lower *Schnorchel* mast."

Kruger moved back to the front of the control room, standing over the control position. Instead of the usual helm position at the forward end of the control room, and two planes controls on the side, *U-2317* had two aircraft-style control yokes, placed side by side against the forward bulkhead. One controlled both the rudder and stern planes, while the other controlled the bow planes. Able Seaman Liebe was on the helm, with Stauber standing nearby, keeping an eye on things.

"How does she handle, Liebe?" Kruger asked.

The seaman looked up from the gyro and angle indicator for a moment. "Very easily, sir," he replied. "But you have to be very gentle at high speed."

"Responsive?"

"Too responsive, sometimes, sir. But you learn, and the controls are much simpler than on other boats."

Kruger nodded. The flat upper deck of a submarine had always been used as a control surface when diving, making it easier to go down quickly. Evidently no one had realised that the deck would have a much greater effect as a boat's underwater speed increased.

"Well, you seem to be doing a good job of it, Liebe. Keep it up."

"Aye, aye, sir."

Kapitänleutnant Rolf Wiegand watched curiously. The new captain seemed to have just the right touch, he thought. Normally, at this point, the men—the more experienced of them in particular—would be starting to get nervous. They'd been through it all before, some many times. The slow approach to the target, the exhilarating moment when the torpedoes were loosed at the unwary victim, and then the relentless hounding as the escorts came sniffing after the killer. In a U-boat, the transition from hunter to hunted was an accepted part of the attack.

It was not something you could ever get used to.

Kruger was probably more nervous than anyone aboard. His was the ultimate responsibility, his skill in evasion the difference between a bad shaking and death. And he had been at it, continuously, longer than many of them had been in the Navy.

"How does it feel, Number One?"

"Sir?"

"Going back into combat. This will be your first brush with the enemy since you were sunk, right?"

"Yes, sir." He frowned. How *did* it feel? "I really don't know, sir. In this boat it feels good. Not like that relic they gave me before. Without a *Schnorchel* it was a wonder we made it as far as we did before the Tommies caught up with us! But going back? I suppose I feel a bit less than completely enthusiastic. I've been sunk once and survived. I don't want to try for a second chance." He looked quickly around the control room, the men all in their places, waiting for the next move. "But I'm not in command this time," he added. "It takes a bit of the nervousness out of the picture. If we screw up this time, someone else takes the blame."

Meaning me, Kruger thought, nodding slowly. "Good answer," he said. "Though you do need to keep in mind that you *could* find yourself in command at almost any time."

"Just don't get in front of any stray bullets, sir."

"I'll try not to." Kruger moved over to von Sänger's little cubbyhole, peering over his shoulder at the glowing screen. "What's the range now?" he asked.

Von Sänger just kept staring at the screen, and after a moment Kruger realised he hadn't heard him. He tapped him on the shoulder, and the sound man turned questioningly.

"Range?"

"Four-zero-five, sir."

"Bearing?"

"Zero-zero, sir." Dead ahead.

"I'm going deeper now. Let me know when we're within range of the enemy's Asdic."

"Aye, aye, sir."

"Take her down," Kruger ordered. "Two hundred metres."

Eisenberg sprang from his seat, taking up a position behind the control position. "Bow and stern planes, down 10 degrees," he ordered. "Zero angle on the boat."

On an even keel, the boat began to swim down to her new depth, her powerful electric motor carrying her closer to her quarry.

Reuter looked up from the plot table. "Should be some worthwhile targets in the area," he commented. "We're damned close to the area where you say you were attacked on the way in, sir."

Kruger walked over to the plot table, studying the chart. They were nearing the mouth of the Skagerrak, about 50 miles south of Grimstad. It said a great deal about the way the war was going that the British were able to maintain a killer group in the area despite the presence of German air units from southern Norway and Jutland.

Was it the same group? The ones who had depth-charged *U-702* as she slipped back into Kiel for overhaul from her operational base at Kristiansand? It was at least possible. Equally, that group might have been replaced by now. One thing seemed certain—those would not be German ships waiting some 40 kilometres ahead.

Kruger slowly paced the length of the *Zentrale*, waiting patiently as the boat steamed ever closer to the waiting enemy. Minutes ticked away on the bulkhead clock, slowly turning into hours.

"Range to nearest target is now zero-five-zero, sir."

A bit over two hours had passed since their first contact. Close enough, Kruger thought, to start taking extra care. "Reduce to five knots," he said. "Rig for silent running."

"Out main E-motor clutch," Eisenberg snapped. "Switch to silent motor."

It was like being in church, Kruger thought. The hum of the main E-motor vanished as the silent motor was engaged. Unlike the main motor, which was connected directly to the shaft through a heavy clutch and also acted as the generator, the silent motor used heavy v-belts to turn the shaft. Together with the cunningly engineered screw, which was absolutely silent at speeds of five knots or less, it could propel the boat at nearly the top under-water speed of most older boats in eerie silence.

An enemy, listening with hydrophones, would hear nothing to warn of an approaching U-boat. The first sound he would hear would probably be the slam of the firing ram as a torpedo was sent on its way.

More time ticked by as they closed the range still further. At last, when they were within three kilometres of the closest target, Kruger moved to the attack periscope. "Take her up to periscope depth," he ordered. "Reduce to two knots." Unlike his old command, *U-2317*'s low, streamlined tower contained only a small escape trunk. Attacks were made from the control room.

Himmler was standing at his computer, ready to work out a target solution once he was given the target bearings.

"What's your load pattern?" Kruger asked.

"Midships tubes are LUT torpedoes, sir," Himmler reported. "The four bow tubes have the G7es. Those are the new models."

LUT torpedoes would travel in a straight line for a pre-set distance, then begin to loop in a carefully-determined pattern, until they encountered something to set them off. The G7es was an experimental type, never before tried in combat, which trailed a thin wire behind it, allowing an operator aboard the boat to listen to the sounds from the torpedo's acoustic sensors, and to adjust the course. Unlike the old T-5 acoustic homing torpedo, the operator could tell the difference between the target's screws and a towed noisemaker, and so insure the torpedo went where it would do some good.

"Be ready for anything," Kruger cautioned. "I'm going to see how close I can get, then we'll decide which torpedo to use."

"Aye, aye, sir."

"Fourteen metres, sir." Eisenberg reported. "Speed is two knots."

Kruger glanced at his watch. It would be dark in another hour, but he didn't want to wait. "Up periscope," he ordered. "Slowly!"

His eye was already pressed to the ocular as the head came clear of the water. "Enough!" he snapped. Only a few centimetres were out of the water. Quickly he walked the periscope in a full circle before letting the cross-hairs settle on the nearest vessel.

"Frigate," he said. "Loch class." He swung the periscope a few degrees. "Another frigate, about two kilometres astern the first." He snapped up the handles and the rating dropped the 'scope into its well. "There is also a small carrier beyond them. We'll go for her first, then worry about the escorts."

"The frigates should give us a chance to see just how well these new torpedoes actually work," Himmler commented. He depended upon the advances in technology that were said to have made the new wire-guided acoustic torpedoes far more reliable than the old types, but he would *trust* that technology only after he had personally seen the results.

Kruger nodded. "We'll use the midships tubes for the carrier. I'm going to try to get in close enough for us to hit him before they start looping."

"What range, sir?"

"Set them to start looping after one kilometer. And be ready to let go a G7 if one of the frigates picks us up in her Asdic."

"Aye, aye, sir."

Kruger looked across the control room at Eisenberg. "Take her down to 100 metres. Increase to five knots."

"Diving, sir. Revolutions for five knots."

Kruger stood rigidly by the attack periscope, expecting to hear the sharp 'ping' of a frigate's Asdic at almost any moment.

Wiegand, standing over von Sänger, looked up. "We're under the screen," he said.

"Five minutes more," Kruger ordered. "Then reduce to two knots and bring her back up to periscope depth."

It was so quiet that he could hear Himmler's breathing, and the occasional splash of condensation in the bilges. How is it that no one has noticed us yet? he wondered. Are they all incompetent up there?

"Time, sir."

Slowly the boat planed up, leveling off at 14 metres, the rounded top of her tower just beneath the ruffled surface of the Skagerrak.

"Periscope depth, sir."

Kruger's eye was fixed to the ocular as the image turned from deep green to pale blue, then dull tones of grey as the head cleared the water by bare centimetres.

"Got her," Kruger said. "She's landing aircraft, so she'll have to hold a steady course for the next few minutes."

He dipped the periscope beneath the surface. "Flood tubes five through seven," he ordered.

"Tubes five through seven are flooded, sir," Himmler reported, after a few moments.

"Open outer doors."

"Outer doors open, sir."

Up with the periscope again. "Target bearing—that!"

"One-six-nine."

"Angle on the bow—red nine-zero!"

"Angle red nine-zero, set!"

"Range—500 metres!"

"Range 500 metres, sir."

"Set depth at 7.5 metres."

Himmler spun his dial. "Seven point five metres, sir. Set."

"Five—loose!"

The boat shivered slightly as the firing ram cycled, shoving the torpedo from its snug tube.

"Five running, sir!"

"Six—loose!"

"Six running, sir!"

"Seven—loose!"

"Seven running, sir!"

Kruger put up the periscope again, swinging it around the check the escorts. Even a deaf man should have heard the torpedoes being fired, he thought. But neither of the visible escorts seemed to be concerned. There were no lights flashing, no running men on their decks.

He swung the periscope back onto the target just as a dirty brown column of water erupted at her waterline, just abaft the forward elevator. *U-2317* shook to the distant concussion, while the escort carrier, build on a converted merchant hull, veered from her set course, forcing a Seafire fighter to pull up awkwardly before slamming into the rear of the island, drenching the bridge and flight deck in blazing aviation fuel.

At five second intervals the remaining two torpedoes smashed into the little carrier's offered flank, tearing her guts out, so that she began to turn turtle in seconds.

Kruger swung the periscope onto the nearest escort, which was now charging down on them, working up to full speed. "Flood one and two!" he shouted.

"One and two are flooded, sir!"

"Open outer doors! Bearing—that!"

"Three-four-four, set!"

"Angle on the bow—zero!"

"Angle zero, set!"

"Set depth to 3.5 metres."

"Three point five metres, sir!"

"One—loose!"

The periscope hissed down into the well. Now came the hardest part. He would have to continue on his present course as the G7 rushed toward the charging frigate, lest any drastic manoeuvres should break the control wire. Nor could they go deep, with the outer door still open.

Wham!!

"Got him!" Himmler shouted.

"Close outer door. Come right, 50 degrees. Take her down to 100 metres." Kruger hesitated. "Turbine. Ahead—full!"

The turbine lit off with a sound like a cannon shot, and the silent hum of the E-motor was replaced by the shrill whine of the turbine and its attendant gearing.

"I'll bet they heard *that*," Wiegand commented.

"One hundred metres, sir," Eisenberg reported.

"Steering zero-one-six, sir," Liebe reported.

"What's our speed?"

"Twenty-four knots, sir."

"Present course and speed for three minutes," Kruger ordered. "Then go back to silent speed."

The frigate was going under. Even without the hydrophones they could hear it clearly. The acoustic torpedo had smashed into the charging frigate, blasting her bow wide open, and now all could hear the sound of her bulkheads collapsing under the impact, the muffled thunder as the sea roared triumphantly into her fire rooms, shattering the red-hot boilers.

"Ship breaking up, sir," von Sänger reported. "Bearing Green one-two-six."

One minute later the turbine was shut down and silence again fell over the boat.

Slowly, as the residual way fell off the boat, Kruger conned her around, back toward the enemy. The frigate was a definite kill, while the little escort carrier, though still afloat, was a total loss so far as the enemy was concerned. When he had ordered the boat down to avoid the charging frigate, the carrier had been floating precariously, her huge single screw uppermost, while her crew—those who had managed to get around in time—clung to her upturned bilges. The others, those in the water, were probably already dead.

Kruger walked over to von Sänger, peering over his shoulder at the ghostly glow of the screen. The image altered as von Sänger touched the key, sending a single ultra-sonic ping into the water. As he watched the newly returned echo appeared on the screen. *U-2317* was at the centre of the screen, with two small pips of light on a reciprocal course. Two other pips, a large and small one, marking the position of the capsized escort carrier and the remaining frigate, very close together, and Kruger guessed that the frigate was trying to take off as many of the carrier's crew as possible before the ship went under.

"Come up to 50 metres," Kruger ordered.

Eisenberg hovered over the controls, his eye on the telltales, as they brought the boat up to her new depth.

Staying by von Sänger's cubbyhole, Kruger looked back at Himmler. For this phase of the attack he would go by the book, making use of the tricks the engineers had dreamed up since his previous command was built.

"Flood tubes two through four."

"Two through four flooded, sir."

He touched von Sänger's shoulder. "Range to nearest targets?"

"Zero-two-seven, sir."

"Range is zero-two-seven. Bearing?"

"Number one is at zero-zero-five, sir," von Sänger replied. "Number two at three-five-eight."

"Number two eel, target bearing zero-zero-five," Kruger said. "Number three, bearing three-five-eight."

"Aye, aye, sir—zero-zero-five and three-five-eight. Set, sir!"

"Set depth at four metres."

"Four metres, sir!"

"Open outer doors, tubes two and three."

"Outer doors open, sir."

"Two—loose!"

At 50 metres depth, the shock of the firing ram was harder, more positive, forcing the 'eel' out against the greater sea pressure. Once ejected, the torpedo planed up to its pre-set depth as it streaked along the course dictated by its whirling gyroscope until it was close enough to the target for the operator to lock onto the noise of the frigate's screws.

"Two running," Himmler reported, as the light flashed on his panel.

Kruger waited impatiently as the first eel streaked on its way. In the bow, the operator would be hunched over his control—a simple, round knob, which could steer the torpedo to port or starboard as he listened to the target on stereophonic headphones. When the volume from both was identical, he would have the proper course. Depth was pre-set, and was not under the operator's control.

The double explosion came a bit over two minutes later, followed at once by the rending agony of the frigate taking her final plunge.

"Three—loose!"

"Three running, sir!"

With the torpedo's counter-rotating screws screaming, Kruger had von Sänger go briefly active on the *Nibelung*, allowing him to observe the second frigate as it started to turn away, as if afraid of hitting some wreckage, moments before the last eel blew her stern off, setting off the ready-use depth charges and sinking her in seconds.

That was it, then, Kruger thought. Time to fall back and consider what to do next. There was still another frigate up there.

"Come to course one-eight-zero," he ordered. "Take her down to 300 metres. Maintain silent speed."

"Three hundred metres, sir," Eisenberg reported.

"Thank you, L.I.. All compartments, report anything that looks to be a problem." They had been this deep before, but Kruger was still nervous. The boat seemed to be taking it well, with hardly any strain on her thick hull. Not like a *Typ* VII, which would be groaning in protest by now—if she hadn't actually collapsed under the enormous pressure.

Himmler was just coming back from the torpedo space when the boat gave a convulsive shudder, as if she had run headlong into an undersea mountain. Von Sänger yelled incoherently, ripping the headphones from his ears and leaping up from his seat.

"What the hell?" Wiegand shouted.

"It's the—the carrier, I guess, sir," von Sänger reported. "She's blown up." He banged his ear with his right palm. "God! You could go bloody deaf that way!"

"She was on fire when she capsized," Kruger mused. "The fire must have continued to burn internally until it reached a magazine, or possibly ignited petrol fumes from her storage tanks."

"Anything on the screen?" Wiegand asked.

Von Sänger resumed his seat, reluctantly pulling on his headphones and keying the *Nibelung*. He studied the screen for a long time, and when he looked up his voice was almost reverent.

"There are no ships in this area, sir," he said.

•   •   •

Captain David Ralston, DSC and Bar, stared dejectedly at the floating wreckage, which seemed to cover the sea for miles in all directions. Five ships gone, and all in no more than an hour. If the man weren't already dead he would have killed his 'best' hydrophone and Asdic operator himself. Only seconds before three torpedoes had smashed into *Snapper*, destroying her even as she attempted to recover her fighters before darkness, the operator had announced that there was no enemy activity in the area.

It had only been the sound of the torpedoes themselves that he had noticed—when it was too late to give a warning.

Nothing around! In minutes destruction was coming from all quarters, blasting apart the killer group he had worked so long to bring up to top-line efficiency. In the short time they'd had been patrolling the mouth of the Skagerrak they had accounted for three definite kills and another four probables.

And now this! *No enemy activity in the area.* Hell, they'd obviously wandered right into the midst of a damned wolf pack!

When his own ship, *Loch Grym*, was blasted apart, Ralston had only just managed to clamber aboard this raft. Two others, almost in reach of it, had gone with only feeble cries, the icy water sucking the strength from their limbs in seconds.

He could still see them, floating silently in their life jackets, the winking red rescue lights making their dead faces seem afire.

Ralston shivered suddenly. An odd rumbling sound from very close made him look around, and he gasped in something like horror, gaping at the slim, black tube of a submarine's periscope. He could almost swear that he could see the commander's eye, pressed against the ocular at the other end of the tube, which was directing its unblinking stare at him.

With a further roaring, the tube rose higher, and then the top of the submarine's fairwater emerged from the black water. Nothing more. Only the upper part of the tower, and the impression of a great mass of steel just beneath the surface.

Two seamen appeared at the front of the tower, each armed with an evil-looking Schmeisser, which was immediately pointed at Ralston. He didn't think they intended to kill him, but they were obviously taking no chances.

A third figure appeared in the cockpit, wearing a heavy leather watchcoat and a white cap, its peak surrounded by brass oak leaves. The captain, presumably.

"Need a ride?" the German called down, his English well accented, sounding vaguely upper class.

"Go to hell!" Ralston snapped.

The German laughed. "I probably shall," he replied. "But not just yet, eh?" The tower was now directly over Ralston's raft. "Come along now, Captain. I'm sure you don't wish to spend the night here!"

Ralston glared at him. Smug, arrogant bastard, he thought. Then he shrugged. The war was almost over, and a brief period behind barbed wire was certainly preferably to dying of exposure on this damned raft.

As one of the seamen helped him up the side of the tower, Ralston blinked, looking beyond him in disbelief at the whirling radar antenna, which bore a striking resemblance to an American unit. When did the Germans get *that* installed in their submarines? Come to that, just what sort of boat was this? The tower looked like nothing he had ever seen before.

"Welcome aboard," the German said. "I am *Korvettenkapitän* Hans Kruger, captain of *U-2317.*" He smiled. "Sorry about sinking your ship. I'm sure you'd have done the same to me, given the chance."

Ralston frowned. "Bloody right." He stamped his feet on the gratings and smashed his hand together. "Cold out here," he grunted.

"Then we shall get you below. I don't care to hang about on the surface in any case."

Ralston looked at him curiously. "Your wolf pack on the way in or out?" he asked.

Kruger said something in German and the others laughed. "What wolf pack?" he asked, in English. "As far as I'm aware, the closest boat right now is tied up in her pen in Kristiansand."

The man was lying, Ralston thought, as they guided him down the ladder and into the tiny escape trunk in the tower. The attacks had come from widely separated points on the compass. No submarine could cover the distances involved in the brief time elapsed.

Then the others were also in the trunk, the captain sealing the hatch, guiding him down a second ladder into the red-lit control room.

"Untertauchen!" Kruger ordered. *"Dreihundert Meter! Steuern drei-sieben-fünf. Walterturbine voraus—voll!"*

Ralston jumped as something gave a great 'bang!' right aft, looking around apprehensively as the boat seemed to leap out from under his feet with the sort of acceleration he was used to feeling in his frigate. He hadn't served in submarines since before the war, but he knew that something was drastically different about this boat. The whine of gears, more typical of a surface warship's turbines than the electric motors of a submarine, added to the sense of unease.

Another thing—all of the officers were wearing dress uniform, instead of the mix of battledress and old civilian clothes he had always seen when they rescued one of their victims after a kill.

A stocky officer, wearing the uniform of a full commander, with an engineer officer's cogwheel over the upper stripe, was watching a dial above the control wheels. The depth gauge, Ralston supposed.

"Dreihundert Meter, Kapitän," the officer said.

Ralston studied the gauge. Three hundred feet. The graduations stopped at 500, he noticed, wondering if they ever actually went that deep. The scale turned bright red at the 350 foot level, so that was probably test depth.

Then he looked at the manometer more closely. *Tiefenmesser*, it was labeled. Ralston had no German, but it was close enough in sound that he presumed it meant depth gauge. But there was a further label. *mWASSER*. Well, 'wasser' was obviously 'water.' Even he could understand that. But the little "m" before it?

Christ! he thought, suddenly. This was a *German* submarine, and Germans, being Germans, didn't use feet in their measurements. They used metres, which meant that it must be 300 *metres* from the keel to the surface! Nearly a thousand bloody feet. It was deeper than any reasonable escort command would ever believe a submarine could dive. Deeper, certainly, than he'd ever set his own depth charges.

"Are we really that deep?" he asked the captain.

Kruger looked at the gauge. "Seems that way," he said. He sounded quite nonchalant, as if there was nothing in the least unusual about a submarine operating at such depths.

"Now," Kruger said, "come along with me, Captain. I'll let my doctor have a look at you and then we'll find you a place to sleep for the next day or two."

"Where are we going?"

Kruger shrugged. "I don't suppose it matters if you know. Bergen. You'll be landed there. Then, I suppose, a prisoner of war camp, once they get any information they need from you."

Ralston shuddered. He'd willingly give the Geneva Convention information of name, rank, and number, expecting it to be duly reported to the Swiss Red Cross inspectors and thence passed back to London, where his family would be notified that he was still alive. His ex-wife, who was still listed as a person-to-be-notified, probably wouldn't give a damn, but he thought that his parents would at least be relieved to hear it.

But there was other information he could also give. Information that he would *not* give willingly. Information they would want.

They would have to torture it out of him. He shuddered again. His captor appeared to be simply a professional Naval officer, and as such quite ready to observe all the rules of civilised warfare so far as they reasonably applied to his particular speciality. Despite the propaganda, he suspected that most U-boat officers were little different from British submariners. But his interrogators? Would they also be Navy?

Or Gestapo?

It didn't bear thinking.

Chapter Four

News From Home

It was exactly one hour after sunset when *U-2317* rose streaming to the surface and made her pre-arranged signal to the pair of powerful fleet destroyers that would guide her into Bergen. The high command was taking no chances this time. The boat had proven her value, and was to be afforded the maximum protection available.

They had been at sea for two weeks, working the last kinks out of the boat, and in that time Kruger had begun to regard the surface of the sea as a place to be generally avoided. With her powerful air search radar, *U-2317* wasn't nearly as vulnerable to surprise attack as the older boats, but Kruger was one of the most experienced captains, and aware that that an equally deadly killer was another submarine. But British submarines could strike only when their target was surfaced, which provided an added incentive to stay down and use the *Schnorchel.*

In any case, in a boat such as his, long submergence was not really a handicap. The carbon dioxide scrubbers kept the air pure and breathable, even when running deep for an extended period.

Even the Englishman, Ralston, who had admitted to being a former submarine commander, had grudgingly said that he'd never seen a finer boat.

Once the doctor had finished with the Englishman, Kruger had put him in the wardroom, with Eisenberg and Reuter, the only other English-speaking officers, keeping an eye on him. The wardroom steward, Seaman Schwartz, had also kept his ears open, having learnt English as a steward in the Hamburg-Amerika Line before the war.

Schwartz was the spy, Kruger thought. Unlike the two officers, he never let on that he could understand what was being said. There was always a chance the Englishman might say something useful when he believed no one could understand him.

"Bridge—radar. Two contacts, bearing Green five-zero, range five-eight-zero. Course is zero-one-two."

Kruger bent over the voice pipe. "Thank you. Keep an eye on them and let me know if you make any more contacts." He turned to a young signalman, who was standing in the corner of the cockpit. "Call up the leading escort. He'll want to know about that contact."

It was probably nothing to worry about, Kruger thought. A pair of friendlies, most likely on their way to Trondheim. Well inland, and therefore no danger unless they changed course.

"Permission to come on the bridge?"

Kruger looked down the hatch at the doctor's smiling face. It was too shallow to dive here, so one more wouldn't make that much difference. "Come on up, Doc," he said.

Zimmerman climbed unsteadily through the narrow hatch and stood next to Kruger. For a moment he said nothing, his eyes fixed on the tiny spot of brilliance winking from the destroyer's bridge.

"Trouble?" he asked.

"Escort says, *Thank you*, sir," the signalman reported.

"Doesn't sound like it," Kruger said, smiling. "But you can never be certain."

"Surely we'll not be attacked here, sir?"

Kruger shrugged. "Why not, Doc? Lately the enemy drop their bombs just about anywhere they like. Just ask the men who were in *Tirpitz*."

"Or my family in Berlin," Zimmerman added, nodding glumly. "Their house was destroyed while I was on leave a few months ago." He frowned. "Luckily, no one was home at the time."

"Yes. Lucky." Kruger thought of another house—one where the family had not been away when their world was blasted into fragments.

"It's different," Zimmerman offered.

"What is?"

"Being in a submarine. I've been in the Navy since I finished my surgical training in 1938, but this is the first time I've ever even been *aboard* a U-boat. Much less served in one."

"You've been to sea before, though?"

"In *Deutschland*—before they changed her name. I was supposed to sail in *Bismarck*, too, but my appendix decided to act up the day before we were to sail. I went into hospital and another surgeon sailed in my place."

"You sound like a lucky fellow, Doc. Maybe we should keep you around."

"I doubt if my replacement in *Bismarck* would have seen it that way, sir."

"Probably not," Kruger admitted. "Still, this boat isn't at all a bad place to be, though I suppose you'd feel a bit safer ashore?"

"I don't think so," Zimmerman said. "Don't forget, sir— when you're operating you can't just dash off to the nearest shelter whenever the air raid warning goes off. You just have to keep working and hope like hell that nothing gets too close."

"At least you've a red cross on your roof. That should help a bit."

Zimmerman laughed. "Doesn't help that much. Particularly at night."

"Well," Kruger said, "you seem to have survived well enough."

"I do my best, sir. But I can tell you, I don't miss that hospital. Not now, not with all the refugees being brought back as the Russians advance."

Kruger nodded, leaning against the screen. "There will be a great many more refugees before long," he said. "I've been told by people who should know that the *Grossadmiral*'s main job right now is arranging for the evacuation of as many people as possible from the eastern provinces." He grimaced. "I suppose they feel the Russians will occupy anything they take forever, if given any sort of chance."

The doctor smiled. "As we would have their country, sir."

"True enough." Kruger looked at him coldly. "We would have been right through Russia and linked up with our Japanese allies at Vladivostok by now if a few men in high places had been less brutal and more intelligent. Did you know that the Ukrainians consider themselves a conquered nation? That they *hate* the Russians? My brother was there and saw it happening. When our armies marched in they were greeted as liberators!

"But the men who came *after* the Army changed all that. I'm told that the *Gauleiter*, Koch, had over 2,000 landowners murdered in order to provide himself with a hunting preserve. That the SS went about slaughtering civilians by the thousands, for no obvious reason except that they were Slavs."

"You hear stories," Zimmerman said. "There are always stories. But are they really true, sir? No one could be as brutal as some people would have you believe!"

"Just what is brutality, Doc? You're a Naval surgeon, so you've been given training in triage techniques, right?"

"Naturally, sir. It's just common sense—when you have a large number of casualties you separate them into three groups. The first will die no matter what you do, so you fill them with morphine for the pain and let them die. The second are in serious need of treatment, but can survive, so you treat them first. The third have only minor injuries and can be safely left for last."

"Which means," Kruger said, "that those with the most serious injuries, those most in *need* of treatment, are left to die!"

The doctor nodded. "Yes. But most would die even if they were treated, and in the meantime you've taken time that means the difference between a less grievously wounded man living or dying."

"How much difference do you think there is, really, between simply letting a man die, and deliberately killing him because you consider him to be inferior? That he is taking up a space that could be better utilised by a superior individual? How much difference is there?"

"Doctors do not kill, sir. It would be against all our training."

"That's not really an answer," Kruger said. "But it tells me a lot about what you might do. You would never intentionally take another human life. You'd also like to believe that no other physician would do so."

"Something like that, sir."

"Which is why you're a doctor and not an SS officer, eh? *They* don't baulk at killing, whether there's a good reason or not."

Zimmerman shivered. It wasn't wise to talk about such things where anyone could hear. "Cold as hell up here, isn't it, sir?" he said.

"You get used to it." Kruger grinned suddenly. He had said much the same thing to Hannah at the Christmas party, on the balcony of Admiral Wünche's mansion in Potsdam. She'd probably be in her quarters by now, perhaps thinking of him.

He had meant every word he said that night. He *was* going to make it back from this job, take her back to what was left of Emden and go into business with his uncle. He had received a long letter from him on the day they sailed from Kiel. The business was still there, languishing at the moment with most of the skilled building workers off in the military, but waiting for the war to end and business to boom as all the work of rebuilding a shattered city began.

It wouldn't be much longer. He was sure of that now. The Ardennes Offensive had collapsed, just as von Saltzmann had predicted, when the supplies had begun to run out. They had been gambling that the enemy would break, but in Belgium they had held, and now it was the German Army that was in retreat.

This time, it appeared, they would at least be allowed to do so. It had been Hitler's obstinate refusal to let Field Marshall Paulus fight his way out of the trap at Stalingrad that had cost Otto his life.

Probably. There was always a chance that he was still alive, but Kruger wondered if it might not be better if he was not. It was said that the Russians did not so much take prisoners as they did slaves.

"Bridge—Radar. Aircraft, bearing Green two-seven. Range zero-eight-six and closing."

"Inform our escort," Kruger snapped.

"Escort's acknowledged, sir."

"Everyone keep your eyes open. We can't dive, so if we're jumped just take cover as best you can."

Zimmerman swallowed hard. "I believe I'll go below now," he said.

"Suit yourself, Doc."

"Escort's signaling, sir. *Aircraft are friendly. Our Hermann is helping tonight.*"

Air cover, Kruger thought. Nice when you could get it, yet it still paid to be cautious. The Luftwaffe had sunk more than one U-boat in this war, but if these planes had been called out purposely to provide air cover then it would be unlikely they would start shooting.

Besides, German aviators weren't the only ones with poor eyesight. There were also a few British submarines on the bottom after an encounter with a 'friendly' aircraft.

"Aircraft," a lookout snapped. "Green two-zero!"

Kruger trained his powerful glasses over the screen. In the darkness the planes were hard to pick out, but after a moment he saw them. Black against the night sky, there were four of them, flying in a loose formation. Bf110G-4s, the heart of Germany's night-fighter forces.

Kruger's friends in the Luftwaffe had ridiculed the twin-boomed fighters during the assault on England in the summer of 1940. Hopelessly outmatched by the Hurricanes and Spitfires thrown against them, they had spent most of their time flying in circles, one behind the other. With inadequate manoeuvrability and an almost useless rearward defence, the only way they stood a chance was to cover each other.

But that had been in daytime. Now, reorganised as night fighters, the *Zorstörers* had shown their true value when thrown against the massive British bomber formations. For if their rear armament of two 7.62 millimetre machine-guns was next to useless, their forward weaponry, a pair each of 30 and 20 millimetre cannon, was formidable indeed.

For the next two hours the big fighters kept watch as the three vessels made their way up channel to the safety of Bergen. Then they flew away, back to their base and a hot supper, while Kruger gingerly conned his command into the submarine base.

Once there, no time was wasted getting *U-2317* beneath the concrete roof of a pen. Norwegian nights are very long in mid-January, but no one was about to leave the most modern U-boat in the fleet out in the open for one minute longer than was absolutely necessary.

• • •

Kapitän von Saltzmann was waiting when Kruger climbed out of the carefully guarded entrance of the U-boat pen. There was an old Volkswagen sedan parked close by. A pre-war model, it was one of the few that had been produced between the time when Hitler had touted Doctor Porsche's diminutive vehicle as an affordable car for the German worker and the day when war production quotas put an end to civilian automobile manufacture in the Third Reich.

"I've got some transport," von Saltzmann said. "Had to pull a few strings, but she's mine—which also means yours— as long as I'm here." He opened the door. "You have your pistol with you?"

"On the boat."

"Never mind. I've got mine, and there's a Schmeisser on the passenger's seat. Any trouble, use that."

The engine started on the third try, and von Saltzmann put the little car into gear. "I don't think I need to tell you just how much of a commotion your signal caused," he said.

Kruger smiled. "I'm not surprised. It's not the sort of thing we've been doing lately."

While they were picking Ralston off his raft, Ostermann, the radio operator, had sent off a coded message to headquarters. *Have sunk one escort carrier and four frigates. No enemy warships remain in Skagerrak. Kruger.*

"All in one day, too," von Saltzmann enthused. "I think there's some sort of record there."

"A little over an hour, actually, sir. One 7,900-ton escort carrier, and four 1,400-ton frigates. Almost 14,000 tons, with only six torpedoes expended. Not at all a bad day's work."

"All warships, too," von Saltzmann added. "It took the enemy six days to replace them, and in that time 17 U-boats were able to sortie from Kiel."

Kruger grinned. "It was astonishing. At speed, *U-2317* is almost invulnerable. And the deeper she dives, the faster she is. At 300 metres she picks up almost a full knot over her trial speed."

The captain nodded. "Which is already faster than most of the enemy's escorts."

Von Saltzmann stopped at the gate, while a Naval Policeman checked their identity cards and made sure that both men were armed. "The Underground has been more active lately," von Saltzmann explained. "Particularly since the collapse in the Ardennes."

"You predicted that."

"I know. I'm not pleased to be proved right, though."

Kruger peered out the windows as they drove into the city. Here and there someone moved about, glancing curiously at the nondescript little car. Their glances made him uneasy. It was just as von Saltzmann had said. Some Norwegians, the government included, were friendly enough. But the majority of the people merely tolerated their conquerors, and were more than willing to do whatever they could in the form of murder and sabotage.

"We brought back a souvenir, by the way," Kruger said.

Von Saltzmann glanced at him curiously, then put his eyes back on the road. "What sort?" he asked.

"A British captain, complete with Distinguished Service Cross and Bar. Policy is against rescuing survivors, of course, but for a full captain I'll make an exception. Particularly if he's by himself on a raft, and there is no real danger in picking him up."

"Did he appreciate it?"

"Not much. I believe him to have been the group's commander. His rank suggests it, at least. When we first picked him up he was convinced that he'd stumbled into the midst of a wolf pack. It gave me an idea, though."

"What might that be?"

"We could use my boat in a wolf pack. A real one."

Von Saltzmann shook his head. "Not practical. There's only one like her, and you can hardly have a wolf pack consisting of a single boat."

"The other boats wouldn't have to be of the same type, sir. If I could operate with several of the new *Typ* XXIs it would be wonderful, but a half-dozen old *Typ* VIIs would do just as well."

"Just what do you have in mind?"

"We form the wolf pack in the usual way, but just before nightfall *U-2317* goes in alone and takes out all the escorts. With those eliminated, the other boats can go in on the surface in safety, so long as we stay out of reach of land-based aircraft."

Von Saltzmann grinned. "It could work," he conceded. "Most enemy merchantmen are armed, of course, but even with Navy gunners they don't exactly have the most modern weapons, and a U-boat doesn't present much of a target in the dark."

"So we can try, sir?"

"I'll have to take it up with my superiors, but I think it's worth a try. Equally, with what you've accomplished, they may want you to just continue what you've been doing. By yourself you're probably worth a dozen older boats."

The planner downshifted around a corner, his eyes darting nervously in all directions as he did so. The damned Underground seemed to have a fondness for blind turnings, and it was not at all uncommon to hear of an official car crashing headlong into a building at one, its driver dead after rounding the corner directly into a spray of machine-pistol bullets. It sometimes seemed that everyone in the bloody country had a Sten gun hidden away somewhere, just waiting for a chance to use it to riddle some poor German.

"How much do you suppose your Britisher knows about your boat?" von Saltzmann asked. "We'll get some useful information out of him, I expect, but there *was* a certain security risk in picking him up."

"Expecting him to get away?"

"I hope not. But you can never be certain. If he *does* manage to escape, I'd like to know just what he might be able to tell his superiors."

"I wouldn't think he knows too much, sir," Kruger said. "He is certainly aware of her diving depth—he was staring at the manometer as if it were about to bite him. I'm sure he's also aware that we are much faster than a normal U-boat, though I doubt he realises by how much."

"Does he understand German?"

"Not that I could tell. His contact was essentially limited to the officers, and besides myself only *Fregattenkapitän* Eisenberg and *Oberleutnant* Reuter speak English. Seaman Schwartz as well, but he was told to keep his mouth shut and his ears open."

"Did he hear anything?"

"No. Nothing of value, at least. Also, if Ralston *does* speak German, he is a man of remarkable self-control, considering the things I've called him, or suggested he'd done with various close relatives and household pets. I might as well have been reciting the alphabet for all the reaction I got."

Von Saltzmann pulled up to the kerb in front of the commandeered hotel that served as quarters for visiting officers and officials. "We're here," he announced.

An Army lance-corporal, carrying his Schmeisser at the ready, came down the steps and peered into the car, nodding when he recognised von Saltzmann as one of the hotel's temporary residents.

"Good evening, gentlemen," he said, as the two officers climbed out of the car.

The two Naval officers returned the soldier's salute, then walked quickly up the steps to the light trap at the door. "That soldier can't be over 18," Kruger commented.

"Probably not even that, Hans." Von Saltzmann looked down the steps for a moment, shaking his head. "Too many men have died in this war. Or been captured. Any real fighting men have been transferred to the two main fronts, so now our Army of Occupation seems to be composed entirely of old men and children."

•   •   •

Fregattenkapitän (Ing) Parsifal Eisenberg made a few final entries in his journal, then undressed and climbed into his bunk. I'm going to miss this boat, he thought. One more patrol, getting the final kinks worked out of her, and then it will probably be back to Danzig, to make use of the experience here to prepare the new generation of boats. This can't last much longer. It's just not normal for a boat to have an L.I. who outranks her captain.

I think I may even miss the Englishman. A bit boring at times, rattling on about how they were certain to win, what with the bloody Yanks pitching in with their men and their so-far untouchable industrial facilities. But he could also be charming when he wanted to be, and his stories of submarine operations between the wars—a period he knew damned well was of no intelligence value, and so could be spoken of with impunity—were fascinating.

Still, for all his bluster, I suspect he was genuinely worried that this boat, and a few more like her, could still turn things around. Unbombable factories are of little value if their products have to be sent in ships that can't survive the voyage across the North Atlantic.

He clasped his hands behind his head, looking up at the sagging springs of the bunk above his. Himmler's. A likeable little man, if you were willing to excuse his tendency to hop into bed with any female who offered. It simply wasn't the sort of behaviour one expected of a married man.

Eisenberg thought of his own wife and four young children. As far as he was aware, they were still in Danzig. Arrangements would have to be made for them to leave. His aunt in Bayreuth would be happy to take them in, if they could manage to get there.

His family had recently become a source of considerable anxiety. Before, they had been as safe in Danzig as they would be anywhere else in Germany. But now it seemed certain that it would be the Russians who eventually marched into that city, and Eisenberg wanted none of his family there when they did.

Not after what had happened at Nemmersdorf. After the East Prussian town was captured, the Soviet commanders had encouraged their troops to do as they wished with the German population. During their stay, indiscriminate murder and rape became the norm. When German troops retook the town five days later there were only a handful of survivors.

Eisenberg was aware that he would not, himself, be given any choice about going back. His capture would be a risk the high command would be willing to take, just so long as his expertise was made available in the U-boat construction programme under way there. A miracle was needed, and only the new boats could provide it. With the Danzig shipyards so far escaping the worst of the enemy's bombs, it was the most logical place for him to be employed.

No one expected to actually win the war now, he thought. Probably not even the *Führer*. But if we can get enough of the new boats ready, deployed at sea and wreaking havoc in the shipping lanes, perhaps we will be able to dictate surrender term that will not fatally damage our country. Perhaps even manage a separate peace with the British and Americans—even gain their help against the Russians.

If not, then Germany is doomed. The Russians will see to it that we're never again in a position to threaten them.

Eisenberg closed his eyes. Just get out, Rosa, he thought. You and the children—get out of Danzig while you still can!

● ● ●

"Is this where the torture starts?"

The young *Korvettenkapitän* studied his prisoner curiously. There was no making sense of their fears, he thought. This irrational terror that all British prisoners seemed to have of being tortured. As if they had been handed over to the

Gestapo, rather than Naval Intelligence. He shook his head, smiling slightly. He would get the information out of this man, certainly. But he doubted that any torture would be needed.

It only needs being smarter than your subject, he thought.

"Just tell me your name." He smiled reassuringly. "No torture, really."

"David James Ralston. And I don't think I believe you."

The young interrogator shrugged, his eyes darting momentarily to the pretty Women's Corps stenographer in the corner, who was taking down every word on her pad. Like him, she had been chosen for her job because of her excellent command of English. She also had very good legs, which he thought of as a nice bonus.

The interrogator had been born in Frankfurt, but spent the first 16 years of his life in London, where his father had been on the embassy staff. There were times when he believed that his English was actually better than his native language.

"Pity," he said. "Rank?"

"Captain, of course," Ralston snapped, glaring at him. "Are you bloody blind?"

"I see four rings on your sleeves, sir. You do not, however, have an identity card, so for all I know you may actually be the captain's steward who nicked his uniform as the ship was sinking in hope of receiving better treatment."

"I was the bloody captain of *Loch Grym!*"

Out of Ralston's sight, the stenographer's pencil moved across her pad. The interrogator suppressed a smile. All it takes is to get them mad at you and they'll tell you their bloody life story. Much easier than torture, really. If he had simply asked the name of the man's ship he would have closed up tighter than a paymaster's pocketbook.

"That remains to be seen," he said. "Number?"

"17783390. And not a bloody thing more!"

"Fine. That's all you're required to tell me, isn't it, Captain?"

"Bloody right."

"In any event, we already know you were just a minor character in this little operation. Captain of a little frigate who couldn't manage to protect the carrier he was supposed to guard."

"We did a damned fine job!" Ralston growled. "Not my bloody fault you Jerries have come up with a weapon we were unprepared for."

"We do our best, sir. And, in any event, as I recall from my history, the last time England was actually *ready* for a war was when Napoleon broke loose from Elba."

"We're prepared now. We're bloody winning, aren't we?"

"Are you? I was under the impression that it was the *loser* of a battle who was generally sunk. Besides—not your fault. You can blame your senior officer for that little fiasco, eh?"

"I *was* the damned senior officer, you bloody squarehead!"

The interrogator laughed. "You? You're only a captain. No, there'd have been at least a commodore, maybe a rear-admiral, in the carrier, running the whole show."

"I was senior officer of the group, damn you. Me!"

"Sure you were. Probably don't even know what the other ships were called, or who commanded them."

Ralston half rose from his chair. "There was *Snapper*, the escort carrier, under Captain Alden. The only other captain, and he was junior to me by two bloody years!"

Behind the British captain, the stenographer was grinning, her pencil flying as the rest of it poured out. The fool was going to tell them every detail they wanted, she thought. But Strasser *was* a master at that sort of thing. Find a weak point and exploit it to the full.

With this man it was obviously vanity. With others it would be fear, or pride, or stupidity, or even—disgustingly—greed.

In a few minutes, she thought, he'll probably tell us the address of his mother's house.

•　　•　　•

Leading Seaman Heinz von Sänger touched the tip of the soldering pencil to the connection, carefully brushing on the flux and then applying the solder. Even in a brand-new boat there were always problems, he thought. This wireless, for instance. It should have been as near to perfect as any, yet there had been this almost hidden fault. Whoever had made the original connection at the factory had failed to heat the wire sufficiently, so that the solder had simply beaded on the joint, but not penetrated. It *looked* solid, but wasn't.

Simple enough to put right—provided you knew where to look for it in the first place.

It wouldn't be long before they had to start assigning an officer to look after all the complex new electronic gear they were stuffing into the latest boats. For the moment Petty Officer Ostermann, the radio operator and von Sänger's immediate superior, was in charge of the electronics, but he did not expect it to last much longer. Any time something started to get very complicated, the Navy would decide it needed an officer to look after it.

Frequently, the officer assigned would know nothing about his new job, and would have to rely on the rating or petty officer he had replaced to get it done properly. But at least the Navy would have found a job for one more junior officer. And, in this boat, there were already several officers doing jobs that would normally fall to a petty officer.

In an odd way, Himmler was an example. In the older boats, the Executive Officer handled the torpedoes and served as attack coordinator, feeding the captain's instructions and bearing into the computer. Now, with the more complex torpedoes and tubes installed in this boat, a separate officer had been detailed to look after them, leaving the Exec to serve mainly as a watch-keeper and administrative officer.

And understudy, in case something should happen to the captain.

Screwing the access panel back onto the wireless, von Sänger packed up his tool kit and smiled. With this job done, he had the rest of the day free. He could even take a run ashore, if he felt like it. There were some lovely girls in Bergen, and not all of them were unwilling to be friendly. He might see what was available, after he finished his letter.

Von Sänger was married. He even considered himself to be a good husband and, in a shore job, would probably never have done more than look at any woman but his wife. But he was a U-boat sailor, and there was never any assurance he would ever see his wife again. No assurance that he would ever see *any* woman. He cared nothing for the prostitutes he slept with. They were just a substitute for his wife—an itch to be scratched, then forgotten.

When *U-2317* arrived in Bergen there had been single letter waiting for him. It was chatty, carefree—as if the war was of no concern to her. He still couldn't understand how she could manage that. With all the shortages, the meager rations, and the constant threat from enemy bombers, it was a wonder she could manage at all.

He knew for a certainty that she had *not* moved from their small flat in Linz due to the availability of something better, regardless of what she put in her letter. A friend had told him the truth—the building had been knocked flat by an American bomb while she was at work.

Yet she had never said so. It was as if she was willing to lie about the problems, the constant worries and miseries at home, so that he might have less to worry about while he was at sea.

Von Sänger wanted to reassure her. To tell her that in this boat he was probably safer than he would be on land. But that was impossible, with *U-2317* still very much on the secret list. Greta would simply have to continue worrying.

The only thing she knew about his present posting was the number of his boat. She knew nothing of its type, nor even where it was stationed. Unlike the Americans, who had numbered all of their submarines consecutively since the first was commissioned, U-boats were numbered in blocks, with each series assigned to a particular builder. A more advanced boat, under this system, could have a lower number than an older type.

He pulled out his pad, and the old fountain pen his father had presented him when he was graduated from Gymnasium. *My Darling Greta*, he wrote. *We are now safe in port...*

• • •

"Careful with those bloody things!" Himmler bellowed, as the working party gingerly guided a new torpedo through the open hatch. It was the one job he always hated. While it was exceedingly rare for a brand-new 'eel' to blow up, it would only take one time to finish both him and the boat.

"Don't blow your stack, Karl," Eisenberg said. "Those things make me nervous enough as it is!"

Himmler shrugged. "So does your turbine."

"True. But it seems to be behaving itself just now."

"So far, you mean?"

"So far." The Chief smiled. "It's actually behaving itself rather better than I'd expected, if you want the truth."

Himmler nodded. "I don't, particularly. You know, Chief, it never fails, does it? Here we finally have a U-boat that's as near to being a true submarine as you could want, torpedoes that work the way they were intended, hydrophones that can pick up an enemy vessel at 50 miles, sound gear that can locate him precisely, and even the ability to dive deeper than the enemy can set his charges." He grimaced. "And to make it all perfect, we also have that bloody turbine, which at any moment may take it into its head to blow up and accomplish what the British escorts can't!"

Eisenberg laughed. "That's not a bad assessment of the situation, Karl. We run Perhydrol through a catalyst, which splits it into water and oxygen, then mix *that* with diesel fuel in a combustion chamber. That creates superheated steam and we use that to drive the turbine. When you stop to think about it, it's a bit like tying down a V-2 and holding a paddle-fan in front of the exhaust. A controlled explosion."

"Just so you keep it controlled." Himmler paused to watch as the crew rigged another torpedo for loading. Another experimental model, this one with an active sonar homing system. With no reloads being carried, loading was somewhat slowed down, as each torpedo had to be loaded into the tube immediately upon being take aboard.

It did leave a bit more room for bunks, though.

"We're keeping a close watch on things," Eisenberg said. "I don't like taking chances. I even have one of my stokers assigned to do nothing but keep a constant watch on the piping system for the Perhydrol fuel. That's where the greatest danger is."

"Just keep a bloody *good* watch on— Hey! Careful with that bloody tackle, you stupid sod! You trying to bash someone in the head with it?"

Eisenberg chuckled. "Well, enjoy yourself, eh? I'm off to town."

Himmler nodded, then turned to glare at the offending seaman. He'd have the bloody lunatic's head if there was an accident. Even if his father *was* an *SS-Obergruppenfüher*.

•   •   •

Kapitän zur See Siegfried von Saltzmann read the decoded signal a third time, wondering what his proper course should be. It was the sort of thing that happened every day, yet this time it might cause enormous problems. Perhaps even destroy the entire project.

Still unsure what he should do, he folded the pink sheet and thrust it into the inside pocket of his reefer jacket. He would walk the whole way from his commandeered office to the pen.

Perhaps somewhere along the way he would find the wisdom to do the proper thing.

•   •   •

Kruger finished his inspection in the tiny sickbay. Two bunks and the doctor's desk, with the cabinets for his instruments and medicines. There was even provision for setting up an operating table, should that become necessary.

After the next patrol Zimmerman was scheduled to go ashore, his place being taken by a petty officer sick-berth attendant, who would be capable of taking care of the majority of injuries likely to be encountered in a U-boat. Even minor surgery, if there was no other choice. It had been done before, and Kruger remembered seeing a captured American film that featured an emergency appendectomy aboard a fleet boat in the Pacific. As he recalled, the boat portrayed was extremely primitive. More so, perhaps, than even the old 'pig boats' of the First War. Security, probably—Hollywood would show old-style techniques, while the actual boats used the most modern equipment available.

No one, after all, was likely to drop real depth charges on Cary Grant.

"Looks fine," Kruger said. "Spotless."

"I like to keep it that way, sir," Zimmerman replied. "More efficient."

"What sort of shape are the men in, Doc?"

Zimmerman thought a moment. "Top condition, sir. Better than you'd expect, really."

"No illnesses?"

"Nothing we need to worry about. One of the stokers is having a bit of sinus trouble, but otherwise everyone is fine." He smiled. "Well—Ostler had the crabs, but that's been taken care of."

Kruger chuckled softly. "Couldn't happen to a nicer chap, eh? What about mental condition? Everyone okay in that department?"

"Like the boat, sir—top line. Not a bit of trouble."

Kruger perched on the edge of the doctor's desk, his heels tapping rhythmically on the metal base. "I thought so," he said, "but I wanted an expert opinion to confirm it. *Most* U-boat sailors generally look like they've been turned loose in a football arena, with marksmen lined up every ten metres around the perimeter, and told that if they can escape between them without being killed they'll be rewarded by getting to try again with the intervals reduced by five metres!"

"Exactly, sir. But not with this crew. The men are all quite confident they'll survive." He grinned. "So am I, for that matter, and I'm certainly no U-boat sailor."

"That may be to your advantage, Doc," Kruger replied. "You've never been through a depth charge attack. That killer group we encountered in the Skagerrak never got a chance to come after us."

"I don't think I want that particular experience, sir," Zimmerman said. "I've heard about it, but I think I can manage nicely without the actuality."

Kruger nodded. He'd survived this long on a combination of skill and luck. Until coming to this boat, mostly the latter. *U-702* had returned to Kiel primarily to make good repairs after a 78-hour depth charging in the Channel approaches.

He still didn't know how they'd survived. It had been like sitting inside an oil drum while an enormous lunatic attacked it with a sledgehammer. The endless banging and shock, the infernal 'ping' of the enemy's Asdic against the hull, the roaring of the destroyer's screws as they passed overhead, followed by more hammering, and the boat shaking like a wet dog.

At one point a stoker had sworn that he had seen one of the huge diesels lifted bodily from its mountings for a few moments before smashing down again. Kruger wasn't sure he believed the man had actually seen it, but when the attack was over at last it was found that that engine *was* loose from its mountings.

He was still not sure of the ultimate cause of their survival. Whether the enemy had at last decided they had been sunk, or if they had simply run out of things to drop on them.

It had hardly seemed to matter by then. Most of the crew were sick to the point of collapse from the foul air in the sealed hull. At most they might have held out for another hour—after that, they would have been forced to the surface, no matter how great the danger. It was possible to release compressed air into the boat to replenish the oxygen supply, but the lack of air wasn't the real problem. After too many hours the carbon dioxide from the men's exhalations would become too concentrated for their systems to tolerate. In *U-2317* there were systems to remove it; in the older boats you either surfaced or died.

When they had finally surfaced the air had been so incredibly sweet that it had been all he could manage to force himself to dive an hour latter, when a fat-bellied Liberator came roaring over the horizon.

After all that time submerged, being killed on the surface had begun to seem almost preferable to diving again!

Oddly, the pounding they had taken in the Skagerrak, on the way back to Kiel, had come closer to finishing them than the long attack, though Ralston's group had given up after only three hours.

"You wouldn't *want* the experience, Doc," Kruger said.

The wardroom steward, Seaman Schwartz, looked in. "Sir?" he said. "*Kapitän* von Saltzmann is here. He said he would wait in your cabin."

"Tell him I'll be there directly, Schwartz."

"Aye, aye, sir."

Zimmerman looked curious. "Orders, do you think?"

"Could be, Doc. We're rearmed and reprovisioned, so sailing orders are all that are wanting."

"If they've decided to pull me off early, sir, would you suggest that I'd like duty at, say, the embassy in Madrid?"

Kruger laughed. "I'll mention it."

With the captain gone, Zimmerman began straightening his desk again. It was almost a compulsion—everything had to be in exactly its proper place at all times. When he was still at the hospital in Kiel some of the other doctors had joked about it, but when there was trouble he was frequently the only one who could always count on laying his hands on exactly what he wanted.

A compulsion was only a problem when it had a bad result, Zimmerman was sure. Otherwise, it could easily become a blessing.

•　　•　　•

Von Saltzmann was standing beside the desk when Kruger came in. The older man looked nervous, uncomfortable, as if he had a great deal on his mind. As he must, Kruger thought, with the major responsibility for this boat and her proper utilisation resting solidly on his shoulders.

"You'd best sit down, Hans," von Saltzmann said.

Kruger perched on the edge of the bunk, studying the captain. Much of the usual bluff joviality was missing today. As if he had suddenly realised that the war was already hopelessly lost. Yet he had already said as much, so it had to be something else.

Perhaps *Konteradmiral* Godt was going to get his way, and the boat would be returned to training duty?

Von Saltzmann pulled the pink signal flimsy from his pocket. "This came in this morning," he said.

"Trouble, sir?"

"Possibly. It certainly isn't good news."

Kruger leaned forward. "Have we been cancelled, sir?"

The pudgy captain shook his head. "Nothing like that. The project will continue as before. This doesn't affect the boat—only her captain."

"What is it, sir?" He was sure he knew already. The rest of his family had finally been killed in a raid. Or they had got confirmation of Otto's death in Russia.

"There was a British raid on Kiel last night, as there usually is," von Saltzmann said. "The usual strategic targets were hit—shops, docks, and the like." He hesitated. "A single stray bomb fell on a barracks and killed 30 Women's Corps enlisted personnel."

It was like a knife thrust into his heart. "Hannah?"

The captain nodded slowly. "I understand she was killed instantly. They all were."

Kruger looked dazed. "We had made plans, you know? She was so worried that *I* would be killed. Like her brothers. Like so many others. But somehow we never thought that she—"

Von Saltzmann dropped the decoded signal onto the little desk. "You never think of that, Hans. In this war U-boat sailors have given far more than anyone could realistically expect of them. We've suffered enormous losses. Yet the people at home have given just as much, and perhaps more." He sighed. "For us it is a war, where we kill them or they kill us, and for both sides there is as much skill involved as luck. But the people at home either live or die, and chance alone is the deciding factor. There's no skill to it, no manoeuvring to avoid the fatal stroke. There is only blind luck. A bomb misses a factory and topples a row of flats, or a hospital. They weren't the targets, but they were destroyed just the same."

Kruger was looking at his leader, but all he could see was that final glimpse of her, standing at the end of the Tirpitz Pier in the near darkness, a white handkerchief fluttering in her hand.

"When can we sail again?" Kruger asked, his voice hard and flat.

"Three days. Orders are being cut now."

"The bombers were British."

"Yes."

"Then we will go where there are British ships, and we will sink them. Every damned one of them!"

Von Saltzmann nodded. "I could arrange to have you flown back to Kiel if you'd like, Hans? You could only stay a single day, but it might help."

Kruger stood and picked up the signal, reading it over slowly. It helped to have it in his hand, he thought, a focus for his anger.

"Thank you, sir," he said, "but that's not necessary. I am just going to get very drunk and plan my plans." He shrugged. "It seems that I have nothing else to do now."

Chapter Five

Convoy

Kruger rested his arms on the screen, hardly noticing the black water rushing past in the night. The lookouts in the cockpit were excellent, and they would also be watching aboard the escorts. Dozens of eyes scanning the dark sky and sea for the first hint of any enemy. The lookouts, together with their own radar, and their covering flight of radar-equipped night-fighters, provided sufficient warning. Enemy bombers might still be a threat, but under the circumstances not a major one.

He slowly shook his head, wondering if he would ever be the same. The most dangerous part of the patrol, steaming on the surface, exposed to the threat of bombs or a marauding enemy submarine, and *U-2317*'s captain was all but asleep at his post!

But Kruger had hardly slept at all since receiving the news from Kiel. His future had all been assured, safe. Working for Uncle Fritz, Hannah waiting at home, and, in a few years, children to make it all complete. Then, in an instant, a single British bomb had ended it all, his safe post-war world blasted apart like the Women's Corps barracks.

After von Saltzmann left, Kruger had hardly stirred from his cabin. He had sat there on the edge of his bunk, staring at her photograph, and pouring himself drink after drink, until at last Wiegand had removed the bottle, ignoring threats of court martial for insubordination.

"Do what you like, sir," Wiegand had said, "but we sail tonight, and you are bloody well going to be sober enough to command us! So say farewell to your bottle and get some sleep. Sir."

Kruger had raged, roaring threats and curses, but Wiegand had been quite unrepentant. What was worse, von Saltzmann had shortly appeared to back him up. There was no brow-beating a captain, so Kruger had gone to bed, muttering to himself.

Now they were under way again, and he had a headache that would have presented a problem even for one of those Nazi 'supermen' Ostler was always carrying on about. The liquor, mostly, he thought—with a considerable measure of grief thrown in.

He would get over her. He knew that, knew that it was inevitable, that the human heart was not intended to carry its burden of grief for an indefinite time. But it would take time. A lot of time.

And time was in rather short supply just now.

Wiegand came through the hatch. "I've been right through the boat, sir," he reported. "The crew seem almost happy to be going out again."

"Makes a change," Kruger said. He frowned. "Look, Number One—try to forget what I said before, right? I'm not usually like that."

Wiegand shrugged. "It was never a problem, sir. *Kapitän* von Saltzmann told me about the girl. You'd had your share of problems already, by all accounts. We all have. Then to throw something like this at you? It's enough to make anyone want to hide in a bottle."

"Even so, there was no excuse for it."

Wiegand smiled. "Just forget it, sir. I have."

"Bridge—Navigator."

"Bridge, aye."

"Position for diving in five minutes, sir."

"Very good. Thank you, Pilot." Kruger straightened from the voice pipe. "I won't be a bit sorry to leave the surface behind for a while," he said.

"None of us will," Wiegand commented. "Not in this boat. It's really wonderful to be able to cruise at a decent speed, running deep, while the air stays fresh day after day."

Kruger smiled. "Tell it to the L.I., Number One. It wouldn't surprise me if he didn't have something to do with that little trick."

"The only thing that would surprise me about him," Wiegand said, "would be if the brass let us keep him."

"Not much chance of that, I'm afraid," Kruger said. "They may send out an L.I. who outranks his captain while a boat is really still experimental, just to see to it that everything is working properly. But once we're fully operational you can expect them to replace him with someone whose rank is a bit more appropriate."

"Meaning also less expert, sir?"

"Something like that."

"I think I'll ask for a transfer once that happens," Wiegand said.

Kruger swung his glasses around the horizon, seeing nothing of interest beyond their escorts, dimly outlined against the dark sky, and the tiny blue sternlight the leading escort was showing for them to follow.

"You've had a command once, Number One. Think you're ready for another?"

The Exec grinned. "I'd not object to it. So long as it isn't another antique with a 20-minute life expectancy."

"Unlikely. *Kapitän* von Saltzmann thinks quite highly of you, and I gather they'll want you to take over another boat like this once one becomes available. After what you've learned here, the job should be a natural."

A light stuttered from the leading destroyer's bridge.

"*Position for diving*, sir," the leading rating reported.

Kruger bent over the voice pipe. "Pilot? Ready to dive?"

"Just crossing the line, sir," Reuter replied. "We can dive whenever you're ready."

Kruger turned to the signalman. "Inform the escort, *Am diving. See you later.*"

"Acknowledged, sir. He says, *Take care of yourself and good hunting*, sir."

"Right. Clear the bridge."

In seconds the rest of the bridge party had vanished into the red-lit world below, leaving Kruger alone. With a grim smile he snapped down the covers on the voice pipes. He was going home, back to the killing ground."

And this time it would be the British who would suffer."

He pressed the button. "Alarm!!!!"

After the chill of the open bridge, the control room seemed cozy. Kruger moved to the periscope, looking at his hands on the grips. In the glow of the night-vision lighting they seemed to be on fire.

"Take her down," he ordered. "Periscope depth."

At his panel, Eisenberg was busily flipping switches. Unlike the older boats, with their manually operated valves, *U-2317*'s diving controls were completely electric. It was one reason for the smaller size of her crew. The L.I. could easily handle the entire diving operation by himself, without having to rely on a trained crew opening and closing valves by hand.

The old-style valves were still there, just in case, but so far there had been no need for them. The boat continued to function flawlessly.

"Fourteen metres, sir," Eisenberg announced.

Kruger swung the periscope around the horizon, then focused on the leading destroyer, which was now making a wide circle as she turned to return to port.

At Kruger's signal the periscope dropped back into its well.

"Normal lights," he snapped. At once, the red glow was replaced by the normal brilliance. They would not surface again this night, so there was no need of keeping their eyes accustomed to darkness.

"All normal, sir," Wiegand reported.

"L.I.?"

"No problems, sir. Batteries are fully charged."

"Sea depth?"

Reuter looked at the echo sounder, then at the chart. "We're in 200 metres here, sir," he reported. "That should increase gradually for about the next 70 miles if we stay on our present course, then drop off to well below our maximum depth."

"Very well. Take her down to 100 metres for the next 15 minutes. I don't want us accidentally colliding with one of our escorts. New course will be two-six-five. Revolutions for eight knots."

"Scotland?" Reuter asked, his mind automatically projecting the course onto the charts stored in his head.

"Close enough. We'll pass between the Shetlands and the Orkneys, then south through the Irish Sea to the Western Approaches. There should be good hunting there." He grinned. "Especially for us."

•   •   •

The old Mercedes saloon rolled steadily south, away from Bergen and the sea. In the rear seat, Captain David Ralston dozed fitfully, pinned between the stocky petty officer who had charge of the detail and a hefty leading hand. By now he had resigned himself to the idea of spending the next few months in a German prisoner-of-war camp. With the realisation that what the interrogator in Bergen had said was true, that no one had any intention of torturing him, it had all become easier to accept.

He frowned, thinking back to the interrogation with a sense of disgust. Name, rank, and number—nothing more. That was the doctrine that had been drilled into him from the time he'd entered Dartmouth as a 13-year-old cadet in 1924. Twenty years of indoctrination, yet in minutes a young German officer had managed to get through his guard and extract every bit of information he had to offer.

It was just as well he'd known no real strategic information, Ralston thought. Otherwise he'd probably have blabbed that as well!

Silently cursing, Ralston dozed off again.

He awoke with a start, to find a P-38 pistol jammed into his side. The car had stopped, and it was dark outside, so he must have been sleeping for some time.

"What is it?" he asked. His first thought had been to say something abrupt, but the pistol had moderated his remarks.

"Road have tree fall on," the petty officer said. The man had some English, Ralston had discovered, but his ideas of grammar were uniquely his own.

"Trouble, do you suppose?"

"Shut keep mouth, *Kapitän*. Is big trouble, kill you is orders mine. *Vehrstehen?*"

Ralston grunted as the pistol barrel explored his ribs. "Too bloody right I do."

The petty officer nodded. The driver and the leading hand were both out of the car by now, trying to remove the fallen tree that was blocking the road, which here ran through the bottom of a narrow valley. With a stream at one edge of the road and thick forest at the other there was no way to drive around.

At last the door opened, and the heavily muffled guard in his Naval greatcoat and coal scuttle helmet started to climb back into the car.

"*Ist alles?*" the petty officer asked.

"*Ja,*" the guard grunted, a heavy pistol appearing suddenly from beneath his greatcoat. "*Für dich.*"

In the confines of the car, the three quick explosions were deafening. It was all over in an instant, the petty officer's gun falling into Ralston's lap while the man himself, the back of his head blasted away, his eyes bulging as if in surprise, lay sprawled against the far door, which was stained bright red with his blood.

"You take his gun, right, old son?" the 'guard' snapped. "And hurry. There's no bloody time to waste."

Ralston stared at him. His first thought had been that the guard had suddenly gone berserk, but this man spoke with an accent that would have been completely at home in the House of Lords. "You're British?" he asked.

"Call me Wilson, why don't you? Now come along, Captain, before Jerry notices that something's amiss. They patrol this road fairly regularly."

"Er—right."

●   ●   ●

Von Sänger looked up from his screen. "Plenty of movement in the area, sir," he reported. "All the close stuff seems pretty small, but there are three vessels with Asdic coming up channel, and a lot of heavy HE beyond, so we may be getting something worthwhile before long."

Kruger nodded. "Keep your ears open, lad," he said. "We don't want to miss our chance when it comes."

They had been on station for three days now, and so far as Kruger could determine the enemy was completely unaware of that fact. Unlike the normal U-boats, *U-2317* was under orders to maintain strict radio silence under most circumstances. Coming under the Admiral's Special Operations venue, rather than the normal Submarine Branch, operating procedures were different.

It was no doubt safer that way, Kruger thought. In the past he had been struck by the enemy's uncanny ability to always appear at just the right place to spring his trap. Most of the experts said that it was a simple matter of triangulation —you got a null on your radio direction finder and it gave you a line, with a U-boat located somewhere along it. A fix from a second station, a good distance away, would give you a second line, and where they came together you would find your U-boat. It was a simple answer, but Kruger had his doubts. More than once he had reached his station to find the enemy already there—*before* he sent his signal.

It was as if they were decoding the signals from headquarters as fast as the U-boat commanders. As Kruger knew that his own side had broken British codes, it seemed likely that the British would be able to return the favour—even if Dönitz's technical staff believed the Enigma codes used by the U-boat service to be unbreakable.

"What would you do now, Mister Schultz?" Kruger asked.

Leutnant Jurgen Schultz looked up from the plot table. "Sir?"

"The sound gear shows nothing in the way of suitable targets above us," Kruger said, "but von Sänger reports three vessels with Asdic coming up channel, and a lot of heavy HE beyond them. What would you do now, if you were in command?"

Schultz thought for a moment. It was the first time since his promotion that anyone had asked him to venture such an opinion, and he wanted to be sure he had considered the available information properly.

"I would go deep, sir," he said. "Get as deep as was safe to avoid being picked up by the enemy's Asdic, then come up to attacking depth under the ships behind them."

Kruger smiled. "Very good, Schultz. That's exactly what I intend to do. You know, Schultz, the British vastly over-estimated the value of their Asdic between the wars. They had their Admiralty all but convinced that it was so good that it had rendered submarines useless as offensive weapons." He laughed. "It took the first few weeks of war to convince them otherwise.

"What they have now is much better than it was at the start of the war, but it *still* has to actually hit a U-boat to reflect back and give them a bearing. For the most part, they simply rely on hydrophone bearings to put them onto us, then pin us down in their Asdic for the attack. But if they can't hear us, then they don't know where to aim their Asdic, and if we're deep enough the beam may reflect back off a thermal layer in the water and never reach us."

"I *think* I understand, sir."

"Good." Kruger liked the dumpy blond officer, almost as much as he detested Ostler—the 'senior' *Oberfänrich*. When he was given authorisation to promote one of them, Kruger had had no trouble making his choice. Schultz was a professional, from an old Naval family, while Ostler was a Nazi.

Politics had no damned business in the Navy, or so Kruger believed. He had never belonged to a political party, nor had any of the men he had served under at the beginning of the war. He had taken an oath of loyalty to the *Führer*, but that was no different from the oath every soldier of every nation took to king, country, or leader. Politics had nothing to do with it, and if Hitler were to drop dead tomorrow and a Hohenzollern was to resume the throne, Kruger would quite happily take a new oath to the Kaiser.

It was the Navy's job to be there, to provide a good defense, and a powerful striking force for Germany's leaders to use. Who those leaders were was not their concern. Only that they be loyal to them and follow orders.

It was only since Rastenburg that these politically indoctrinated young officers had been forced on the U-boat arm. Before that, the Navy's loyalty had been taken as a right. Kruger saw nothing strange in his loyalty and obedience to the *Führer*, although he considered the man's political and racial theories absurd.

He bent over the intercom grill. *"Achtung! Achtung!* Diving stations!"

The off-watch men scrambled to their stations in an orderly stampede.

"Boat closed up at diving stations, sir," Eisenberg reported.

"Very good, L.I.. Take her down to 300 metres. Silent running."

"Out main motor clutch," Eisenberg ordered. "All stop main E-motor. Engage silent motor, revolutions for five knots. Bow and stern planes down ten degrees. Zero angle."

"Carry on, L.I.. When we are at 300 metres you may fall out diving stations. Mister Schultz, you have the watch."

"Aye, aye, sir."

"I'll be in my cabin. Inform me when we are within attacking range of the enemy convoy. *If* that's what we're heading for."

Kruger walked forward, bending low as he passed through the circular door of the control room and into the narrow passageway beyond. Once in his cabin he hung up his service dress jacket on its hook, then sat at his desk.

The pink signal flimsy was still there, pushed to one corner. He wanted to keep it, as a reminder of just why he was now creeping along the ocean floor some 50 miles southwest of Land's End. That the enemy had taken too much from him in this war. First his family, and now his hope of a new one. It was too much to expect from one man. Too much.

And someone, he thought, was going to have to pay.

•   •   •

The wind was out of the west, bitter cold. The sort of wind that would cut through the thickest watchcoat like a hot knife through butter. The sort of wind that would make a man wonder why any sane human being would ever make his life at sea, when with the same amount of ambition he could as easily have found himself comfortably ensconced in some warm office in the city.

Captain Thomas Sykes stood stiffly, ignoring this wind, as he had so many like it over the last 30 years at sea, scanning the waves with his powerful glasses. Here and there the wind whipped at the crest of a wave, the flying spray presenting a constant worry for Sykes and every other captain in the convoy. It was too easy to grow complacent, mark every plume of spray as the result of wind and wave. When that happened you would not react quickly enough when the spray came not from the wind, but from a submarine's extended periscope. A moment's inattention was all it took.

Just now, Sykes decided, it was only the wind. He sighed, the sound inaudible more than inches away. A few more hours and it would all be finished. Ten safe trips in this ship. Compensation, he thought, for other convoys and other ships, when he had landed in England alone, his command resting at the bottom of the Atlantic.

Sykes had commanded freighters during every month of the war, and in that time had had his ship sunk beneath him four times. No fault had ever been laid to him—it was just poor luck. In a convoy, he suspected, even the enemy commander didn't always know which ship his torpedo was going to hit.

The First Mate, Andrews, emerged from the wheelhouse, carrying his sextant.

"Noon already?" Sykes asked.

"Yes, sir."

"About seven hours, then," Sykes commented. "Then we'll be in Falmouth." He grinned. "Never thought I'd see us make it this far again, but we seem to have done it."

"No thanks to Jerry," Andrews grunted. "You'd think he'd have sense enough to know he's beat and leave us in peace, wouldn't you?"

"Not bloody likely, I'd think. After all, *we* didn't give in when we were in the same fix, did we? Maybe Jerry thinks he can make a comeback as well, eh?"

Andrews nodded. There was some sense to that, though the conditions were quite different. England had had help available—the Germans did not. But, he thought, there was little difference between the English and the Germans in any case. Since Britain's rightful monarchs had lost their last chance at regaining the throne in 1746, the difference was even less so, with the Hanovers and their equally Germanic descendants on the throne. The Kaiser had been Queen Victoria's grandson, for God's sake.

If only James Stuart hadn't been a bloody Catholic, he thought.

He scanned the thin clouds, trying to get a fix on the sun. It *had* been a good crossing, he thought. Forty-seven ships had left New York with their escorts, and 46 were still steaming along at eight knots.

The ship that had been lost, a gasoline tanker, had gone up like an exploding sun the first night out. Torpedoed, struck a mine, or a stray spark. No one seemed to be too sure, and it hardly mattered to the men whose lives had ended in a single instant.

The escorts had milled about after the explosion, dropping depth charges and generally raising hell, without seeming to accomplish anything. If there had been a U-boat, it had either escaped, or been sunk without anyone noticing.

After that, the crossing had been as close to boring as was possible with a war on. Two fighter-bombers from their American escort carrier had caught a U-boat napping on the surface about 50 miles ahead of the convoy and promptly attacked with machine-guns and depth charges, sinking it.

And that was that. The rest was routine, and, as Sykes had said, seven more hours would see them safely in Falmouth, where their cargo of light tanks and tinned rations would be off-loaded for shipment to Patton's advancing army on the Continent.

The voyage is already finished, Andrews thought. This area is so heavily patrolled that no Jerry will dare to bother us. The skippers may be bold, but they're not bloody suicidal!

●   ●   ●

The telephone buzzed insistently, dragging Kruger up from his dream as he snatched it from its hook. He had been back in Potsdam, in that little hotel, and waking seemed all the more bitter for the realisation that he would never see Hannah again except in dreams.

"Captain," he said.

"Schultz here, sir. Von Sänger is getting a good return from his sound gear now. He estimates about 60 ships, moving in formation."

"I'll come," Kruger snapped, replacing the handset. Smiling, he sat on the edge of his bunk and pulled on his shoes. A convoy at last! It would be a chance to show what a Walter boat could do.

It would also be a chance to begin his revenge.

"Course is two-six-five, sir," Schultz reported, as the captain stepped into the control room. "Speed five knots, silent motor. Depth 300 metres."

"Very good, Mister Schultz. I have the deck."

Kruger walked slowly to von Sänger's little cubicle, leaning across his shoulders to watch the screen. "What's the range?" he asked.

"Three-two-zero to the nearest vessel, sir."

Kruger nodded, moving slowly back to stand beside the lowered attack periscope. "Reduce to dead slow," he ordered. "We will wait until the convoy passes over us, then come up to 50 metres and make the attack using the *Nibelung*." He smiled. "It's time to discover if the theories concerning all this equipment will work out in actual practice."

The second hand on the bulkhead clock ticked slowly around, time seeming to hang almost suspended as *U-2317* idled along at a bare one and a half knots while the convoy steamed toward them.

Wiegand stood with Schultz beside the plot table, feeling the tension as the time for action drew slowly closer. It was as if time had stopped, the men in the control room unmoving statues.

Wiegand glanced around. Eisenberg was sitting, looking very content, at his control panel. Forward, von Sänger was hunched over his sound gear, while Reuter stood over him, calling out minor course corrections from time to time. There were few of these, Wiegand noticed, as would be expected at their creeping speed.

Kruger was still standing beside the periscope, unmoving, his face fixed in a grim smile. There was a look of fanaticism about him now, Wiegand thought. A sudden dedication to the task of taking the war to the enemy.

He remembered the first time he had seen the captain, back in Kiel, when he had come aboard with von Saltzmann, still filthy from his last patrol, his eyes ringed with dark circles, looking like a hunted animal.

Now it was very different. Kruger was obviously the hunter, like a lion who, after surviving a long chase, suddenly finds himself in a safe place to rest and wait for his tormentors, who are moving, all unknowing, within reach of fang and claw.

He did not seem to be the same man who had plucked a British escort commander from the Skagerrak, seemingly as much for sport as to serve any military function. That Kruger had been a skilled U-boat commander, but still willing to hold on to his humanity. *This* Kruger would probably have left the Britisher to freeze to death.

"Forward escorts are passing over us now, sir," von Sänger announced.

"Mister Reuter?"

"Sir?"

"What speed are the enemy making?"

"About eight knots, sir."

Kruger nodded. "Good. In fifteen minutes we will come up to 50 metres. Mister Himmler?"

"Yes, sir."

"What is your load pattern?"

"Bow tubes are 'wrens,' sir. All midships tubes have LUTs."

"Very well. We will attack with tubes five through ten first, and hold the bow tubes in reserve—just in case we have any problems with the escorts."

"Aye, aye, sir."

"Now, Number One—send the crew to attack stations, then close off for depth charging." He glanced at the bulkhead clock. "In twelve minutes we will start the attack."

• • •

"Are you *sure* this is going to work?"

"Trust me, Captain," Wilson said, grinning. "We've been using it for some time now, and no one has been killed yet."

Ralston frowned. "I wish you hadn't said 'yet.'"

"It works, Captain. Don't worry."

Ralston's frown deepened, then he added. "You're sure you can't arrange for a boat? I'm more than willing to take my chances with the German coastal patrols, but I'm just not very good with aeroplanes."

Wilson laughed and shook his head. "London wants you back in a hurry for some reason. This is the quickest way."

"I hope you're right." Ralston shook his head, looking at the arrangements of line and poles laid out on the floor of the little hut where Wilson had his current headquarters. "Now, once again, how does this bloody thing work?"

"It's a bit like parachuting in reverse," the Commando officer explained. "You put on this harness, then we attach it to a loop of line, which is hung open between two long poles. All you have to do then is sit on the ground while an aeroplane flies past, catches the line, and hoists you up. Simple as that." He grinned. "They use it all the time to pick up downed fliers."

"Sounds bloody insane," Ralston offered. "But I don't suppose we have much choice, do we?"

Wilson laughed. "*I* have a great deal of choice, old son," he said. "*You*, on the other hand, are going flying tonight."

"Bloody wonderful."

•   •   •

The control room was silent, but for the soft ticking of the bulkhead clock, and the hushed breathing of the men. Now and then there would be the brief hiss of compressed air, or the subdued rush of water, as Eisenberg made some minor correction in the trim.

The silent motor, driving the screw through its heavy belts, was something that was felt through the soles of the feet, but not actually heard. A faint vibration and no more.

"Time, sir," Reuter said.

Kruger moved over to von Sänger's station and peered down at the glowing screen, nodding to the operator for a single ping. The convoy was spread out around them now, with *U-2317* hovering silently, 300 metres beneath them.

"General course of convoy?" he asked.

"Zero-six-zero, sir," Reuter replied.

"We will conform," Kruger said. "Come around to zero-six-zero and increase to five knots."

Stauber slipped into the helmsman's seat. "Course is zero-six-zero, sir," he reported.

"Speed five knots, sir," Eisenberg said.

"Bring her up to 50 metres. Mister Himmler, stand by for firing orders."

As *U-2317* planed up from the depths, sailing on in complete silence, Kruger found himself smiling. *Only in this boat*, he thought. We're directly under the centre of a fat convoy, sailed right under her escorts, and not a thing has been done to chase us off—or even to discourage us. They just steam on, in complete ignorance of their danger.

By God, with a hundred boats like this one we could still turn this war around, he thought. The enemy armies would be stranded in Europe with their supply routes completely severed, impotent against a resurgent Wehrmacht.

He sighed. It was too late now, of course. Fate. No matter what Hitler or Goebbels, or even the base chaplain back in Kiel might have to say about it, God had no favourites in any war.

Six months earlier, it might have made all the difference. But those six months had passed like all the months before them. It was all fate. God didn't care who won. Not since Joshua, at least.

"Fifty metres, sir," Eisenberg reported.

"Mister Himmler, bearing and angle on the bow are zero. Set your depth at three metres. LUT torpedoes will be set to run straight for 600 metres, then loop, maintaining our present general course.

"Depth and run are set, sir."

"Very well. Flood tubes five through ten. Open outer doors and fire when you are ready." Kruger turned to Eisenberg. "L.I., stand by for full speed when I give the word. Once we've fired they'll know we're here!"

"Ready when you are, sir."

At two minutes past four, on a Friday afternoon, *U-2317* shivered as the first torpedo was ejected from its tube.

• • •

Sykes tumbled from his bunk as the first detonation rolled across the choppy waters of the Western Approaches. In a moment he was through the door and into the pilot house.

"What the hell was that?" Sykes demanded.

Andrews was staring off to port. "Over there, sir," he said, pointing. "Another liberty ship. Took a hit smack on her bow, from the look of her."

"Torpedo?"

Andrews shrugged. "Mine, more likely. We're too close to home for U-boats to be mucking about. And besides, if it was a U-boat he'd have waited until dark, when he'd stand a better chance of getting away."

Sykes nodded. "I expect you're right. Better alert the lookouts to keep a sharp watch for anything in the water, though. If there's one mine about you can bet there'll be more."

"Aye, aye, sir."

The telephone began buzzing even as Andrews reached for the handset.

"Bridge."

"Well, what is it?" Sykes demanded, as Andrews replaced the handset. "You look like you've just seen your own ghost."

"I think I have," the Mate replied. "That was the forward lookout. He said a torpedo just passed directly up the port side of the ship, about ten feet abeam, then veered to starboard and crossed our bow no more than five feet ahead!"

•   •   •

The thump of a distant explosion brought a grim smile to Kruger's face. Another enemy damaged, and at minimal risk to his own command.

On the intercom, Himmler was talking excitedly to Schwartzkopf, his petty officer. The last of the 'eels' had been fired no more than three minutes ago. If only they had room for reloads! But now the six aft-firing midships tubes were empty, while the four bow tubes, with their acoustic homing torpedoes, remained in reserve.

It seem ironic. *U-2317*'s hydraulic loading gear made the job almost effortless, and the great speed of operation was obvious, but the tubes were normally only reloaded in port, where speed was of questionable utility.

The hull trembled slightly, and von Sänger looked up from his screen. "A second hit, sir," he reported.

"Give them another ping, see what the escorts are doing."

"One escort from the inner screen has closed on the first ship, sir, but none of the others seem overly bothered."

"Probably thought the first ship hit a drifting mine," Wiegand offered. "They've no reason to suspect a U-boat. It's been months since anyone has dared to operate in these waters."

Kruger nodded. It made sense, when you considered it. There had been nothing to warn the enemy that *U-2317* was slipping under their screen. At 300 metres they had probably been beneath more than one thermal layer, which would have reflected any Asdic beams. And their silent motor and superbly engineered screw would have made no obvious sound for enemy hydrophones to pick up.

The torpedoes would change all that. While the boat was still slipping beneath the convoy at silent speed, the fast turning screws on the four 'eels' that were still running would be clearly heard by any alert hydrophone operator.

"We still have the bow tubes, sir," Himmler commented.

Kruger looking up at the chubby officer's beaming face. Himmler was obviously pleased with his crew, and with the results of his first spread.

"Quite so, Mister Himmler. My compliments to your crew on their performance, eh?"

"I'll pass them along, sir."

"You may flood tubes one through three. I'll have firing instructions in a moment."

"Aye, aye, sir."

Kruger moved back to the sound cubicle. Above them, the convoy's orderly progress had been disrupted by the need to avoid the two stricken ships, while from the outer edges of the convoy several points of light were moving purposefully through the formation. Escorts, Kruger thought, at last awake to the presence of the enemy in their midst.

U-2317 had dropped back from her first firing position, the convoy moving ahead at an average of three nautical miles in each hour. Even so, the boat was still well inside the limits of the convoy, which stretched over several miles of ocean.

"Same settings as before, Mister Himmler," Kruger said. "Independent guidance. You may fire when you are ready."

Two more distant explosions, one following the other by only seconds, shook the hull. Four hits from their first six torpedoes, Kruger thought. It was an average that would have been considered good even with a carefully aimed salvo. With the LUTs, which had merely been fired in the proper direction and left to luck, it was an incredible result. The convoy was spread out over a large area, and it would not be at all unusual for a torpedo to make repeated loops across its path without ever striking a target.

Even without hydrophones, Kruger could hear the scream of a ship as it began to sink, the crash of machinery ripping loose inside the hull and tearing through the bulkheads, hastening its demise. There was a muffled blast, sounding quite different from a torpedo, as the boilers were plunged into the chilly water and blew themselves apart.

How could men sail on those freighters? he wondered. Every waking moment spent with the knowledge that only thin steel plates excluded the sea. That at any moment a torpedo might crash through the side and blow the guts out of the ship and everyone aboard her.

"All torpedoes away and running, sir," Himmler reported. "Outer doors closed."

Kruger nodded. "Very good. We're going to get out of here now." He smiled. "We'll come back later and finish the job, eh?"

There was another distant detonation. Von Sänger looked up, shaking his head. "Terminal detonation," he said. The torpedo's batteries had run down and it had blown itself up. Normally, they would have set the 'eel' to simply go dead and sink, lest the explosion alert the enemy to their presence, but inside a convoy there was always the chance that it might be close enough to do some damage when it ran down, so the mechanism was set to detonate the warhead when the motor stopped turning. The enemy already knew that they were there.

"Four of the first six hit something, " Himmler commented. "That's not a bad average for pure luck, eh?"

"Not bad at all," Kruger agreed.

There was another blast, and this time von Sänger was smiling. A half second later the pressure hull trembled to a terrific concussion. Von Sänger ripped off his headphones, cursing."

"Must have been an ammunition ship," Himmler said.

Ping!

Ping! Ping! Ping! Ping!

"Asdic contact!" Wiegand whispered. "They've found us!"

Above them, the powerful screws of the escort were clearly audible as it charged in for the kill. Her captain might already be congratulating himself on finding the U-boat that had so disrupted a convoy almost within sight of Land's End.

"Two escorts, sir," von Sänger reported, sounding as calm as if he were giving the results of a football match pitting

Germany against a kindergarten team. "Listener is at Red four-five, attacker at Red two-zero."

"Come left to three-three-zero," Kruger ordered. "Turbine, ahead full! Take her down to 300 metres."

For a moment the boat seemed to hang suspended, and then the turbine was lit off with a bang and the deck seemed to leap from beneath their feet as *U-2317* tore around onto her new course.

"Depth charges coming down," von Sänger announced, pulling off his headphones to avoid being deafened by the blasts.

The boat shivered violently as a full pattern exploded about 50 metres astern. But it was merely a shaking—uncomfortable, but no real danger.

Kruger picked up the telephone handset and spoke briefly. Moments after he replaced the handset the intercom popped loudly, and music began blaring out at full volume.

Kruger grinned, while most of the others merely gaped in astonishment. Every enemy hydrophone in the area would certainly pick up the noise, making them an easy target to track. Then, slowly, the others began to smile as they realised what their captain was doing.

U-2317 was already passing through 250 metres, her streamlined hull slipping through the water at almost 26 knots. Even without the music, her powerful turbine was making such a racket that only a deaf man would be able to miss it.

Only a hedgehog bomb could touch them now, and that would have to actually strike the hull to do any damage. At their speed and depth the risk was minimal. Depth charges, which could not be set to detonate at these depths, were no longer a factor.

It was a gesture, Wiegand thought. A gesture of defiance from a nearly beaten, but still deadly, foe. *Here I am—catch me if you can!*

At the end of the first chorus the music was cut off abruptly.

Kruger and Reuter were both standing over von Sänger, shouting occasional course changes to keep them from running directly beneath any enemy ship. From this point on, until the convoy sorted itself out and the patterns were re-established, they would assume that anything on the screen was an escort and simply stay out of the way.

In the distance, two more ships blundered into torpedoes and began to settle.

"That's it, then," Himmler mused.

"Yes," Kruger said. "Seven hits, and two have blown themselves up at the end of their runs. So that's all nine eels accounted for."

"Ship breaking up, sir," von Sänger reported. "Bearing Green six-nine."

Kruger took a further look at the glowing screen. "Come round to one-eight-zero," he ordered.

"Course is one-eight-zero, sir," Stauber reported.

As more depth charges blasted apart the water well astern, *U-2317* slipped between a pair of wing escorts and raced off into the depths, leaving behind a bewildered and furious escort commander.

•   •   •

The room was a concrete bunker, buried deep beneath the old Admiralty building. One entire wall was dominated by a huge chart of the North Atlantic, stuck full of coloured pins indicating the known positions of Allied and the estimated positions of German units.

Captain David Ralston stood silently before the metal desk, duly impressed with the efficiency of the organisation that had whisked him back to London in less than 24 hours. True to Wilson's prediction, the pick-up gear had worked perfectly. A small aeroplane had plucked him from a Norwegian pasture, carrying him over the North Sea to a tiny airfield in the Shetlands. There he had been transferred to a larger transport for the flight to London, stopping only briefly in Glasgow to take on fuel and a pair of passengers. Specialists from Naval Intelligence, who had begun debriefing him on the flight back.

And now, after stopping off on the drive in from Gatwick at his flat, where he had shaved and put on a clean uniform, he had been brought here.

They'd kept him waiting only briefly, while a Wren second-officer, who bore an uncomfortable resemblance to his ex-wife, glared at him over her glasses.

Admiral Sir Alexander Taunton looked up from the hand-written report, gesturing for Ralston to have a seat. "This is a very interesting story," he said. "It has perhaps explained something I've been puzzling over since yesterday."

"Sir?"

The admiral shook his head. "Later, Captain." He smiled. "Did you have a good trip back?"

"Bloody efficient, at least, sir."

"I'm sure you were in good hands. The Special Air Service handled the operation. The chap you met in Norway was one of their lads."

"I felt a bit like a football while they were picking me up," Ralston admitted. "But once I was actually *inside* the plane it wasn't so bad."

"I understand you don't care to fly?" the admiral said.

"Not much, sir, no. I'll gladly take my chances on a ship, but in my opinion only animals who have their *own* wings belong in the sky."

The admiral laughed. "I doubt if anyone in the RAF would agree with you on that, Captain, but I'll try to keep you out of aeroplanes from now on, right?"

"Fine, sir."

"Now," Taunton said, tapping the report, "there was something you said about the man who captured you. You said he had a tendency to show off his boat?"

"Yes, sir. He was obviously very proud of his command. An understandable trait, I might add. She was far superior to anything I've ever heard of before. Deep diving, and obviously very fast underwater."

"How fast?"

"I'm not sure of the speed, sir," Ralston said. "I never saw an indicator, or, if I did, I didn't recognise it. But I *did* recognise the depth gauge, and at one point it was showing 300 metres."

Taunton nodded. "What's that in feet?"

"Nine hundred eighty-four, sir."

"Deep enough," Taunton admitted. "No idea of his speed, eh?"

"Very fast, sir. I've never felt that sort of acceleration in a submarine. It was more like what you'd expect in a destroyer. Just from the feel of her, I'd say at least 18 knots, and possibly more."

"Well, that may very well explain what happened yesterday," the admiral said. "A convoy was attacked about 40 miles southwest of Land's End. The first report said that a freighter had struck a drifting mine and been sunk. Unfortunate, but it does happen."

"Of course, sir."

"Well, Ralston, that was the *first* report. The opinion changed a few minutes later when another ship reported sighting a torpedo passing close aboard. By the time the attack had ended, seven ships had been hit. Five were sunk, and the other two will be out of the war for months."

"And you think it was Kruger, sir?"

"It seems possible. For one thing, the escort commander was in complete ignorance of a submarine in the area until after the attack had started. Not, in fact, until the *second* ship was hit."

Ralston said. "It sounds like Kruger," he said. "They spent some time at silent speed while I was aboard, and you couldn't hear the motor or screw *inside* the boat. If they're that quiet at the source, a hydrophone operator would be very unlikely to pick them up. Asdic would be the only way, and that could happen only if they happened to blunder into the beam."

"Sounds right," Taunton replied. "Your report mentioned some sort of advanced detection gear, too, I believe?"

"Yes, sir. They have some sort of sound gear rigged to a screen, like a radar scope. The operator works it with a key, so they only send out a ping when they require it. It seems to give them the position of everything around them in the water, and I imagine it would be quite useful for avoiding escorts."

"Exactly. Still, it was your remark about showing off which really makes me think we're dealing with the same man. The escorts *did* pick up a single U-boat in their Asdic shortly after the start of the attack. The *boat* may have been silent, but her torpedoes were not. Several operators were able to get a bearing on the sound of them being fired, and once in range made a positive Asdic contact. They *tried* to attack."

"Tried, sir?"

"The U-boat took off at a very high speed, and at least two hydrophone operators reported that it sounded as if she was powered by turbine machinery. He was also reported playing *Deutschland Über Alles* at full volume on his Tannoy!"

Ralston smacked his fist into his open palm. "Kruger!" he snapped. "No one else would do something like that. He's got a turbine of some sort, I'm sure. But the bloody music is just the sort of thing he'd do."

Taunton nodded. "I'm inclined to agree, Ralston. We know of Kruger, of course. He's probably the most decorated U-boat commander still at sea, with a reputation for ruthlessness when it comes to attack. He also has a reputation for daring, even against heavily-defended convoys."

"I really didn't know about his reputation, sir," Ralston said. "But he was wearing the Knight's Cross, complete with oak leaves and swords, so I'll go along with the decorated part. As to daring? He came after my killer group without any hesitation, while normal submarine doctrine would have been to avoid contact with warships, which present an obvious danger, and save your torpedoes for cargo vessels. I've been told that their tendency to attack only warships has been a major fault with Japanese submarine doctrine in the Pacific— they sink the escorts, and then allow the freighters to get through, without realising that the freighter's cargos are the real threat. You can't take an island with a destroyer, after all."

Taunton smiled. "Well, Kruger seems to be aware of that detail."

Ralston frowned, shaking his head. "He's good. Damned good."

"Quite. And just now you probably know as much about him as any officer in the Navy. You've met him personally, talked to him. So far as I know, you're the only one who has. Everything else we have on him is what Intelligence has come up with—mostly from German newspapers and radio broadcasts. He's their last 'ace,' so when he sinks something it's news."

"Yes, sir."

"I want you to get him for me, Ralston. We're forming a new killer group, Number 65. You'll be senior officer."

Ralston nodded, astonished. After the destruction of his old command he'd been expecting a court martial, not this. A new killer group, new ships and men to command.

"You'll be appointed captain in *Apache*, with three other tribal class destroyers and the escort carrier *Vicious* under you. I'm giving you destroyers, rather than frigates or corvettes, because of the speed of this U-boat. Your estimate was 18 knots. The convoy escorts' hydrophone operators put his speed in excess of 20 knots. So you'll need something fast enough to counter him, and a 36-knot destroyer should be just the ticket. You know the procedure; one or two ships get a fix on him, another makes the attack."

Ralston grinned. "It should work, sir," he said.

"It had better. We're gambling that there is only one of these new boats around right now. If there are more, then it could be 1941 all over again. Our armies are advancing in Europe, and we can't afford to have them halted by a lack of supplies."

"I'm game to give it a go, sir," Ralston said. He frowned. "Besides, I want another crack at him!"

"Then you shall have it. My flag lieutenant has your orders. A car will take you to Portsmouth. You'll be based there until this operation is concluded. Another convoy passed through the same area today without incident, so I suspect your friend may have returned home to rearm. If so, I want you to have your group ready to meet him when he returns."

"You can count on me, sir."

"I intend to, Ralston. Now, off with you." He smiled. "And don't come back until you've sunk him!"

Chapter Six

A Second Chance

Von Saltzmann arrived on board *U-2317* an hour after she had safely been tied up in her pen in Bergen. A young seaman followed him aboard, loaded down with a magnum of good French champagne, packed in ice.

Behind von Saltzmann and the champagne-laden seaman followed a tall, very thin, and rather studious looking *Oberleutnant*, blinking through his wire-framed spectacles at the still crowded control room.

"Bloody good work," von Saltzmann enthused, after the champagne had been safely placed on the wardroom table and the seaman sent ashore. "This boat is setting a remarkable record! Five ships sunk, another two damaged and probably out of the war for good!" He touched the huge bottle. "I thought a little celebration might be in order, eh?"

Himmler was grinning broadly. "That's even better than we thought, sir," he said. "We knew that we had several hits, but it's very difficult to confirm anything when you never go nearer than 50 metres to the surface! You can tell something has been sunk, but you can't tell just what—and there's no way to assess damage at all."

"It's been confirmed now," von Saltzmann assured him. "Our agents in England have confirmed the sinkings and identified the victims. For that matter, so has the British government, making their normal announcements of losses."

"Have they said anything about us, sir?" Kruger asked.

"Nothing specific, at any rate. They're attributing the losses to a wolf pack." He grinned. "They also claim to have sunk one U-boat. An interesting accomplishment, as there were no other boats within 500 miles of that spot."

"Probably sunk one of their own," Himmler quipped.

"As long as they don't know about us," Kruger said. "The longer we stay on the secret list, the better our chances will be."

"A touch of bravado nonetheless, surely, sir?" Schultz offered.

"That, too," Kruger agreed. "Yes."

Wiegand laughed. "Well we bloody well managed *that*, I'd say."

"God, yes," Himmler said. "When the national anthem started blaring out of the intercom speakers as we were clearing away— Probably drove the escorts stark, raving mad."

Von Saltzmann looked curiously at Kruger. "National anthem?"

Kruger shrugged. "A bit of nose thumbing, I suppose you could call it. Go haring away at full speed, making a lot of patriotic noise in the process. Here I am, what do you propose to do about it? That sort of thing."

"What *did* they do about it?" von Saltzmann asked.

"Dropped a few hundred depth charges, from the sound of it. Except for the first pattern, which they obviously plotted just before we went to turbine power, none were even close enough to shake us up." He grinned. "To be honest, sir, if I had been the escort commander, I suspect I'd have dropped dead on the spot!"

"I might have done the same," von Saltzmann agreed. "Particularly if I'd been *in* this boat at the time. A U-boat announcing itself by playing music under water has to be a first." He smiled. "Still, the propaganda people will no doubt love it."

"I expect it's really safe enough, sir," Kruger said. "The turbine makes so much noise that a deaf man could track it in any case—a little more noise hardly matters. And when we shut down the turbine at depth, we can still coast at a very high speed for well over two miles."

"Do as you wish, Kruger. But try to remember that this boat needs to remain secret for a while longer."

"Until we get more like her into service, you mean, sir?" Reuter asked.

"Something like that, yes."

Kruger gestured at the studious-looking young *Oberleutnant*, who was standing near the door, a stranger in the midst of these old friends. "Who's our guest?" he asked.

"Your new L.I.," von Saltzmann said.

Eisenberg looked up from his chair. "I don't *want* to be relieved," he muttered. "I like it here."

Von Saltzmann held up his hand. "Not my idea, L.I.. But they want you back in Danzig, working on more of these boats. Personally, I'd rather have you stay a while longer. Until we're sure there will be no more teething problems."

"This chap any good?" Eisenberg asked.

"Klaus? Come join us, will you?"

The new L.I. ambled over, walking slightly stooped, as if fearful of bashing his head on some projection. "Sir?"

"Let's have your qualifications, shall we, lad?"

"Sir! Three years service, all spent in the engineering branch, with practical experience in both diesel and steam propulsion, as well as a six-week course on a prototype Walter turbine, with the emphasis placed on potential problems. Also, I hold a degree in mechanical engineering from the University of Berlin, and had begun advanced studies toward a Masters in the same subject when I joined the Navy."

"Why did you join up?" Kruger asked. "If you were still in school, I mean?"

"My uncle is one of the officials charged with keeping the services adequately manned. He warned me that I was about to be conscripted for the Infantry unless I volunteered for some other service first. With my education, the Navy seemed the most logical place."

"Shows some common sense," Wiegand mused.

"He is about the best man we have for the job," von Saltzmann said. "Perhaps not as experienced as *Fregattenkapitän* Eisenberg, but unquestionably the best qualified man of appropriate rank."

Kruger studied the man, who was standing uneasily before him. Only a bit shorter than himself, with blond hair and pale blue eyes, his wire-framed spectacles adding a scholarly touch, as did the slight slouch, which was probably the result of service in U-boats or coastal forces in the recent past. There were plenty of things for a tall man to bump his head on in either, as Kruger knew from painful experience.

The man's qualifications sounded good. Von Saltzmann and the Admiral would both have insisted on that. But he wasn't Eisenberg. In the brief time they had served together, Kruger had grown to like the big engineer. More, he trusted him. Next to the captain, the L.I. was probably the most important man in any U-boat. The captain commanded, but it was the L.I. who actually ran the boat, handled the diving, and insured that every piece of machinery was functioning at top efficiency. The IWO, nominally the second-in-command, was really just the senior watchkeeping officer. In *U-2317*, with a specialist torpedo officer, his job was mostly administrative and disciplinary.

"What are you called, *Herr Oberleutnant?*" Kruger asked. Somehow he wasn't quite ready to begin addressing the new man as 'L.I.' Not with Eisenberg still there.

"Döring, sir. *Oberleutnant* Klaus Döring."

"Where are you from?"

"Emden, sir."

Kruger smiled. "So am I. Where?"

"Just outside the Navy Yard, sir. My father owned a butcher shop about 200 metres from the main gate. Rudi's Pork Butcher?"

"I know it." He nodded slowly. "My family used to trade there." Kruger nodded again. "Well," he said, "it is good to have you aboard."

Döring smiled. "I'm glad to be here, sir."

Von Saltzmann grinned. "Good. Now, L.I.," he looked at Eisenberg, "and L.I., this bottle is still unopened, eh? Let's all have a drink to celebrate your successful patrol. Then *Fregattenkapitän* Eisenberg can report to the base Personnel Office. Your new orders will be waiting for you there."

"Schwartz!" Wiegand called.

The steward put his head in the door. "Sir?"

"Open this bottle, will you, lad?"

"Right away, sir. Just let me get a towel. You won't be wanting champagne all over the overhead, I imagine."

"Good lad. Hurry now."

Schwartz returned with a clean towel in a few moments and carefully extracted the cork from the big bottle, then poured the sparkling wine into each officer's glass. "No proper champagne flutes, I'm afraid, sir," he said. "Just have to make do with Navy issue water tumblers."

Von Saltzmann laughed. "This is supposed to be an excellent vintage, so I don't suppose having to drink it that way will be too great a problem." He lifted his glass. "To *U-2317*, gentlemen. May her record continue to mount."

"Good stuff," Reuter commented.

"It is that," Eisenberg said, standing up. "Well, I'm off then."

"I'll see you over the side, sir," Kruger said. Now that the big engineer was no longer under his command, he automatically reverted to the more respectful form of address. Rank aside, until now Eisenberg had been one of his subordinates — now he was again a superior officer.

Von Saltzmann was waiting at the base of the ladder when Kruger returned. "I *could* have told you this earlier," he said, "but you've had enough to worry about without being the bearer of bad news as well."

"What is it?"

"*Fregattenkapitän* Eisenberg." Von Saltzmann hesitated. "He had been urging his family to leave Danzig for some time now. Arrangements were eventually made, and they were taken across the bay to Gotenhafen for evacuation to the west."

"What happened, sir?"

"His family was put aboard the *Wilhelm Gustloff*. The ship sailed on schedule. Four nights ago she was torpedoed by a Russian submarine. A few hundred were all that were rescued."

"And Eisenberg's family?"

"His daughter, Irma, was picked up. The others were all killed." He frowned, shaking his head. "There were over 7,000 refugees aboard that ship when she went down. Most of them went with her."

"Good God!" Kruger rubbed his eyes. How did you comprehend a tragedy of that magnitude? "I remember the ship," he said. "I was quartered in her while I was in Gotenhafen on my commanding officer's course. But I wouldn't have thought she'd have held 7,000 people."

Von Saltzmann nodded. "That was the *official* figure, Hans. I've heard reports that there may have been as many as 10,000 aboard. The ship was packed with people—civilian refugees, wounded, submarine crews from the training establishment. The loss of life is incomprehensible."

"A Russian submarine did this?"

"So it seems. Since we've had to withdraw from the Gulf of Finland they've been active in the Baltic. Ivan doesn't have much of a Navy, but we have very little to throw against him at the moment."

Kruger walked slowly across the control room, standing over the darkened plot table for a moment. Was there to be no one left untouched by this war? Now it seemed that even rescue attempts were doomed to failure.

And the toll. Even apart from Eisenberg's family, there had never been anything like it in Naval warfare. All those thousands of people, killed by a single torpedo. How could anyone accept such losses? Compared to what had happened to that ship, his own losses were as nothing. Less than nothing.

He turned back to von Saltzmann. "I should have been the one to tell him, sir."

The captain shrugged. "You have enough to worry about, Hans. And *Fregattenkapitän* Eisenberg has been reassigned." He smiled. "Look, there's good news as well. These last two kills have given you a higher tonnage figure than anyone in the war. One or two more ships and you'll have your diamonds. As it is, you are now the top U-boat 'Ace' of the war."

"Somehow," Kruger said, "that goal no longer seems as important."

"Well, you'd best get used to it. The propaganda people have scheduled a news conference for you tomorrow afternoon."

"I thought we were still secret?" Kruger objected.

"You are, Hans. But the news conference is for *you*, not your boat. You have sunk more enemy shipping than any other commander. Very soon you will probably earn Germany's highest honour as well. It's all news." He smiled. "Besides, you've had the treatment before. You should know how to handle it."

"That was a long time ago, sir. And I didn't like it then."

Von Saltzmann shrugged. "Well, Hans, you're a bloody hero now, so you may as well get used to it."

•   •   •

His Majesty's Destroyer *Apache* tore through the choppy waters of the Saint George's Channel, smashing back the waves at her full speed of 36 knots, the spray surging back in a solid fountain from her raked stem. A few hundred yards abeam, *Gurkha* idled along, her captain relaying instructions from his Asdic operators.

As *Apache* charged past, a string of depth charges rolled lazily from her stern racks, while several more were fired out abeam. A few seconds later, the pattern detonated, throwing up great fountains of dirty water and dead fish in her wake.

A pair of Swordfish torpedo bombers, their bomb racks filled with depth charges, roared overhead, while their covering flight of four Seafire fighters milled about above them. The escort carrier *Vicious* was by now over the horizon, with only the upper part of her mast visible from the destroyers.

Ralston picked up the TBS microphone. "Leader to Ears," he said, using *Gurkha*'s call sign, which had been chosen for the unusual skill of her chief Asdic operator. "Did we accomplish anything?"

"My chief operator says he got away again, Dave. We're tracking him how. We place him at Green two-oh, range 4,000 yards."

"Port fifteen," Ralston ordered. Then, into the microphone, "I'm coming around to engage him. Blackie, come in from your side and we'll hit him with a double pattern."

"On my way," 'Blackie' replied.

"Midships," Ralston snapped. "Steer zero-five-nine."

The navigator, Lieutenant Geoffrey Walsh, moved to the front of the open bridge. "*Kikuyu* is helping on this one is she, sir?"

"Right. We'll hit the bastard with a double pattern and give ourselves twice the chance of a depth charge exploding within fatal distance of his hull."

"Do you think it's your friend, sir?"

Ralston shook his head. "He's manoeuvring too slowly. If it was Kruger he'd not hang about and let us batter him. He'd just fire up his turbine and clear out."

"Ears to all units!" the TBS speaker crackled. "The bastard's just fired a torpedo!"

"Where's it going?" Ralston demanded.

"Fired from Green two-oh," *Gurkha*'s captain reported. "Fish is now at Green three-five."

"Blackie!" Ralston snapped. "Break off and run for it!"

"Already done so, Leader," *Kikuyu*'s captain responded.

"There he goes," Walsh said.

"Ears to Blackie—the fish is following you around."

"I'm going to full speed. I'll see if I can outrun the bugger."

It was a reasonable risk. The electrically powered torpedoes the Germans used had a speed virtually identical to a Tribal class destroyer at full speed, which meant that with a sufficient lead the greater endurance of the destroyer should allow it to stay far enough ahead for the torpedo's batteries to run down before it could catch up. And provided the destroyer actually steamed at her design speed.

"Ears to Leader, you are approaching release point in five-four-three-two-one…"

"Release charges!" Ralston shouted, his finger mashing the button under the screen. Aft, the firing gong clattered and the waiting seamen pulled the lanyards of the depth-charge throwers and tripped the release levers on the racks, dropping several more over the stern.

The two explosions were almost simultaneous. Astern *Apache* the water boiled up as the depth charges reached their set depths and exploded, while half a mile away *Kikuyu* lurched violently out of control as an acoustic torpedo blasted away her stern. A moment later, the powerful destroyer went up in a single, massive explosion as her ready-use depth charges were set off in a sympathetic detonation.

One moment she was there, the next there was only a scattering of floating wreckage, and a great mushroom cloud of smoke and fire as her magazine joined the depth charges in completing her destruction.

Apache was already swinging around for a new attack when the stern of the U-boat broke surface amid a great welter of foam.

"U-boat on the surface at Red nine-oh!" a lookout shouted.

"All guns," Ralston ordered. "Open fire!"

Apache and her remaining consorts opened fire with everything that would bear, while overhead the old 'stringbags' swept down and dropped their charges right alongside the stricken U-boat, assuring her destruction.

"They're bailing out, sir," Walsh shouted.

"Direct hit!"

The rear of the U-boat's conning tower was shredded by the exploding shell, and the white-capped officer who had been encouraging his crew grabbed his leg and pitched over the side.

"Cease fire," Ralston ordered. "She's going down. Stand by to pick up survivors." He walked across the bridge. "Yeo, signal *Gurkha* to conduct a search for any survivors from *Kikuyu*."

"There she goes, sir!" Walsh shouted.

Ralston recrossed the bridge, watching with grim satisfaction as the U-boat began her final dive. It was a definite kill, he thought, but not the one he wanted more than anything. Not Kruger.

Just an old Type VIIc, the mainstay of the German U-boat arm, but still obsolete—good only for committing suicide.

The first lieutenant came up onto the bridge. "Good work, sir," he said. "Our first kill, eh?"

Ralston nodded slowly, gesturing first at the floating wreckage that moments before had been a powerful Tribal class destroyer, and then at the sinking U-boat. "And his last."

The shattered conning tower lingered a moment longer, listing far to starboard, so that the last anyone saw of the U-boat was the slime-covered grey tower, with its Popeye-like sailor insignia, and the depth charge scarred number, *U-702*.

•   •   •

Korvettenkapitän Hans Kruger stood at the window of the big conference room, his hands clasped behind his back, studying the people moving about the crowded streets just below. It was still early, but already the light was going. At this time of year the day never lasted long in Norway.

A rating moved past him, pulling down the heavy blinds. "Sorry, sir," he said. "Have to black out now."

Kruger nodded. "Carry on."

Von Saltzmann came over. "They're ready to begin," he said.

"Waste of time," Kruger commented. "I'm a Naval officer, not a bloody film star."

The pudgy captain shrugged. "Heroes are hard to come by lately, and you've accomplished more in your last sortie than most commanders manage in half a dozen."

"That simply makes me an efficient executioner," Kruger stated, "not a hero."

"Well, the Admiral has approved this, so there's not much you can do about it."

Kruger walked over to the long table that had been placed at the front of the room and took a seat. "I don't suppose there is," he said, "so why don't we just get it over with, right?"

"Right." Von Saltzmann nodded to the rating, who was now standing at the door. "Let them in," he said.

To Kruger it seemed that hundreds of people were crowding into the room, though he supposed there were really no more than 25 or so. They entered in a great rush, jostling each other, all trying to get the best seats, flash lamps popping, notebooks and pencils ready. In the rear of the room, a man was setting up a heavy cine camera on a tripod, while his assistant brought a microphone up to the podium and set up a pair of powerful lights.

When the newsreel photographer was set up, and the others had at last quieted down, von Saltzmann went to the podium and glared out at the group. He was used to the disciplined world of the Navy, and though he had dealt with people like these many times in the past, he was no more used to them than Kruger.

"I am *Kapitän zur See* Siegfried von Saltzmann," he began. "As you are probably aware, our U-boat forces have suffered setbacks recently in their battles with enemy forces in the North Atlantic."

One of the reporters groaned audibly. There was nothing newsworthy in *that*. It was by now an all too familiar story.

"But this time," von Saltzmann continued, "we have had a major success. During the day and evening of 18th January, *U-2317*, under the command of *Korvettenkapitän* Hans Kruger, made an attack on a fast convoy in British coastal waters. Before he withdrew, after expending all of his torpedoes, a total of seven enemy vessels had been hit, with five sunk. One of those sunk was the cruiser HMS *Curacoa*."

They were listening now, he thought. After the depressing string of German defeats on all fronts, even a small victory was something to savour. And this was a major accomplishment. Would have been, even in the early part of the war, when the U-boats were still the scourge of the convoy routes.

"I will now turn this over to *Korvettenkapitän* Kruger, who will be happy to answer your questions."

Kruger forced himself to smile as he took his place at the podium. 'Happy' was not quite the right word, he thought. 'Resigned' would be more like it.

A fat little man, with a notebook and pencil in his hands, stood up. "Krause," he said, adding, rather pointlessly, "of the Propaganda Ministry. Could you tell us, *Kapitän*, what was the total tonnage sunk on this patrol?"

"Approximately 36,000 tons."

The questions continued for almost an hour before von Saltzmann declared the news conference to be finished. Kruger watched them go, shaking his head. It had been more difficult than either of them had imagined, for so many of the reporters' questions could not be properly answered without giving away details of the boat's performance. Details that were still secret.

"Back to Berlin for me," von Saltzmann said, as they left the building. "I have to make my report to the Admiral. We're going to keep you in our section as long as possible, Hans. *Konteradmiral* Godt is very eager to get his hands on your boat. Particularly since your convoy. However, our Admiral outranks him, and just now Dönitz is too busy with other matters to worry about a single U-boat, so for the moment the problem is settled." He smiled. "And very soon you should receive your diamonds, eh? God knows, you deserve them."

Kruger laughed. "I'd settle for a nice, long leave."

"Wouldn't we all? Well, if I get back here before you sortie, I will see you then. Otherwise, when you return, eh?"

Kruger saluted. "Have a good trip, sir."

He had gone only a few metres when he heard someone calling his name. Even without the big camera in her hands he could remember her from the news conference. Ingrid something or other.

"I have nothing more to say," he grunted, as she caught up with him.

The girl smiled, falling in step beside him. "No more questions," she said. "Besides, I already know more than most of the others."

"Do you, *Fräulein?*"

"I'm not with a newspaper or service," she said. "I work directly for the Propaganda Ministry."

"So do all the others. What makes you special?"

"My job gives me access to information the others never see. Details of your boat, for instance."

"That information is secret," he reminded her.

"And it's going to stay that way, *Herr Korvettenkapitän*. Besides, it's not the boat I'm interested in, but the man."

He stopped walking. "How—particularly?"

"You have accomplished something no U-boat commander has done in years. Perhaps never in a single day. The public is desperate for some bit of hope, for some hero to look up to."

"And I'm to be him?"

"Yes."

"No." He shook his head firmly. It was obvious what was intended, and he wanted no part of it. Her ministry was planning to give him the full build-up—perhaps try to make another Prien out of him

But he wasn't another Prien. He had done nothing that any other commander, given the same boat, could not have done as well or better. The real hero, if there was one, was the boat, not her captain. Given such a command even an idiot like Ostler could have become an ace.

"I'm not a hero," he said.

"That doesn't matter," the girl said. "You soon will be, to a great many people. The fearless U-boat 'Ace,' slapping the enemy in the face, defying them to accept his reckless challenge!" She laughed, brushing a wisp of blond hair back from her face. "You *are* going to be a hero, *Kapitän* Kruger, whether you like it or not."

"I don't think I do."

She shrugged. "You have very little choice in the matter, I'm afraid."

He looked at her, hearing the steel in her voice. She can't be more than 20, he thought, but something has hardened her, made her tough beyond her years.

She was a small woman, quite slender, but with a good figure, and very attractive in a casual sort of way. Blond, with very blue eyes, and a good smile.

"I don't have to cooperate with your hero-building efforts," he said.

"True enough," she laughed. "*We* can do it without you, just so long as you continue to sink enemy ships."

• • •

Captain David Ralston threw the newspaper onto his bunk in disgust, wondering again if some of these so-called journalists were actually on the same side in this war.

'RALSTON GETS SECOND CHANCE,' the headline declared.

It was true enough, he thought. So was the story. But the emphasis seemed all wrong to him.

He frowned and picked up the paper again, sitting down on the bunk to read it through more carefully. Around him the ship was silent, with only the faint vibration of the generator motors to convey a feeling of vitality, as they rested alongside the old depot ship in Portsmouth Harbour.

'After having his ship sunk beneath him off Jutland,' the article said, 'Captain David Ralston, RN, DSC and Bar, was able to accomplish a daring escape while being transported to a prisoner-of-war camp in southern Norway. Upon his return to England, Captain Ralston was appointed to the command of a new Killer Group, which promptly put paid to an enemy submarine last week in the Irish Sea.

'On the same day, at a Bergen press conference, the German Naval Command announced that the same U-boat that had been responsible for the sinkings of HMS *Loch Grym*, Captain Ralston's former command, along with her sister frigates HMS *Loch Katrin, Loch Fanich*, and *Loch Seaforth*, and the escort aircraft carrier HMS *Snapper*, was also responsible for the destruction of the anti-aircraft cruiser HMS *Curacoa*, along with four freighters, on 18th January. The responsible U-boat has been revealed as *U-2317*, under the command of *Korvettenkapitän* Hans Kruger, who is said to be Germany's most highly decorated submarine commander still on sea duty.

'The German Propaganda Ministry are touting Kruger as the new ideal of the U-boat "Ace," an understandable campaign as his boat has been responsible for the sinking of 37,600 tons of badly needed shipping during a single day, as well as the damaging of an additional 14,100 tons. The damaged ships are not expected to be repaired before war's end, although government sources indicate that it had been possible to salvage much of their cargo.

'During his time in submarines, Kruger has reportedly been responsible for the sinking of 490,000 tons of Allied shipping, a total which includes a large number of merchant vessels, as well as four frigates, an escort aircraft carrier, an anti-aircraft cruiser, and the heavy cruiser HMS *Bedford*.

'British seamen have nicknamed Kruger "the Bandmaster," in response to his daring act of playing the German national anthem at full volume on his intercom while eluding the convoy's escorts, who were evidently unable to destroy him even with his boat loudly announcing its position.

'It is expected that Captain Ralston's new Killer Group will have, as one of its primary tasks, the detection and destruction of U-2317.'

Bloody Rubbish, Ralston thought. Except for the first paragraph it was all Kruger. As if the British press was as bent on building the man's image as the Germans were.

Very little was mentioned of Ralston's own past record, which he thought was odd, as the article purported to be about him. Kruger's list of kills was well documented, while his own were seemingly ignored.

He was surprised the writer had failed to mention *Kikuyu* being sunk along with the U-boat last week. That event had ruined the successful attack, but pointed up a new danger posed by the improved model acoustic torpedoes the Germans were using. Even the sight of the enemy commander moaning on the table in the sickbay had not made up for the loss.

They had picked up 30 survivors from the U-boat, but *Kikuyu* had taken her entire crew with her to the bottom of the Irish Sea.

He tossed the paper across his sea cabin and lay back on the bunk. A few hours in harbour, replenishing their stock of depth charges and 4.7-inch ammunition, and the ships would be off again. At some point a fourth destroyer would no doubt be provided, but for now they would operate with what they had, and if Kruger came into their snare it would be the end of him.

Ralston had no doubts as to who the ultimate victor would be. This new group would see to that, given a chance. Not even Kruger, in his astonishing boat, could outrun a destroyer at full speed. And the group was getting better by the day, honing their skills against the day when *U-2317* would fall into their net.

They had sunk another boat the previous day, using the same techniques. One boat listened, while the others made the attack at high speed, and the carrier's planes hovered over head, ready to help if an opening presented itself.

The weapon was forged and ready. Now all he had to do was find Kruger again.

• • •

Kruger looked up from his novel as someone rapped on the cabin door. It never ended, he thought. With a sigh, he slipped a scrap of paper into the book and tossed it onto his desk.

"Enter."

It was Döring, the new L.I., looking rather disgusted. "Sorry to disturb you, sir," he said, "but there's a problem."

"Serious?"

"Potentially, yes. We've discovered a fault in one of the Perhydrol lines."

Just what we needed, Kruger thought. "What sort of fault, L.I.?"

"A leak, sir." He spread his hands. "This is in the line itself, I'm afraid, so it presents a major problem."

"Can you repair it?"

"Yes. But not easily and not quickly." He shrugged. "If it was a fitting, we could probably manage without any real trouble, but this is a fault in the fuel line itself. It means flying in a part from Kiel. When that arrives there's still the job of purging the line and getting it installed."

Kruger looked up, curiously. "What do you mean, purging?"

"The lines have to be absolutely clean of any grease or oil," Döring explained. "I expect you've seen how peroxide reacts when you put it on a wound, sir?"

Kruger nodded. "Little bubbles," he said. "Lots of fizzing."

"Exactly, sir. But with the commercial preparation used for treating wounds, you have only a 3% solution—it's mostly distilled water. The Perhydrol fuel is 95% *pure* hydrogen-peroxide. A bit of grease in a fuel line and you'd have an explosion, which would probably rupture the line."

Kruger frowned. They had completed reloading an hour ago, and their escorts were already laid on for that night. Now, it seemed, there would be a delay.

"How long to make repairs?"

"Perhaps a week, sir. *If* we can get the part here."

"The fuel line, you mean, Chief?"

"Yes, sir."

"Can't you just make one up? I expect you'll be able to find sufficient pipe or tubing on a base like this."

"I *could* make one up, sir," Döring replied. "But I'd not be able to guarantee the repair for more than a day or two. Perhydrol is extremely corrosive, and the proper fuel lines are lined with glass to keep it away from the metal."

Kruger nodded. "Very well, Chief. Put through a request for the part." He thought a moment. "No, write up the request, then give it to me and I'll send it through the Admiral's office. We'll probably get faster results that way."

"I'll take care of it immediately, sir."

Kruger picked up his novel, but found that he couldn't get himself interested again.

The bloody delay! he thought. At this stage of the war every minute was precious. With the enemy closing in on all fronts there was absolutely no time to waste.

Döring returned with the requisition and Kruger reached for his greatcoat. Right now it would do him good to get out of the boat for a while. Let the fresh, cold air clear his mind.

He found Wiegand in the control room. "Did our new L.I. tell you what's come up, Number One?"

"Yes, sir. He said there'd be a delay."

"He estimates a week." Kruger held up the requisition form. "I'm going ashore, to put this through direct to the Admiral. With any luck he can expedite things."

The IWO shook his head. "Not fast enough to suit me, sir," he said. "This town is damned depressing. I like a bit of sunlight from time to time."

Kruger laughed. "You'll see bloody little of that once we're under way, Number One."

"You know what I mean, sir," Wiegand asserted. "When we're out on patrol there's plenty to keep you occupied, but just sitting around bloody Bergen—"

Kruger walked to the ladder. "I see your point," he said. "I'm off now. You can make up a roster for local leave. As we seem to be stuck here a bit longer, we may as well allow the men a bit of freedom."

"I'll see to it, sir."

•   •   •

"Do you mind if I join you?"

Kruger looked up from where he had been brooding over a
beer in a little tavern that had been more or less taken over by
the Navy since their arrival in Bergen. It was noisier than he
liked, and at the moment he would have preferred getting
completely away from uniforms. But the civilian bars were too
dangerous for a lone German, no matter what Quisling and his
government might wish.

And now this! It was the girl from the Propaganda Ministry, well-muffled in a heavy fur coat. What was her name?
Ingrid something?"

"Does it matter if I do?"

She smiled. "Not much. I wish to speak with you, and if I
can't do it here, then I'll simply see your *Kapitän* von Saltzmann and make an official request."

Kruger shrugged. "Then, by all means, sit down, *Fräulein*,
er?"

"Brenner. Ingrid Brenner." She slipped off her coat and
hung it over the back of her chair before sitting down. Kruger
could almost feel the other men in the smoky room watching
her. Her dress was of flame-coloured silk, and left her slender
arms bare. The smooth material seemed to glow in the subdued light, moulding itself to the sleek curves of her body,
while in the front it was cut quite low, showing off the upper
curves of her breasts.

"You don't like me very much, do you?" she asked.

"Not particularly."

A waiter appeared at the table, saying something in Norwegian. The girl looked at him curiously. "What?" she asked, in
German. "Sorry, I don't speak your language."

"Of course, Miss. Excuse me. Would you care for a drink?"

"Beer will do."

The waiter bowed slightly. "Right away, Miss. More for you, sir?"

"Not just yet."

"Why did he do that?" Ingrid asked, after the waiter had gone.

"Do what?"

"The man seemed somehow relieved when he discovered I only understood German, yet he speaks with a terrible accent. Why?"

"He thought you were Norwegian when you first came in, I suppose. Even the people here, who have known Germans for years, are still upset when one of their girls goes around with a German. They don't like collaborators very much, but, as you are German yourself, there's no objection."

"It sounds idiotic."

He shrugged. "It is. But I suspect we would feel much the same if it was *our* country that was occupied."

The waiter returned with her drink, then went back to the bar.

"Why don't you like me?" she asked.

"I really have nothing against you. But you've decided to make a hero of me, and I don't see myself in that role. You're doing something I consider objectionable, and so I naturally dislike you for it."

"And how do you see yourself, if not as a hero?"

"I'm a rather ordinary man with a job to do. It happens that my job is to sink enemy ships, which means that it's also to kill enemy sailors. I can assure you that not all of them die easy deaths." He frowned. "You don't always think about it when you see it in a photograph, or even while watching it through a periscope. That gives it all a rather detached, almost impersonal feeling. But the death is still there. In a freighter you kill a few men with every torpedo—in a large warship you may kill hundreds, or even thousands. Always there are those deaths—men, sometimes women and children as well. The lucky ones are killed instantly, or simply drowned. But others may be scalded by an exploding boiler, or broiled alive by burning fuel. Some are left to freeze in water where no one can last more than minutes. This is war, which is at best a form of legalised murder.

"But *your* job," he went on, "is to somehow make all of that slaughter glorious. Well it's not! It's merely killing now, and long past the time when there's any real purpose to it!"

She regarded him curiously. How old was he? Twenty-seven? There was a sense of bitterness in his voice, even of despair. As if he had long since had enough of killing and war. Like an old man who no longer cared if he saw his next birthday.

It was said that there was a limit to just how much any man could do. This man, she thought, was very close to reaching it.

"Did you know," she asked, "that Captain Ralston—your former prisoner—has escaped, and been put in command of a special group whose primary job seems to be killing you?"

He looked up. "No. I didn't know that."

She nodded. "It's all over the English newspapers. They say he's been given a second chance. As I understand it, his group has already sunk two U-boats." She paused. "One of them was yours."

"Mine?" He looked at her, puzzled. "My boat is tied up exactly where I left her."

"No, captain, not your *present* command. Your previous boat—*U-702*."

Kruger took a long pull at his beer, wondering why he didn't feel a greater sense of loss. He had been in that boat for nearly two years, and knew every man in her as a friend. But all he felt was a certain numbness—as if it no longer mattered.

"Most of her crew were captured," Ingrid added, softly.

"And her captain?"

"The Red Cross tells us that he's alive." She paused, watching him for any hint of remorse. "They also say that he will be repatriated as soon as it is practical."

Repatriated? Kruger thought. That meant a man so grievously wounded that he would be unable to remain in the military. "How badly was he injured?" he asked.

"He lost a leg and one eye." She was watching him intently. Wondering. "Was he a close friend?"

Kruger shrugged. "He was my Executive Officer for two years. We made a very good team." He nodded. "I suppose he was also my friend, yes."

But had he been? Kruger wondered. A captain and his IWO were necessarily close. The daily routine, to say nothing of emergencies, required it. But did that always make for friendship? Sometimes they could hate each other, but still make a good team.

He smiled suddenly. Perhaps that was to be the case with this girl. She intended to make a hero of him, and what he thought of it didn't seem to matter. She would simply do her job, while he would do his, and in the end they would most likely both benefit.

"How old are you?" he asked.

She looked startled. "Does it matter?"

He grinned. "I seem to be stuck with you," he said. "So I'm naturally curious. You don't seem old enough to be such a nuisance."

She laughed. "I'll be 20 in June."

"You're a bloody infant. Such dedication in one so young is—well, either encouraging or daunting. I really don't know which."

"You're not so old yourself, *Kapitän* Kruger."

"Twenty-seven going on 90," he replied. "Old enough." He frowned and held up his empty glass in a gesture to the waiter, who nodded and turned to the barman. "My entire generation—what there is left of it, that is—is much older than it should be. I was born during a war that destroyed much of a generation. I may well die in one that's even worse."

The waiter came and placed a fresh drink in front of Kruger. When he was gone, the girl said, "I expect you'll manage to live to a good old age, with a crowd of adoring grandchildren gathered at your feet, every one of them full of questions about what it was like in these days." She lowered her voice. "The last days of an empire—aborted before it was ever truly born."

He studied her, surprised. "And I thought you were a dedicated Nazi!"

"I am dedicated to only one thing," she stated flatly, "and that is to surviving this war. If that means working for a lecherous old degenerate like Doctor Goebbels, then I will work for him. And I'm quite good at my job, by the way. But I come from a very large family—four brothers and seven sisters—and I'm the only one still alive." She paused, sipping at her beer. "My parents died before the war, the others in combat, and in air raids."

Kruger nodded. "My family is gone, too," he said.

"My oldest sister was an Army nurse," she said, "on the eastern front. Somehow there was a mistake, a communications breakdown that prevented the evacuation order from being received. The Russians captured the hospital. They slaughtered most of the doctors and patients. The nurses they kept as toys. When our forces re-captured the hospital my sister was still alive, but was also quite insane. I'm told she was raped at least 50 times. The Russian officer simply gave her to a platoon as a present, and they all took turns with her." She looked directly at him. "A week later she killed herself."

"I'm sorry," he said. It seemed totally inadequate.

She signaled the waiter for another beer. "I've learned to live with it." She smiled weakly. "Besides, with all the losses we've suffered, it will soon be over in any case. Then will come the *real* task, *Kapitän*. Building a new Germany from the ashes of the old."

Kruger shook his head. "Unlikely. I think the Allies have learned their lesson. They'll never permit Germany to become strong again. The Russians will see to that."

"Churchill is not a fool," Ingrid said. "Neither is Roosevelt—though I suspect he's the more naïve of the two. If Germany was *once* bent on world domination, Russia still is. The Yanks and Tommies will need this country strong again to help stand against them. And you can tell your grandchildren I predicted that."

"No grandchildren," Kruger said. "Once, not so long ago, I thought there might be a family after the war." He shook his head. "She was killed in a raid."

"So now there is no one?"

"No."

The waiter placed the beer in front of her. A very beautiful girl, he thought. It was a pity she was German. He didn't like Germans very much, though he had once, before the war, when they had come as tourists and not as conquerors. A bit arrogant sometimes, but never so bad as some others. The English, for instance, who seemed constitutionally incapable of ever learning any language but their own, and completely unconcerned with the fault. Most Germans would at least make an effort—the English insisted that everyone else learn to speak *their* language.

The girl was interesting, but the snatches of conversation he had heard were unimportant. Sometimes he could pick up useful information, when the right German officers had had a bit too much to drink.

"Will there be anything else?" the waiter asked. "He gestured at the clock behind the bar. "We close in ten minutes."

"Nothing else, thank you," Kruger said.

The waiter nodded and disappeared into the back of the bar.

"I think I'll go back to my boat now," Kruger announced.

"Do you have to?"

He looked at her curiously. There was something odd in her voice. "Why?" he asked. "More questions about my so-called heroism?"

Ingrid shook her head. "Nothing like that. I just don't want to be alone right now. It's all this talk of war and killing. It reminds me of things which were better forgotten." She sighed. "Some memories are not to be savoured."

"True." He thought of Otto, looking quite grand in his dress uniform, a newly promoted captain of infantry. He had been ready to march off and win the war single-handed, destroying the Bolsheviks now that most of Europe was under German control. Even after fighting in France and the Low Countries Otto had been so sure of himself, so proud of his promotion, and the Iron Cross First Class he wore on his breast.

A few months later, back on leave, Otto had tried to show the same cheerful, optimistic spirit, but it hadn't worked. He had looked haunted, old before his time.

Now he was probably dead.

"Where are you staying, *Fräulein* Brenner?" he asked.

"A little hotel." She smiled suddenly. "I can't even attempt to pronounce the name, but it's quite close to here."

"Fine. I'll walk you there."

"There will be no promises. No commitments."

"I'm only walking you home, *Fräulein*, nothing more."

"Are you sure? And call me Ingrid, will you?"

I don't even like this girl, he thought. Or do I? Somehow she seems more human now. Her family would explain her attitude. Anyone could grow hard with such experience. He shrugged, smiling.

"I'm not really sure of anything just now," he said.

Chapter Seven

Endless Nights

U-2317 cruised slowly northward, her extended *Schnorchel* supplying fresh air for her throbbing diesel, which was pushing her streamlined hull through the frigid water at an economical nine knots. All around them the sea was empty, the occasional pulses of the *Nibelung* reflecting back nothing more ominous than the odd chunk of floating ice. So close to the surface the range was limited, but it was adequate, and unlike the hydrophones was not rendered useless by the diesel's noise.

In the wardroom, Himmler was frowning at the chessboard, wondering how he could possibly extricate himself from the trap into which Reuter had so skillfully baited him. The two had been playing since the day they both arrived on board, before the boat was commissioned in October. In that time Himmler figured they had probably played at least 300 games.

He could remember winning two.

In the engine room, Döring and the Master Mechanic, Petty Officer Braun, were carefully inspecting the Walter turbine. The fuel line, which had been replaced in Bergen, was showing no further signs of giving trouble.

"Probably cracked the glass lining in that first depth charge pattern," Braun said. "That could have started the problem."

"Or there might have been a tiny flaw in the lining right from the start," Döring offered. "Time and vibration would have done the rest."

Braun grinned. "Anyway," he said, "everything looks fine now, sir."

Döring nodded agreement. Walter turbines were never more than a calculated risk, even on their best behavior. Temperamental, prone to breakdown and the risk of explosion, the fuel highly corrosive. But at the moment everything seemed to be in order.

"I don't see any problems now," Döring said. "I'm going forward to check the trim. Why don't you have a look at the diesel? I thought I noticed a little roughness a few minutes ago."

• • •

Petty Officer Willi Dorfmann dipped his wooden spoon into one of the big pots he had boiling on the galley stove and stirred carefully. He was a bit of a perfectionist, insisting that every meal he served be as nearly to the class of *Der Schwarze Adler*, the wonderful first-class restaurant in Potsdam where he had been second chef before the war, as was possible under existing conditions.

None of the men seemed to have any complaints. Even in a time of chronic shortages and *ersatz* everything, Dorfmann could usually manage to turn out a meal to satisfy the most demanding gourmet. The only complaints came from *Oberfänrich* Ostler, who preferred to emulate his beloved *Führer*'s vegetarianism. Not an easy task in a U-boat, where nearly everything was either tinned or smoked. *U-2317* also boasted the luxury of a freezer, giving Dorfmann a better choice of meats than in older boats.

Testing the sauce, Dorfmann smiled to himself. It was quite good. He was forced to work with the same standard foodstuffs issued to all U-boats, much of it seemingly left over from the Great War. But it wasn't so much the food, he thought, as knowing what to do with it. You could just open the tins and throw it all together, the way many Navy cooks did, or you could exercise a touch of creativity and produce something quite fine.

Dorfmann was an excellent chef, and he had a fine, modern galley to work in. Until the war ended, and he could go back to his old life, he was quite content.

•　　　•　　　•

Oberfänrich Gerhard Ostler paced slowly from one end of the control room to the other, his mind working on the problem of his daily column for *U-2317's* little two-page mimeographed newspaper. Something stirring, he thought, and patriotic. It wasn't easy to come up with that sort of thing day after day. Perhaps, he thought, he could quote something from *Mein Kampf* again, if he could find anything that sounded relatively literate.

What would the others think, he wondered, if they knew what he *really* thought of their beloved leader? What it felt like to constantly glorify the man who had been responsible for the deaths of most of his family? His dedication was protective, he knew, meant to disguise his real feelings and beliefs, which were dangerous to hold.

Seaman Schmitt, who was messenger during Ostler's watch, looked up from the technical manual he was reading. "Time to change course in five minutes, sir," he said.

Ostler nodded absentmindedly. "Inform the captain," he said, still pacing. He was beginning to get an idea for his column.

Schmitt looked at his officer curiously, then put down his manual and started forward. Ostler was a strange bird in any case, he thought. So wrapped up in his Party nonsense that he completely lost sight of what it was all about. The man actually seemed to think there was still a chance of winning!

• • •

Korvettenkapitän Hans Kruger put down his pen at the sound of a rap on the doorframe. "Enter," he called.

Schmitt stuck his head inside. "Mister Ostler says that it will be time to change course in five minutes, sir," he said. Ostler, Schmitt thought, had said nothing of the sort, and probably didn't even know they were actually going to change course, but this was the proper way, and he would try to keep his watch officer out of trouble if he could. It was like caring for an injured bird, or a lunatic relative. A nuisance, but something you did out of basic compassion.

Besides, there were those odd times when he seemed to see through the Party rhetoric into a totally different person. Someone human.

"I'll be there directly," Kruger said. "Is *Oberleutnant* Reuter in the control room yet?"

"No, sir."

"Find him then, and have him report to me there."

"Aye, aye, sir."

Schmitt hurried away, letting the curtain fall back across the opening. Kruger rarely bothered closing the sliding door unless he was working on coding. Keeping it open could save a few seconds in an emergency.

Kruger glanced at the letter he had been writing, still wondering if there was any real sense in it. He had never really intended to go up to the girl's room that night in Bergen. His plan had been to escort her safely back to her hotel, then return to the base. It was the sensible thing to do. His experience with Hannah had driven home the danger of any sort of emotional involvement during wartime. You could never be sure that anyone would still be alive *tomorrow*, to say nothing of the distant future.

But in war there were always surprises.

Three men had come out of an alley moments after they left the tavern. Kruger still wasn't sure just what it was that had warned him. Some almost inaudible sound, he thought, or perhaps the extraordinary sensitivity to danger that every successful U-boat captain was forced to develop just to stay alive.

Without thinking he had shoved the girl roughly to the pavement, rolling over and jerking out his pistol at the same time. While they were still falling a dozen 9-millimetre slugs had chirruped over their heads, whining away into the night and pelting them with chips of shattered brick from the tavern's wall

Then Kruger's heavy automatic was out and firing. His first two shots took the man with the Sten gun full in the chest, dropping him like a stone. The other two, armed with captured German pistols, turned to flee after firing a few poorly aimed shots.

Very deliberately, Kruger lined up the sights of his big Browning automatic and squeezed the trigger.

The second Resistance man screamed, the bullet taking him high in the back, and collapsed in a moaning heap, his P-38 clattering away in the gutter, out of reach of his groping fingers.

The third man vanished around the corner as a dozen Naval officers poured out of the tavern, their pistols drawn and ready.

Kruger got to his feet, then helped the girl up, while the other officers crowded around, asking questions. A moment later an Army patrol came clattering around the corner.

"Are you all right, sir?" the lieutenant asked. He was an old man, Kruger noticed, a veteran of the last war recalled to serve in this one now that five years of fighting had taken its toll on the younger men.

"Fine," Kruger said. "Another one got away, 'round that corner."

"Corporal, take three men and get after him," the lieutenant snapped. "Quickly!"

"*Jawohl, Herr Leutnant!*"

Kruger turned to the girl. "You all right?" he asked.

"I feel like I've been run over by a lorry," she said, "but there's no damage." She smiled. "Thanks to you."

The Army officer put the toe of his boot under the man with the Sten and rolled him over onto his back.

"My God!" the girl gasped.

"You know him?" the lieutenant asked.

"He was our waiter," she said. "In the tavern there."

After that, it had been natural enough for Kruger to go with her all the way to her room. In the end, he had spent the night with her, never quite sure just why.

He was equally unsure why he was writing to her. Ingrid Brenner. A lovely girl, but he still thought of her as rather too hardened by the war.

He shrugged. It would all work out for the best, he decided. Either they would never see each other again, write it all off as a pleasant interlude amidst the harshness of a world war, or they *would* get together again, and perhaps something good would come of it. It was all up to the same implacable Fate who decided whether he would be one of those who survived, or one who went down to a cold, wet grave on the ocean floor.

He stood up, sliding the half-written letter into the desk drawer, and started for the control room. The boat was the immediate concern. His personal life would just have to wait.

•   •   •

The ice was still well south in late February, the darkness almost constant. But the giant four-engined *Condor* had had little trouble finding the darkened convoy as it steamed purposefully around the North Cape and into the Barents Sea, on the final leg of the Murmansk run.

Three Seafire fighters from an escort carrier had taken off to intercept the moment the huge patrol bomber was sighted, but it took time to climb to altitude, and more time to work their way through the hail of defensive fire and shoot it down. By the time they had, the Focke-Wulfe had radioed a message to its base in Tromsk.

The convoy was located, its escorts identified, and the message sent out to all units in the area. Find the convoy and destroy it.

•   •   •

The decoded signal lay at the top of the plot table while Reuter worked over the unrolled chart with his dividers and parallel rules. After what seemed an eternity he stood up.

"Well?" Kruger asked.

"We are here, sir," Reuter said, tapping a spot on the chart. "The last reported position of the convoy was here. So allowing for the necessity of rounding the North Cape, they are about 90 miles ahead of us."

Kruger picked up the signal. "The convoy is estimated to be averaging 12 knots," he said. "So we should be able to overtake them if we use the turbine and run deep."

"Yes, sir," Reuter replied. "If we can maintain a steady 26 knots we should cover the 90 miles in about three and one-half hours. In that time the convoy will have traveled an additional 42 miles."

"Total time to intercept, Pilot?"

"About five and one-half hours."

"Total run?"

"I should estimate 150 miles."

Kruger shook his head. "That doesn't leave us much reserve for the attack," he said. "Ten nautical miles at full speed. Perhaps a bit more—or less."

Wiegand had been studying the chart. Now he looked up, wondering if the decision made now might be the one that would end his life. "What will you do, sir?" he asked.

Kruger studied the chart and Reuter's penciled figures. "It's worth a try," he said. "We'll be arriving in the operations area with a minimum of Perhydrol left in the tanks, but once there we'll probably operate at silent speed for the most part. What fuel we have left, we'll save for use in emergencies." He grinned. "Pilot, give me a course and we'll be on our way."

Reuter glanced at the chart. "New course is zero-seven-five, sir."

"Come to zero-seven-five, Coxswain," Kruger ordered. "Chief, we will dive to 300 metres and go to the turbine."

"Aye, aye, sir," Döring said. He turned to his crew. "Out main engine clutch. Shut down diesel."

The powerful engine clattered to a halt as its fuel was cut off, the boat gliding forward on her residual way.

"Close main induction and exhaust," Döring ordered. "Main E-motor, ahead one-half. Lower *Schnorchel*. Bow and stern planes down ten degrees. Zero angle."

"Course is zero-seven-five," Stauber reported.

"Passing through 100 metres, sir."

Kruger slowly paced the length of the control room, waiting, as the boat planed down to her most efficient operating depth.

"Three hundred metres, sir," Döring reported.

Kruger nodded. "Very well, L.I.. Turbine, ahead, full."

"All stop. Out E-motor clutch. Ignite! Engage turbine clutch."

The turbine lit off with a loud bang. "Full power on turbine," the L.I. said. Silently he watched the pointer creep around the dial. "We are at full speed, sir," he reported. "Twenty-six point six knots."

"Thank you, L.I.. Let me know if you have any problems with the turbine. I don't want to lose this convoy," Kruger asserted, "but neither do I suddenly want to find myself without power at a crucial moment."

"I'll keep an eye on things, sir," Döring assured him. He glanced at his panel. Everything *looked* correct, but you could never be sure with these engines. The design was a sound one, so far as it went, but it was also subject to more than its share of problems. Minor flaws were a constant. In his brief time aboard he had grown used to those, even learned to anticipate some of them.

But at the moment everything seemed perfect. He found that perfection made him more nervous than a constant flow of minor irritations. As if the power plant had decided that it would hoard all its little problems, saving them up as fuel for a major disaster instead.

The signal had come a few minutes earlier, and after decoding it Kruger had responded with his present grid location and *U-2317*'s newly assigned call sign, *Musikmeister*. He grinned suddenly. The radio call sign was like a deliberate challenge to the enemy. It was the British who had invented the 'Band Master' nickname, after that astonishing convoy battle in January. Now the high command was throwing it back in their faces.

Even Kruger found he enjoyed the taunt.

He almost laughed. I'm beginning to sound like Ingrid, he thought. Playing the National Anthem while they raced away from the convoy had been more of a lark than anything else. A playful gesture from a man who, after years of creeping blindly through the depths, groping away from countless depth charges, has suddenly regained the upper hand.

But not this new call sign. This time it was a deliberate taunt.

Even breaking radio silence was a part of it. They were taking precautions, though. The Enigma machine used to code their messages used a different coding sequence than other submarines, with special care taken to insure that the initial sequence was as complex as possible. The chart grid was also different from the standard one. That had been Kruger's idea. Despite assurances that it wasn't possible, he suspected that the enemy had got their hands on a chart and were using it to send their planes directly to where they would find a German submarine.

Would Ralston and his new killer group be with this convoy? he wondered. Probably not, but it was always possible. More likely, though, he would be lurking about the Western Approaches to the channel, where *U-2317* had last struck.

Where poor Konrad had lost a leg, an eye, and his first command. Ralston would have to pay for that, Kruger thought.

"Do you think we'll be able to implement your wolf pack idea, sir?" Wiegand asked.

"I don't know yet, Number One," Kruger replied. "There should be other boats about. There are usually some in that general area, just waiting for these arctic convoys to be sighted."

"Will that put our boat in command, sir?" Ostler asked.

"Perhaps. Normally, the first boat to actually sight the convoy will signal any others to converge on the area. But the actual command is usually by radio from headquarters."

"You know, sir," Reuter said, "if we sink almost anything you'll get your diamonds."

Kruger fingered the Maltese cross shaped medal at his throat. "It'll give me something of value to pawn once the war's over, I suppose."

The others laughed, except for Ostler, who looked hurt and slightly offended. A mandatory attitude, he thought.

"Well, my department is top line," Himmler chimed in. "My men went over the torpedoes earlier today, and they are all in perfect condition." He smiled. "So, I might add, is all the related equipment. You tell me where to aim and when to fire and I'll give you the hits you need."

"Excellent." Kruger pulled his empty pipe from the pocket of his reefer jacket and clamped the bit between his teeth. Smoking was never permitted with the boat submerged, but he had long ago discovered that it was not always necessary to light a pipe in order to enjoy it.

What did the others really think? he wondered. From the look of the man, Ostler was yearning after some sort of glory. Perhaps even death in battle, which for some reason so many otherwise intelligent people seemed to consider a great honour. It wasn't, Kruger was sure. It was simply one of any number of ways to die.

And there would be more than enough dying soon. It was inevitable, Kruger realised, once the attack began. Though you never really saw the slaughter in a U-boat, it was always there. The sudden, shattering detonation of a torpedo, red-hot boilers bursting violently as the cold sea poured in, the released steam scalding and flaying anyone within reach. The slow, horrible death of those trapped behind watertight doors in a sealed compartment, the water inching higher and higher, until the last of the air was displaced and drowning brought an end to the struggle. Or the slower, more horrible death when the compartment held, and you were trapped in a sealed chamber with the air turning foul, gasping for breath as the last of the oxygen was breathed away.

For those on deck there was the endless wait in a small boat, or bobbing about on a Carley float, waiting for the rescue that never came, clenched fists brandished in fury as the other ships steamed heedlessly past. Thrown into the water, death would be quick, freezing in the frigid waters, or being gutted like a dead fish as the escorts laid down a pattern of depth charges, ignoring the havoc they might be causing amongst the survivors. Or the screaming agony as the flames forced you higher and higher up the tilting deck of a sinking ship, the tremendous heat scorching the hair from a man's face, turning buttons and fasteners into instruments of torture, before the last flames licked out and you went plummeting into the sea, your clothes burning like a torch, to die in horrible pain, half-submerged in a lake of burning fuel and oil.

And all that suffering, Kruger thought, was merely to buy a little time. Each convoy to reach Murmansk drove another nail into the coffin of the Third Reich. The Russians manufactured a considerable supply of armaments in their own factories, hidden well behind the Urals, out of reach of German air power. A great deal more came across the sea, from the huge armaments factories in the United States.

"The destruction of this convoy is vital," Kruger said. "It will buy us time." He frowned. "Not much time, I'm afraid, but even a little will help now." He looked at each of them in turn. "Time is the one thing we don't have enough of just now."

"Then we will gain it, sir," Ostler said. "Given time we can still prevail."

"Lord," Reuter said, "preserve us from misguided optimists."

"German victory is inevitable," Ostler insisted. "The *Führer* will find a way—or a weapon."

"The only secret weapon *I've* heard of lately is us," Wiegand commented. "And we can't win the war single-handed."

The 'Commissar' frowned petulantly. "We may have to," he said.

Kruger stuffed his unlit pipe into his pocket. "When you have all finished, gentlemen?" He looked around the plot table again, at the circle of waiting officers, the penciled notations on the chart that might soon define their fates.

"We will probably be in battle some time early tomorrow morning," he went on. "We will all do our best, after which we will try to return to Bergen in one piece so that we may rearm and go out to do the whole thing all over again. So I would suggest that anyone who has nothing vital to do just now get some sleep. It may be your last chance for a while."

●   ●   ●

Kruger slowly walked the powerful night periscope around the horizon, then signaled for it to be lowered.

"Couldn't see a bloody thing," he said, as the periscope hissed into its well. "There's a full scale blizzard up there."

Himmler looked across the control room from his torpedo computer. "That's to our advantage, surely, sir?"

"I think so. We know they have an escort carrier, but this storm should keep their planes grounded. Besides the snow, it also looks to be blowing a full gale. No one in his right mind would want to fly in it."

"If it's bad enough, it should effect the efficiency of their defenses as well," Himmler commented. "Hard to get a good contact when your ship is pitching about like a feather in a whirlpool."

Kruger grinned. He'd almost forgot Himmler's earlier service in a destroyer in the Med. Then his job had been to kill submarines. Now it was all reversed, with anyone on the surface a potential enemy.

"With this storm," Kruger said, "we'll be better off attacking submerged and using the *Nibelung* to get our bearings."

"Going deeper, I hope, sir?" Döring asked. In the heavy seas it had been a daunting task to keep the column of water in the Papenberg at the proper level. One moment the boat was balanced perfectly at 14 metres, the next the tower was almost out of the water.

Kruger nodded. "There's a gale *and* a blizzard up there," he said. "Take her down to 50 metres."

Wiegand was standing nearby, watching closely as Döring skillfully took the boat down into quieter water. Kruger wondered when another *Typ* XXVI would be ready, knowing Wiegand was more than prepared after his experience in this boat. Certainly the man was due for another command.

But a new boat. One like this one, or perhaps a *Typ* XXI, where he would at least stand a good chance of surviving the war. The older boats, even with *Schnorchel* fitted, were still little better than death traps.

Like *U-702*. She had crippled Konrad, costing him an eye and a leg in return for his first command. Yet even in more experienced hands, even if he had remained in command himself, instead of being transferred to this boat, the old *Typ* VIIc might have fared no better.

It might have been worse. The fractional difference in reaction time that had forced *U-702* to the surface after depth charging under Konrad's command might equally have found the old boat one or two metres closer to the exploding charges, rupturing her pressure hull and sending her straight to the bottom, with no chance of escape.

But Konrad was at least alive. Even without his leg, he had survived, and might even be on his way home by now. Many others were still with their boats, resting forever on the bottom in a thousand metres of black water.

Kruger moved forward, peering over von Sänger's shoulder to watch the shimmering spots of light on the glowing screen as they firmed up with the increasing depth.

"Which are the escorts?" Kruger asked.

Von Sänger indicated several small points of light on the phosphorescent screen. "Probably these, sir," he said. "The others are keeping station, but these are moving about the formation, like a shepherd's dog trying to keep the flock together."

"What are you getting on hydrophones?"

"A great deal of slow reciprocating, sir. Also, about here, where this large return is located, I can hear heavy turbines, and probably three shafts."

Possibly a light cruiser, Kruger thought. Or perhaps a small attack carrier, either of which might have three screws. A heavy cruiser or battleship, or a big fleet carrier, would have four shafts. It was odd, he thought. A cruiser was vulnerable to a U-boat, but presented almost no danger to her submerged attacker. She had no way of attacking anything she couldn't see. Likewise, a carrier was no threat as long as the U-boat remained deep enough to be invisible from the air.

"Keep your eyes and ears open," he said. "Let me know the moment anything unusual happens."

•   •   •

It was as if no one had moved in the last hour. Her turbine still, slipping along quietly on her main E-motor, *U-2317* had crept closer to the unsuspecting convoy.

Kruger intended to go for the escorts first, using the three G7es and the single active-homing torpedo in the bow tube. It was a violation of doctrine, but one he thought logical under the circumstances—and then use his remaining 'eels' to attack the freighters.

"Sir!" von Sänger shouted. "Two escorts have broken off from the outer screen and are heading directly for us."

Kruger hurried over to the sound cubicle, looking across the control room at Himmler.

"Flood tubes one and two! Open outer doors!"

"One and two flooded, sir. Outer doors open."

"Closest ship?" Kruger demanded.

"There, sir. Red seven-zero."

"Port fifteen! Midships! Steer zero-two-nine."

"Course is zero-two-nine, sir," Stauber reported.

"Bearing on nearest target?"

"Three-five-eight, sir."

"Target bearing is three-five-eight. Set depth three metres."

"Three-five-eight, aye. Depth three metres."

"Angle on the bow?"

"Zero angle, sir."

"Angle on the bow is zero."

"Zero angle, aye. Set."

"Set active homing after 300 metres." Tube one had the experimental eel, with an active sonar transponder in the nose.

"Set active homing, aye. Set."

"One—loose!"

"One is running, sir!"

"Starboard twenty."

"Twenty degrees of starboard wheel on, sir."

"Steer two-one-zero. Silent running."

• • •

Lieutenant-Commander Ian Rodgers pulled his chin deeper into the collar of his heavy watch coat and silently cursed the weather. In this wind and snow, and with the constant darkness at this time of year, it was hard to see anything past the muzzle of the forward gun.

He leaned over the voice pipe, connecting the open bridge with the Asdic compartment. That individual, at least, was out of the wind, hunched over his equipment like some electronic monk. "What's happening down there?" the captain demanded.

Of all the nights to pick up a contact! Black as a boot, and the wind howling down from the polar ice cap, thick with snow and ice. It had been all the crew could manage to keep everything free of ice, and the steam hoses were busy cutting away at the accumulation one hour out of every three.

The merchantmen probably considered the storm a blessing, Rodgers decided, but pity the poor escorts. Most of the freighters in this convoy were new, running between six and ten thousand tons, and well able to weather these conditions. But his little frigate was another story. Ramming herself through the waves by the sheer power of her engines, her radar screen a confused mass of confetti as the beam was reflected back by the storm and the sea. In this mess a bloody U-boat could probably come steaming up alongside and no one would notice until a boarding party came storming over the bridge!

"Target has altered course toward us, sir," the Asdic operator reported.

Rodgers blinked. I don't care for the sound of that, he thought.

"Bridge—Asdic! Target has fired!"

Bloody hell! "Bearing."

"Green two-five, sir."

"Port twenty!"

"Twenty of port wheel on, sir!"

Rodgers watched the gyro repeater ticking around. "Midships!" he snapped. "Both ahead, full!"

"Torpedo has changed course, sir! It's following us!"

So it's a bloody acoustic fish, is it? Rodgers thought. It's following the noise of the screws. No time to stream a Foxer, and it was probably too rough for the noisemaker buoy to do much good.

"All stop," he ordered. Deprived of a source of noise, the torpedo would home on the nearest engine sounds. Perhaps, if he was lucky, the boat that had fired it.

"Torpedo is pinging, sir!"

"What?"

"The bloody torpedo has an active Asdic sender in its—"

It was like running into a brick wall, Rodgers thought. It shouldn't have happened, but the torpedo had homed in even with the engines shut down, slamming into the ship on her starboard quarter. A torpedo with Asdic guidance? How did you counter something like that?

Within seconds the ship was starting to settle, and Rodgers was suddenly very glad he had shut down the engines before they were hit. With the screws still turning at high speed, the extra force might have torn the ship in half, or driven her bodily under.

Rodgers pushed himself away from the rail. The First Lieutenant would still be aft, he thought. The Yeoman of Signals lay sprawled in one corner of the bridge, blood pouring from an ugly gash where he had hit his head against the pelorus stanchion. Near him, the midshipman was just getting to his feet.

"Mid!" the captain snapped. "Get yourself aft and see what's happened to Number One! While you're there, make certain that all the depth charges have been set on 'safe!' I don't want them going off if we go under!"

"Aye, aye, sir."

If. Not quite the correct word, he thought. Not if, really, but 'when.' His ship was doomed. He could tell by the feel of her. He doubted there would be any survivors. Even without the storm there was little chance of being picked up. The rescue ship had been the first to be sunk, within a day of leaving Reykjavik. Not that it mattered—no one could live more than a few minutes in the water up here.

The midshipman ran back onto the bridge, looking ill. "Number One has bought it, sir," he gulped. "There's a piece of deck planking the size of a dustbin lid sticking out of his chest."

"What about the depth charges?"

"The gunner's already taken care of them, sir. All on 'safe.'"

The little ship rose sluggishly in a swell, seeming to hang forever before sliding down the other side, her list increasing as she did. It wouldn't be long now, Rodgers thought.

"Very well," he said. "Pass the word to abandon ship."

•   •   •

"First target is dead in the water, sir," von Sänger reported.

"What about number two?"

"Still coming, sir, but more slowly. I don't think he had as good a fix on us."

"Bearing?"

"One-five-six, sir."

"Target two," Kruger said. "Bearing is one-five-six. Set depth at three metres."

"Bearing one-five-six, aye. Depth set—three metres."

"Set torpedo for self-guidance. If they're not streaming a decoy I see no reason to hang about and let the operator play with the guidance controls."

"Self-guidance set."

"Two—loose!"

"Two is running, sir."

"Come left to two-seven-zero. Take her down, L.I.. Two hundred metres."

"Bow planes down 15 degrees," Döring ordered. "Stern planes, down five degrees."

U-2317 drove smoothly down into the frigid water, while above her the second eel sped on its way, the sensitive homing gear locked onto the charging frigate.

The blast came as the boat was passing through 170 metres, and just starting to level off. Even without using the hydrophones the sound was chillingly clear, followed at once by the terrible, grinding screams of a ship breaking up as it sank deeper and deeper into the black waters of the Barents Sea.

"Two hundred metres, sir," Döring reported.

"Very good. Maintain this depth for ten minutes. Then we will go back to 50 metres and resume the attack."

Schultz watched the lighted 'bug' of the dead reckoning plotter moving slowly across the chart. Outside the hull, the sound of the sinking frigate was still clear. Schultz thought that it sounded very much like a subway train rounding a curve. He had heard that sound often enough, when he visited his cousin in New York in 1936. He'd still been a child at the time, but he remembered the screech of the steel wheels. This sounded much the same, but much more frightening.

That could be *us*, he thought.

"Do you suppose there will be any survivors?" he asked.

Reuter shook his head. "Not likely. If they weren't drowned, or killed when the torpedo hit, the water will finish them quick enough. It's so cold that it will freeze you solid in a few minutes. Anyone who didn't make it into a boat is probably doomed."

"Or a raft?"

"Maybe." The navigator looked doubtful. "Rafts are really for warmer waters. Even if you make it into one, the odds are your arse and feet will be in the water. You'll freeze both."

"Two other ships have separated from the convoy, sir," von Sänger reported. "Converging on the area we fired from."

Let them, Kruger thought. They can blast the hell out of where I *was*, so long as they ignore where I *am*.

It seemed an eternity as the control room clock ticked around to the appointed time. In the distance, the rumble of depth charges was almost constant, the detonations so concentrated in a small area that Kruger found himself wondering if another U-boat had blundered into the enemy's Asdic.

But that wasn't it, von Sänger assured him. He *had* picked up a second U-boat, but her bearing was well away from where the British escorts were wasting their depth charges.

"They seem to be killing ghosts," the sound operator said. Either that, or they were depth charging the hulk of one of their own consorts as it sank.

"Any other U-boats in the area?" Kruger asked.

"No, sir. Just the one I mentioned before." Von Sänger slowly turned his hydrophone controls, listening intently. "No other U-boats, sir," he said. "But I'm picking something up at extreme range, coming from the west at high speed."

"Opinion?"

"Still pretty faint, sir. But probably heavy turbines, which means it's likely a heavy fleet unit."

"Any idea who she belongs to?"

Von Sänger shook his head. "Can't tell, sir. At least, not yet."

"Very well. Keep listening."

Reuter looked up from the plot table. "Time, sir," he said.

Kruger walked over to Döring, who was still watching the diving panel intently. "Take her back up to 50 metres, Chief," he ordered. "And be ready to go to turbines if necessary."

"Aye, aye, sir."

Kruger thought about the still unperfected power plant. To this point, it had proven reliable enough, if you ignored the leak that had surfaced while they were in Bergen. But how much longer could it last? Throwing *U-2317* into operations had been at best a calculated risk. Von Saltzmann had said as much when Kruger assumed command back in December. A very advanced design, but also one with sufficient teething problems to be months behind schedule for production and deployment.

Much of that, he knew, was because of the *Führer*'s short-sighted view of planning, which overlooked the long-term strategic advantages of lengthy development projects. What couldn't be completed within a year was often neglected. But for this, there could have been a fleet of a hundred *Typ* XXVIs at sea by now, and things might be very different.

If the present emergency didn't require that extra risks be taken, the boat would still be in the Baltic, used for training. And, in any case, the risk of the power plant blowing them up was still less than the risk of being killed by the enemy in a conventional boat.

"Fifty metres, sir."

The boat slipped through the icy water in total silence, her cunningly engineered screw making no sound at all as it drove her along at a steady five knots.

Kruger walked over to the sound cubicle. "What looks promising?" he asked.

Von Sänger keyed the *Nibelung*, then touched a spot of light. "This one, sir. Probably a warship. Twin screws, turbines, and from the return signal quite a bit larger than anything else close by."

Kruger turned to Himmler. "Flood tubes five and six."

"Five and six flooded, sir."

"Open outer doors."

"Outer doors are open, sir."

Kruger looked down at the screen. "Bearing?"

"Zero-three-zero, sir" von Sänger replied. "Range zero-zero-nine."

"Bearing is zero-zero-three," Kruger said. "Range 900 metres. Set depth 3.5 metres. Straight run."

"Angle on the bow?"

"Green four-five, sir."

"Angle on the bow is green four-five."

He waited tensely while Himmler fed the information into his computer. Inside the computer, a complex collection of gears, motors, and servos whirred softly, and then displayed the results, which Himmler relayed to Schwartzkopf in the torpedo room, who set the gyros in the torpedoes' guidance system.

Using the acoustic eels, particularly the wire-guided type, this information did little more than set the initial course. With the LUTs in the midships tubes, set to run straight, precise guidance was needed.

"Ready, sir."

"Five—loose!"

"Five is running, sir."

"Six—loose!"

"Six is running, sir."

Kruger watched the second hand on the control room clock moving slowly around the dial. Himmler was doing the same, timing the run with a stop watch, counting the seconds as the 'eel' rushed through the frigid water in search of its victim.

Von Sänger looked up suddenly. "First torpedo has struck, sir," he reported. "No explosion."

Kruger frowned. Failures had been common enough early in the war, but most of those problems had been sorted out long ago. Yet it could still happen, and a dud was a menace to his own command, for it announced his presence as surely as would a successful attack.

A moment later, the hull shuddered to a powerful detonation as the second torpedo smashed into the target. A detonation that seemed to grow in power, rolling on in increasing fury for what seemed an eternity.

"I don't think that was a warship," Kruger commented.

Von Sänger nodded. "It sounded like one, sir." He smiled. "But whatever she was, I'd say she's been destroyed."

"Probably a petrol tanker," Reuter said. "I saw one of those torpedoed once. She went up like a huge bomb. Worse than an ammunition ship."

"Could be," Kruger agreed. "A modern tanker could be turbine powered, and the newest ones are damn big vessel. As much as 15,000 tons, some of them."

Everyone looked up as the hull echoed to the sound of a distant explosion, well away from them. So it seemed the other U-boat was taking a hand now.

"The other U-boat," Kruger said, touching von Sänger on the shoulder. "Can you pick her out?"

"This return, sir."

"Keep an eye on her. If she seems to be getting into trouble we may have to lend a hand."

Wiegand was at his side now. "Can we do that, sir?"

"If necessary, Number One, we can set ourselves up as a decoy and lure the escorts away from the other boat. With our speed, and the help of our detection gear, we should be able to pull it off."

Döring looked up from his panel. "Keep in mind, sir," he said, "that we have only a limited amount of Perhydrol fuel remaining."

"How much, L.I.?"

"I can give you about 15 miles at full speed. If you keep your speed down to, say, 15 knots, then I can probably give you another ten or twelve miles."

"I'll keep that in mind, L.I.."

"The other U-boat has company, sir," von Sänger reported.

"What's he doing?"

"Taking evasive action. But very slowly, sir. Not more than six knots, and making a fair amount of noise in the process."

Which meant she was an older boat, Kruger thought. A new one would be taking advantage of her larger battery capacity to make off at a respectable speed. One which, while it might not leave the escorts lagging behind, would at least make their efforts to kill her much more difficult.

"Is he being attacked yet?"

"Not yet, sir. But the enemy are manoeuvring to do so."

Kruger nodded. "Pilot?"

"Sir!"

"Lay off a course to intercept."

"Course would be zero-five-seven, sir," Reuter reported, after a brief look at his chart and the *Nibelung* screen.

"Make it so."

U-2317 swung round onto her new course, still slinking along at a bare five knots on her silent motor, some 50 metres beneath the surface of the Barents Sea, the ultrasonic pulses of the *Nibelung*, keyed at 90-second intervals, giving a clear picture of activity above them as they moved beneath the convoy.

In the distance, a pattern of depth charges rumbled through the sea. The hunt for the other boat had begun in earnest. This late in the war, it was unlikely she would be permitted to escape. The British seemed to possess an unlimited number of depth charges, and they had all the time in the world to do their killing.

Once they had a solid Asdic contact it was usually all over for the hapless U-boat. The enemy would keep him pinned down, impotent, until he was either sunk, or the air became so foul that the only alternative to suffocation was to surface and face the enemy's guns.

"Range to other boat?"

"One-five-zero, sir," von Sänger reported. Fifteen kilometres—a bit over eight miles.

"Chief! Go to turbine. Revolutions for 15 knots."

"Aye, aye, sir."

Wiegand grinned. "We're smack under the middle of the convoy," he observed. "This should get an interesting reaction from someone!"

The turbine lit off with its usual loud 'bang!' and the boat began to pick up speed as the silent motor was disengaged and the turbine took over.

A sudden thought intruded. Kruger walked across the control room to the torpedo officer, who was standing by his panel, looking very pleased with himself after speaking to his petty officer in the bow compartment.

"Mister Himmler?"

"Sir?"

"We are going to the assistance of an older U-boat, which is now under enemy attack. I expect to use one of the remaining G7es eels, possibly self-guided. Is there any chance that it will accidentally home onto her, instead of the escort?"

Himmler shook his head. "Not so long as they're set to run at a specified depth, sir," he replied. "If I set them to run at 3.5 metres, they will not lock onto anything below that depth. They *can* be set to run at an indeterminate depth, but we would do so only if our target was a submerged submarine. And I, for one, wouldn't really trust them for that unless we were using positive guidance. They just might turn around and come back."

Kruger nodded slowly. "Good."

"What are we going to do, sir?"

"We will attempt to take the other boat's place as a target and give her the chance to slip away. Once she's out of danger, we will attack the escorts and destroy them."

"We'll be using the bow tubes, then, sir?"

"Yes. A LUT would do the job, but the acoustic eels are more certain."

"You can count on me, sir."

"You know there was a dud earlier?"

Himmler nodded. "They were all checked earlier and gave no hint of problems. But you can never be sure. It might even be sabotage—a firing pistol manufactured without powder." He shrugged. "I'm told that much of the labour in the armament factories is now supplied on 'contract' by the SS. Political prisoners and others—little better than slaves. They have no great love for their country after the way they've been treated, so these things can happen."

Kruger smiled. "That was not a criticism, Karl. Just something that we will have to be wary of in the future. I intend to close to within about 1000 metres of the enemy, then fire one bow tube to get their attention. Go ahead and flood three and four. Once we start this, it's going to have to be fast."

"Aye, aye, sir." In the distance, another pattern exploded around the hunted boat.

Kruger glanced around the control room, aware of the sudden tension. Since taking command he had always relied on his boat's unique ability to slip away from the enemy at high speed. Now they were deliberately heading into danger, and that knowledge could be plainly seen on the faces of his subordinates. They had all been through the claustrophobic hell of a severe depth charge attack before.

It was not an experience you would willingly repeat.

• • •

Kapitänleutnant Heinrich Ulbricht ducked involuntarily as a pattern of 18 depth charges threw his old boat around like a child's toy in a bathtub. More flakes of paint drifted down from the overhead, and his thick-soled sea boots crunched on the shattered glass that littered the control room deck.

The British had been at it for 20 minutes now, and would no doubt be happy to continue for as long as it took.

The IWO replaced a telephone handset, frowning. "Petty Officer Giese reports a leak in the after torpedo space, sir," he said.

"Bad?"

"He says that he believes it can be controlled, provided nothing happens to make it worse."

A British frigate churned overhead, its racing screws sounding like a record that had played past the end of the music and was now waiting noisily for someone to lift the arm.

"I'm not sure he'll give us that chance," Ulbricht remarked.

"Depth charges coming down," the sound operator shouted, whipping off his padded headset to avoid being deafened by the blasts.

"Hard left, both ahead full. Take her down to 90 metres."

The boat twisted through the turn, the needle on the patent log creeping up to a full eight knots as she tried to manoeuvre out of the way.

It was like running smash into a brick wall. The boat jerked and pitched violently, throwing Ulbricht, and everyone else who was not holding securely to something, onto the littered deck.

"Damage report!" the young captain shouted, pulling himself to his feet and calmly plucking a sliver of glass from a shattered gauge out of his palm. Strangely, it didn't hurt, and he wondered if he would live long enough for the pain to begin.

"All compartments report no further damage," the Exec informed him. "Petty Officer Giese advises that the leak has increased, and says it might be best to abandon the after torpedo space now, sir. While they can still get out."

"Tell him to do so, Number One. L.I., be prepared to compensate for the extra weight of water if the space fills."

The sound operator looked up. "Fast HE approaching, sir. About Red nine-zero."

"Another frigate?"

The operator shook his head, twisting the hydrophone dials. "I don't think so, sir. It doesn't sound like anything I've ever heard before."

Ulbricht looked at him curiously. "What's that supposed to mean?"

"Just that, sir. HE seems to be coming from a submarine, single screw, probably at a depth of about 50 metres. But the engine sounds resemble those from a surface warship. Turbine powered, from the sound of it. And much too fast. Maybe 15 knots or a bit more."

"Keep your ears open."

The Exec put down the telephone. "After torpedo space has been abandoned, sir. The hatch is sealed."

Ulbricht nodded. By rights he should never have permitted the watertight door to be opened at all, even to allow the crew to escape. They should have been left to either stop the leak or drown, their deaths written off as necessary for the safety of the boat. But he had decided to risk it. They would hear if any depth charges were on their way down, and it would have taken no more than seconds to get the men out. And Giese would never have suggested abandoning if there was any danger of flooding the motor room, which was just forward of the after torpedo space.

The war was nearly finished now, Ulbricht thought. If he was going to survive, then he would have to do his damnedest to keep his crew alive as well.

All of them.

"Torpedo running, sir," the sound operator reported. "Fired from the same bearing as the new HE."

"Coming our way?"

"Yes, sir."

"Take her down to 100 metres. Hard right for ten seconds, then come left 20 degrees and damn the batteries."

The seconds ticked by. Perhaps the British had a submarine with their convoy escort. Such a boat could theoretically stalk a U-boat far better than any frigate, being able to match her depth before firing. He had never heard of them using such tactics, but the Americans had made an attempt to integrate submarines into their main battle fleet a few years ago. The result had been the modern 'Fleet' submarines, which the Americans had decided to name after fish and marine animals, discontinuing the previous custom of giving each new series a sequential letter designation and hull number. One wit had argued that the Americans had no real choice but to begin naming submarines, as the last series was "T," and they simply refused to continue to the next letter.

Wham!

The detonation seemed to be almost directly overhead, and was followed at once by the grinding noise of a ship breaking up, driven under by its own momentum.

"What was hit?" Ulbricht demanded.

"One of the escorts, sir," the sound operator said.

The Exec smiled. "Then our company must be a friend."

The sound operator looked up curiously. "Sir," he said, "the other U-boat is behaving very oddly. He's making a great deal of noise."

"The escorts will be after him like a shot if he gives them anything to target on," the Exec commented.

Ulbricht smiled. "Well, Number One, he has given *us* a chance! L.I., dead slow. Absolute silence in the boat. Come to course one-five-five. We will see if we can slip away while our friend keeps the enemy busy, eh?"

•   •   •

The other boat has changed course, sir," von Sänger reported. "He's getting out of it, creeping away at about two knots."

"What's the enemy up to?"

"Number two is circling now, sir. Probably getting ready to make his run. Number one is still on station, pinging away."

"Have they got us?"

"It appears so, sir. Yes."

Kruger smiled. "Belay the noise," he ordered.

A young rating ceased banging on a metal fitting with a spanner, a technique Kruger had felt certain would attract the escorts' attention away from their previous target. As the clattering stopped, the 'ping' of the Asdic pulses against the hull became clearly audible. *U-2317* was creeping along at about seven knots, using her turbine, doing her best to draw the enemy's fire. Except for the obvious noise of the turbine, he was doing a fair job of imitating a conventional U-boat under attack, changing course and speed frequently.

He had done it many times before, in a boat far less able to stand the punishment of a close attack. The toughened steel of *U-2317*'s hull was almost twice as thick as that of a conventional boat.

"Open outer door on tube four," Kruger ordered.

"Outer door is open, sir."

"Bearing on number one?"

"Zero-one-four, sir."

"Bearing zero-one-four. Depth three metres."

"Bearing is zero-one-four, aye," Himmler responded. "Depth is three metres."

"Angle on the bow?"

"Zero angle, sir." The escort was charging directly at them.

"Angle on the bow is zero," Kruger repeated. "Self-guidance."

"Zero angle, aye. Set. Self-guided."

"Four—loose!"

"Four is running, sir."

Von Sänger looked up from his screen. "Number two is starting his run, sir."

Kruger nodded. "Come right 90 degrees," he ordered. "If one of the others picks us up, I want them to think we're still the same boat. We will use our speed judiciously, and for the rest act the part of a conventional boat."

"Damn!" von Sänger growled.

"What is it?" Kruger demanded.

"Another dud, sir." He listened intently, then suddenly smiled. "Christ, sir!" he shouted. "Someone must like us!"

"What do you mean?"

"The torpedo was a dud, sir, but from what I just heard it homed on the escort's screws perfectly. She sounds as if she's lost a blade and probably bent a shaft. Our 'eel' sounds to be wrapped about a screw."

"I'd be a lot happier if it had blown her bloody stern off," Reuter commented.

"Depth charges coming down!" von Sänger warned.

"Full speed!"

With a roar the turbine spun up to full power, the boat leaping forward as her screw wound up to maximum revolutions.

The main lighting went out as a perfectly timed pattern of 10 depth charges exploded around the racing boat, her stern slewing round to port while her bow tipped suddenly downward with the pressure.

After a moment, the lights returned as a stoker back aft reset the breakers.

Döring glared at the angle gauge, the tell-tales above the helmsman and stern plane operator, and the depth manometer, which was dropping much too rapidly. "Bow planes, up five degrees," he ordered.

Stauber strained at his yoke. "Won't respond, sir," he gasped.

"She's out of control, sir," Döring shouted.

"Two hundred metres!"

The bow planes were locked in a seven-degree dive, shoving the bow down, the boat sinking rapidly with her screw still racing at full speed.

"Back emergency!" Kruger snapped.

Back aft, the gears screamed in protest as the screw was reversed.

"Three hundred fifty metres!"

That was it, Kruger thought. The boat had reached her design depth and was now plunging past it, out of control. They were already much deeper than any conventional boat could have survived.

"She's slowing," Döring gasped.

"Four hundred metres!"

"Oh, shut up, dammit!" Reuter shouted.

"All stop. Level off."

Kruger looked at the manometer. The needle was resting solidly against the peg, stopped at 500 metres. We have no business being alive, he thought.

"Good Christ!" Wiegand shouted. "Look at that!"

He was pointing at the bridge ladder. The steel rails had bent in a shallow curve as the hull was compressed under the tremendous pressure.

We are deeper than any man has ever been in a submarine, Kruger thought. At least, any *living* man.

"What do we do now, L.I.?" he asked.

"Blow. If we were closer to the surface we could compensate by making use of the stern planes. But we need to clear the bow planes, and at this depth I wouldn't want to use any manoeuvre that might drop us even a single metre lower."

"What do you think is wrong with the bow planes?"

Döring shrugged. "Could be anything, sir. A fragment from one of the depth charges lodged between the planes and the hull. A fault in the electrical system. Anything."

Kruger nodded. "All right, L.I.. Blow main ballast, but see if you can keep us from breaking surface."

"Aye, aye, sir. Blow main ballast tanks!"

Petty Officer Braun, the master mechanic, looked up from the diving panel. "They won't blow, sir," he said. "The sea pressure is greater than the air pressure."

Döring cursed. "Start pumping them out, then. And put Mertens to work on the circuits to the bow planes."

Kruger shivered as the powerful pumps began to force the water from the saddle tanks. The racket would be clearly audible on any escort's hydrophones, though they were well below the depth where an Asdic beam—or a depth charge—could hope to reach.

Then, very slowly, as the water was pumped out and compressed air reluctantly admitted to the tanks, the boat began to rise. But it was a full 20 seconds after they could feel a perceptible upward motion before the manometer needle came off the peg and began to climb round the scale. We will never know exactly how deep we were, Kruger thought. But we have learned something very valuable from this—the boat will take a much deeper dive than anyone had really considered possible.

"Give me a 15 degree down angle on the stern planes," Döring ordered. "Silent motor ahead, revolutions for five knots."

Now the inclinometer showed a slight up angle on the boat, the stern planes pressing the stern down at a greater rate than the jammed bow planes, causing the bow to rise.

But now the boat was rising too fast, threatening to pop to the surface under the enemy's guns. "Belay pumps and blowing!" Döring ordered. He touched the coxswain on the shoulder. "See if you can move them now, Stauber."

"Nothing, L.I.. Still jammed solid."

"Watch your depth!"

With a roar of cascading water, *U-2317* thrust her 850 tons to the surface.

"Red lights!" Kruger snapped, starting up the ladder. "Lookouts to the bridge!"

The storm was still raging on the surface, huge waves rolling across the battered casing. As he climbed up into the cockpit, Kruger swung his powerful glasses around the horizon. There was nothing to see but a blinding white curtain across the darkness of the arctic night.

"Mister Schultz," Kruger shouted. "Bring a damage control party up to the forecasing. Immersion gear and life belts."

Wiegand had joined him in the cockpit. "Suddenly I find myself wishing we actually had a deck gun," the Exec said. "At least we'd have something to shoot back with."

Kruger frowned. "There are still four eels left in the midships tubes. We can strike back if we have to."

"At least the weather is still bad, sir. If we can't see, neither can the enemy."

"*They* can't," Kruger agreed. "I'm not so sure about their radar."

Schultz scrambled back along the casing, holding on to the grab rail at the base of the tower. "It's the starboard plane, sir," he shouted. "Jammed inside the casing."

"Christ! Can you fix it?"

"I think so, sir. Mertens says he can see the trouble, and should be able to clear it with the electric cutter. But he'll have to go inside the casing to do it."

"Do what you can. We can't dive safely without that plane operating properly."

Through the whirling snow, Kruger watched as the heavy electric cutter was brought up and connected, while two seamen, shrouded in their insulated rubber immersion suits against the icy water, freed a section of decking and lifted it free.

Mertens, the second mechanic, was wearing his escape gear, Kruger noticed. The space between the outer casing and the pressure hull was open to the sea, probably flooded as often as not, and it would allow him to breath. But even with the breathing gear and immersion suit he would not be able to work inside the casing for more than a few minutes.

There was a glimmer of light now, as someone played a torch inside the opening, and from forward came the reassuring chatter of the cutter as it slowly bit away at the misshapen fragment of superstructure plating that had jammed the plane.

A light flared, well off to port, and moments later a shell roared past the cockpit like a freight train, plunging into the sea half a cable beyond the boat.

"Someone has noticed us," Kruger said, his voice somehow remaining calm.

"What the hell do we do now?" Wiegand asked.

Kruger bent over the voice pipe. "Main sight to the bridge!" he yelled. "I'm going to take a bearing on the next gun flash," he explained to Wiegand. "Then we'll fire an eel on that bearing. With any luck, it should discourage them a bit."

The powerful bridge sight was passed up through the hatch and Kruger secured it to its mount. He grinned suddenly. It was the first time he had attempted a surface attack in this boat. He didn't even know for sure if the target-bearing-transmitter worked properly. No one had ever expected to use it, and it had not been adequately tested.

The escort fired again, this time a pair of guns, with the shells falling no more that 20 metres beyond the hull. Water and splinters cascaded across the casing, and one man fell writhing to the deck.

"Bearing is three-two-five," Kruger snapped.

"Bearing three-two-five, aye."

"Angle on the bow zero."

"Zero angle, aye."

"Set depth 3.5 metres."

"Range zero-one-five."

"Set, sir."

"Eight—loose!"

The water boiled momentarily along the starboard side as the 'eel' was thrust from its tube, curving rapidly to port as it passed the stern and streaking off toward the escort, which put another pair of shells at either side of the bow, in a perfect straddle.

Another man fell on the casing, pitching over the side, where he was held, thrashing lifeless against the hull, by his safety line.

The light went out inside the casing, and the others scrambled back, leaving the unbolted piece of decking where it lay.

"Bow planes tested and correct, sir," Döring shouted up the voice pipe.

"Get that man below," Kruger yelled. "Hurry!"

The injured man was passed up the ladder to the cockpit, and then lowered down the hatch. Two men hauled the other casualty up onto the deck, then cut his safety line and let him drift astern. "Dead, sir," a seaman yelled. "Half his head's gone!"

"Right. Get below. Clear the bridge!"

The snowy curtain was ripped apart by a flash of flame and smoke as the hastily fired torpedo found its mark. A second, more powerful blast followed at once, the escort torn apart by its own depth charges. Considering the hasty targeting setup, Kruger could only conclude that either he had been very lucky, or the escort commander's time had simply been up. Fate striking yet again.

"Alarm!!!!"

A moment before Kruger dived for the hatch, he saw the thick darkness dissolve in a tremendous flash, several miles to the west. After an eternity of waiting, the sound of the guns, and the shells, arrived at almost the same moment, smashing into the centre of the convoy with devastating effect.

Then he was down the hatch and spinning the wheel as the boat tilted down beneath him and sought the safety of the depths.

"What was all the noise up there?" Wiegand asked.

"We have company. From the sound of the shells, I'd guess *Hipper* or *Prinz Eugen*. It would appear the high command has decided to let one of our remaining heavies make a sortie against this convoy."

"About time," Reuter commented. "All they've been good for lately is sitting in their fjords, providing target practice for enemy bombers!"

"Fifty metres, sir."

"Who was injured?" Kruger asked, remembering the muffled figure being passed down the hatch.

"Seaman Gorch, sir. He's with the doctor now."

"Will he make it?"

Wiegand shrugged. "Doc says it's too soon to tell." He frowned. "The other was *Leutnant* Schultz."

"Killed?"

"Yes, sir."

The telephone buzzed softly and Wiegand picked it up. He listened for a moment, then replaced the handset.

"Mister Himmler reports that the remaining three torpedoes have been checked and appear correct, sir."

Kruger nodded. Schultz was dead, another man seriously injured, but they had survived. Perhaps that was all that really mattered.

"Very well, Number One," he said. "Let's see if we can find a target for them!"

Chapter Eight
Diamonds

Kruger studied himself in the mirror, smiling at the rather dashing figure looking back at him. The new uniform had been whipped up almost over night by a harried little tailor in Bergen, but the fit was superb.

He raised his hand to adjust the knot in his tie, still feeling oddly surprised at the extra strip of narrow gold lace that had been added to his sleeves, separating the two lower stripes from the upper. A *Fregattenkapitän* now, he thought. The promotion orders had been waiting for him when *U-2317* docked in Bergen to make good the damage sustained in the depth charge attack and the subsequent shelling.

The other boat, *U-1296*, had also made it back safely, and Kruger's boat had been credited with a 15,000 ton petrol tanker, four modern frigates, and two cargo vessels, so all in all it had been a very successful cruise.

The promotion orders had shaken him at first. When the base captain handed him the neatly typed sheet, his first thought had been that he would have to give up his command. U-boat captains were usually ranked *Korvettenkapitän* or below, so his new rank might be considered too senior for the post he was filling.

But events proved that the high command intended this promotion purely as a gesture of confidence in his skills, and not as a prelude to some training or staff posting. A special boat like *U-2317* deserved a senior commander, they seemed to feel. Kruger could stay right were he was, so long as he continued to get good results.

Zimmerman had gone ashore once they returned to Bergen. He had been aboard long enough to compile all the data he would need to write his reports. Now he was to be transferred ashore to do so.

He had not been happy to go. His only real patient, Seaman Gorch, had died several hours after being carried below, without ever regaining consciousness. The following evening, with the blizzard still raging, Kruger had surfaced just long enough to put him over the side.

Ostler had taken advantage of the situation to make a speech. Earlier in the war it might have gone over well, for it was filled with all the stirring phrases of patriotism, love of *Führer* and Fatherland, the inevitability of German victory, and so forth. Now it all seemed little more than empty words, exhorting further effort in a cause that was hopelessly lost. Even the ardent Ostler had sounded like he was just going through the motions, managing to sound sincere only when he added a few brief words suggesting that the best memorial for Gorch would simply be to remember him as a good man and a good friend.

And Schultz was dead, too. Which meant that unless he could get a qualified lieutenant from the base, he would have to promote Ostler. Schultz had been, above all else, a professional Naval officer. Ostler was a politician, and Kruger still did not believe politics had any place in the Service. But Ostler had sufficient time in grade, and had passed the appropriate tests, which meant he was qualified for promotion, so there might be no real choice.

He walked slowly to the window and peered through the curtains. It was the same room he had occupied on his last visit to Berlin, but this time the scene below was quite different. The almost carefree air of normalcy under fire was gone now, replaced by a quiet desperation which said better than words just how close to the end it was.

For it was mid-March, 1945, and the beleaguered *Heer* was only just holding back the rampaging Red Army. How much longer Berlin could hold out was anyone's guess. As it was, the city was subject to almost constant air attack, with the Luftwaffe and Flak gunners seemingly powerless to do anything about it.

Someone rapped at the door.

"Come in."

It was von Saltzmann, looking, Kruger thought, much older than when he had left Bergen a few weeks earlier.

But the chunky captain seemed to perk up at the sight of his protégé. "You look damned good, Hans," he said. "The new rank suits you."

"It does now, sir." Kruger replied.

"Now?"

Kruger shrugged. "I thought at first it would mean giving up my command for other duties."

Von Saltzmann laughed. "Not a chance of that ever happening, I can assure you. You are now much too famous to be relieved, even for promotion." He smiled. "Besides, your boat is special, so why not her captain?"

Kruger sat on the edge of the bed, shaking his head. "It sounds damned strange, doesn't it?" he mused. "Could you imagine me objecting to being sent ashore a few months ago?

We counted our lives in days then. Now I feel more confident at sea than I do ashore."

Von Saltzmann nodded. "Your boat has certainly made the difference. The attack on the Murmansk convoy may have been vital. It may even be the reason we're still holding the line in the East. The Russians needed those supplies, and now they will never get them."

"I've never heard the final results, sir. Only what my boat was credited with."

"I think it's safe to say that your boat made the difference. What you did to the escorts was of inestimable value. There was also the other boat—her captain reported what you did." Von Saltzmann grinned. "In addition, the *Führer* was somehow persuaded to allow *Prinz Eugen* to sortie. With the escorts already crippled when she arrived, and the storm preventing the carrier from launching any planes, she more or less had everything her own way. Only two ships made it safely to port, and our intelligence people tell us that one was packed with winter uniforms and the other entirely filled with tinned rations. So Ivan is well-dressed and fed, but perhaps a bit short on the guns, ammunition, and aeroplanes the other ships had been bringing him."

Von Saltzmann glanced at his watch. "Well, my friend, we had best be going, eh? With these constant air raids it can take hours to travel even a short distance, and it wouldn't do to keep the little *Gefreiter* waiting, would it?"

"Lead on, sir," Kruger replied, smiling, as he picked up his hat. Like the uniform it was new, the blue cover spotless, the brass oak leaves around the peak shining like gold.

Kruger found the drive to the Chancellery depressing. Everywhere it was the same, with row upon row of bombed-out buildings. The destruction had been very thorough, with seemingly no thought of confining the targets to military or government ones. Yet Berlin had not been hit so badly as Dresden, where a rain of incendiaries had started a firestorm that had literally melted building stone, leaving thousands dead, and destroying most of the old city. When the war ended, it would all have to be built up again from the ruins.

If Germany was lucky, he thought, the job might be finished by the turn of the century. *If* they were lucky. The last war had shown what a defeated Reich could expect, with the victorious Allies bleeding the heart out of their demoralised foe. And that had been with an armistice and a negotiated peace treaty. With this new doctrine of 'unconditional surrender' it was likely to be very much worse.

At last the old Mercedes staff car pulled up in front of what was left of the Chancellery and von Saltzmann led the way into the building. Nothing of any utility remained above ground, but the business of government was carried on in a bomb-proof bunker beneath the garden.

A smartly uniformed SS orderly inspected their identity cards and papers, then led them down into the bunker. "Wait here, gentlemen," he said, showing them into a Spartanly appointed anteroom. "The *Führer* will see you shortly."

"That could mean anything up to several hours," von Saltzmann said, when the man had left.

Kruger frowned. "I think I'd rather be back in Bergen with my boat. The value of all this ceremonial escapes me."

"It has its value," von Saltzmann assured him. "For morale purposes, if nothing else." He grinned. "Besides, you should be happy. How many other U-boat commanders have ever received the diamonds?"

"How many others have survived that long?"

"Well, you're a bloody hero now, Hans, and at the moment we need all of those we can find."

"I can't help it, sir. I feel as if I'm being decorated for killing honest seamen. Didn't you ever wonder how many your torpedoes had killed? Or how many simply drowned, or died of exposure in some lifeboat?"

"Sometimes," von Saltzmann admitted. "But it does you no good to dwell on it. And you can always console yourself with the knowledge that you have killed no one who would not gladly have done the same thing to you, given the chance."

The orderly opened the door. "Come with me, gentlemen," he said. "The *Führer* will see you now."

The two officers followed him along a concrete walled corridor and into a large office. As they entered, the *Führer* rose from behind his desk and stepped forward to greet them.

Kruger was shocked. Hitler had looked older than his years at the Christmas party, but that had been nearly three months ago, and in that time he seemed to have aged tremendously. The hand he shook was trembling uncontrollably.

This man cannot possible live much longer, Kruger thought, no matter *how* the war goes.

"I understand you have been very busy lately, *Herr Fregattenkapitän*," the *Führer* said.

"Busy enough, sir."

"The destruction of the Murmansk convoy was a pleasant change from the usual dreary news," Hitler said. "Your promotion is well deserved, as is the award we are presenting to you today." He frowned. "I only wish I could be certain that you'll have the full benefit of both."

"I'm sure I will, sir."

"We're fighting for time now, Kruger. My staff tells me only what they think I want to hear, but I am not a fool. I was just a common soldier in the last war. I like to think that I was a good soldier. Certainly I was a lucky one. But this is a different sort of war, and now we are fighting for our very survival as a nation!" He paused, his eyes bright. "Germany will *never* surrender, Kruger. *Never!* We will fight until either a miracle occurs, or until we are destroyed! And if the country falls, then there must be nothing left for the enemy to capture!"

"My men and I will continue the battle until the last second, sir," Kruger promised. "That is our sworn duty, and we will abide by it."

Hitler nodded. "Just be sure that you carry it out. We cannot afford another 1918. If she is to fall, Germany must go down fighting the *enemy*—not herself!"

Kruger nodded slowly. He had been barely a year old when the Great War ended, but his father, at the time a newly-promoted *Oberleutnant* in the Imperial Navy, had told him more than once about the disgrace of the fleet mutiny at Kiel. It was understandable that the *Führer* would not wish to see it happen again.

To lose a war, to be forced to give in to a more powerful enemy, were things he could understand. But for an entire fleet to mutiny, to refuse to put to sea and face the enemy, was more than any normal man could tolerate.

Hitler looked irritated. "Höst!" he snapped.

The SS orderly jerked to attention. "Sir?"

"Where is that photographer? Or is this award to be top secret for some reason?"

The orderly stepped out of the office for a moment. When he returned he was frowning.

"The Propaganda Ministry is sending another photographer, my *Führer*," he reported. "It seems that the usual fellow drove over an unexploded bomb and was blown up on his way here."

"How much longer?"

"They said someone should be here momentarily, my *Führer*."

The dictator sighed. "Well, there's no sense standing here while we wait. Sit down, gentlemen. While we are waiting for this new photographer to arrive you can tell me all about your boat." He smiled suddenly. "It will be interesting to speak with an officer who has been *winning* battles lately!"

• • •

"But your engine troubles have all been corrected now?" Hitler asked.

Kruger nodded. "So far as we know, sir, they have. But the whole system is very temperamental." He grinned. "It's a great improvement on the older boats, but I'm still glad to have my diesel and batteries when I need them."

"Engines are always a problem," the *Führer* commented. "I can still remember the first time I was at sea in *Grille*, my official yacht. The engines broke down." He allowed himself a small smile. "I have never entirely trusted a ship since."

There was a soft rap at the door and Höst, the SS orderly, ushered the photographer into the office. Kruger smiled when he recognised her. He had written before the patrol, and sent off the long letter written during the patrol as soon as they docked. But there had been no mail waiting for him when they returned to Bergen. No mail for anyone, the bags evidently having been sunk with the torpedo boat that had been bringing them from home.

He had no idea if she had received either letter, nor if she had ever responded.

"I'm sorry to be so late, my *Führer*," she said. "But by the time we found out about poor Fritz it was already time to be here."

"Well, you are here now, *Fräulein*," he replied. "Please set up your camera and we will begin."

"*Jawohl, mein Führer*."

Kruger watched her as she set up the heavy tripod and lights. So she had at least survived this long, he thought. Perhaps her prophecies of doom were a bit premature?

She had taken off her jacket when she arrived, working in a fitted silk blouse and a dark skirt. Kruger could see her slim, youthful body moving beneath her clothes. She looks wonderful, he thought. Only her eyes show the worry—the constant strain of living under bombardment every day and night.

The way I used to look, before I got *U-2317*.

The Naval Adjutant, von Puttkamer, came in while she was setting up, carrying the formal orders and the flat, leather-covered box. Once Ingrid was ready, the camera was started, and while von Puttkamer read the orders, the *Führer* somehow managed to fasten the ribbon at the back of Kruger's neck, his hands shaking as if he had the palsy.

The brief ceremony was finished, and Kruger was one of the true elite. A holder of Germany's highest honour; the man who had destroyed more enemy shipping than any living U-boat commander.

Ingrid found him near the entrance to the bunker, waiting until it was safe to return to his hotel. Overhead, a flight of B-17s was adding to the destruction.

"I told you that you were going to wind up a hero," she said.

"Whether I liked it or not? Wasn't that what you said?"

She smiled. "Probably." Sighing, she sat on the heavy camera case. "I didn't know you would be here, Hans," she added. "My boss just told me that someone was to receive a medal from the *Führer*, and to get here as quickly as possible."

He nodded. "Did you receive my letters?"

"One. I wrote back on the same day."

"I never received it. Some mail was sunk—perhaps it was on that boat?"

"Maybe."

"Will I see you again?" he asked. "Before I go back, I mean?"

"If you like. How long do you have?"

"Not long. Perhaps two days. It depends on how long it takes to arrange air transport back to Bergen."

"Then see me tonight." She pulled a notebook from her purse and scribbled an address. "This is where I live. Also, the telephone number, though most of the time it doesn't work. Come by at seven and supper will be ready."

"I could eat first," he offered. "I don't suppose you have much to spare. Or we could go to a restaurant."

"You will eat at my flat," she said, firmly. "You can't find decent food in a restaurant these days, and I can manage to find more than enough for what I need." She smiled. "There are certain advantages to working where I do, after all."

Outside, the all-clear was sounding, and von Saltzmann was tapping his watch impatiently. "Come on, Hans," he said. "We have to take advantage of any lull we can find!"

"I'll see you tonight, then," Kruger said.

"I may not want to let you leave."

"I'll remember that. Tonight, then."

"Until tonight."

•   •   •

His Majesty's Destroyer *Apache* tore furiously through the choppy waters of the Western Approaches, her powerful turbines screaming as she worked up to her full speed of 36 knots. Close behind, the other two destroyers struggled to keep pace with their leader, while farther back the little carrier forged ahead at full speed, slowly falling back from the faster destroyers.

On *Apache*'s open bridge, Captain David Ralston sat stolidly in his high wooden chair, squinting across the screen against the glare of the sun on the water, an unlit pipe clamped firmly between his teeth.

The first lieutenant replaced a telephone handset in its bracket. "We'll not get more out of her," he reported. "The chief is already screaming bloody murder over what he thinks we're doing to his engines."

Ralston grunted noncommittally. Didn't that bloody Welshman realise there was still a war on? Just like a bloody plumber, though, he thought, to go rabbiting on about his engines when a few miles ahead a convoy was under heavy enemy attack. He would slow down when they got there, sure enough, but not before.

"Bridge?"

Ralston got down from his chair and bent over the voice pipe. "Captain here."

"We have the convoy on radar, sir," the operator reported. "Range is about 25 miles."

"Thank you. Keep me informed."

Ralston leaned against the screen, considering. At their present speed it would take just under three quarters of an hour for the group to come up on the convoy. A great deal could happen in that time, he thought. Ships could be sunk, countless men killed, and many tons of valuable supplies lost forever at the bottom of the sea.

In a bit more than a third of that time his old group had been destroyed, blown to bits by a mad German in a miracle boat.

I'll get that bugger, he thought, even if it's the finish of me in doing it! Or the bloody war doesn't end first.

He picked up a handset. "Sparks? Signal *Vicious* to launch a flight of Swordfish to cover the convoy. And have him send along some fighters, too."

Ralston put down the handset. It was quite possible that the war *would* end before he could get his chance at Kruger. And then—what? Considering that they had both made a fair try at killing each other, it was still possible that they might end up friends. *If* they ever met after the war, which was hardly a certainty.

There was nothing really strange about the idea, he thought. He was not himself a political person, and from what he had gathered while a prisoner, Kruger didn't give a damn *who* ruled Germany, so long as there *was* a Germany. They were simply professional Naval officers, each with a job to do. Without a war to keep them apart, they had more in common than many Englishmen. A love of the sea, and a common profession.

It was not unusual for former enemies to become the best of friends. England had fought two brutal wars against the United States, even more with France, yet both were now friendly powers. At least, the Yanks were, in their own rough, uncultured way. The French were *friendly*, and they were allies in this war, but it didn't seem to be in their nature to actually be friends with any other country. Hell, Parisians didn't even like other Frenchmen.

But friends could also become enemies. England and Japan had been on excellent terms since the last century, with most of the early Imperial Navy either built in British yards, or built in Japan to British plans. Even now, a few British built ships remained in her fleet, and the organisation of her Naval Staff and fleet was along British lines. But now the two countries were bitter enemies, fighting a vicious war for control of the Far East. Britain had the colonies, and the Japanese wanted them and were now in control of them, and it was going to be hell getting them back.

At the moment, the Yanks seemed to have things more or less under control out there. But Britain would be joining in the fight with her full strength very soon, once Hitler had been beaten for good, and she could spare the men and ships from this North Atlantic nightmare.

The telephone buzzed and Ralston picked it up. "Captain here."

"Signal from convoy commander, sir. They've just lost a bulk cargo ship."

"Thank you, Sparks. Have you got that signal off to *Vicious* yet?"

"Yes, sir. *Vicious* says he will launch immediately he gets into the wind."

"Fine. Keep me informed."

A bulk cargo ship. It could be almost anything, Ralston thought. Wheat, perhaps? Or coal, or iron ore. The only thing certain was that no ship of that type had ever been designed to stand up against a torpedo. The holds were too big.

But even a warship, with its intricate water-tight division, could be sunk. Sometimes in a matter of seconds, like *Hood*, early in the war, with the loss of all but three of her crew.

He had lost more than one friend when the great battle-cruiser was blown up in the midst of a long range gunnery duel with *Bismarck*. A stupid loss, he thought. The old ship had no business trying to fight it out with a modern battleship. Beautiful she may have been, but her day was long past when she was destroyed.

The first lieutenant moved to his side. "Do you suppose it's him, sir?" he asked.

"Kruger?" Ralston shrugged. "Possible, but I doubt it. He was last reported up past the North Cape of Norway, and even with *his* boat I doubt he could get here so quickly. No, Number One, I expect this will just be one more conventional boat, and our group will notch up another kill." He frowned. "But we'll be no closer to ending the real menace than we were when this group was formed."

"He's bound to return to this area surely, sir?"

"It seems likely. But likely isn't really good enough." He laughed bitterly. "I've got a score to settle with that man, but I often suspect the war will end before the chance comes!"

"Would you mind, sir?"

Ralston considered for a moment. Settling a grudge was fine, but not at the cost of extending the war, or having a few thousand more killed in the process.

"No," he said, "I don't suppose I'd mind at all."

•　　•　　•

The flat was the smallest Kruger had ever seen. Located in the basement of a partially bombed apartment block, close by the Kroll Opera House, it consisted of one room and a bathroom. Kruger immediately found himself seated on the edge of the bed. There was nowhere else to sit.

The old fashioned bed took up most of the room, with just enough space remaining for a large, iron-bound chest, a tall wardrobe, and a tiny, varnished-wood icebox. A hot-plate, resting on the chest, its cord depending from an adapter in the light socket, served as the kitchen. At one side of the room a door opened into the narrow bathroom, which also contained the only window—a tiny, very dirty one. Kruger wondered if the dirt on the window wasn't intentional, as it appeared to be of clear glass, and there was no curtain for privacy.

"It's not very much," Ingrid said, "but at least it hasn't been blown up yet."

Kruger nodded, wondering just how much longer that would be true. So much of the city had already been destroyed that it seemed likely to be no more than a matter of time before the rest was also leveled.

"A bit small," he said, "but I suppose it's adequate if you live alone."

She grinned. "For now. But I want something more, Hans. After the war, perhaps, when things are back to normal."

The kettle began whistling, and Ingrid walked quickly across the room and removed it from the hot-plate. It was replaced at once by a large, cast iron pot.

"What will you do after the war?" she asked, sitting beside him on the bed.

"Go back to Emden, I suppose. My uncle will take me in with him. He's a builder. Housing is in short supply now, and will be even more in demand once the military is demobilised. We should prosper."

"What about the Navy?"

He shrugged. "I don't suppose there will still *be* a Navy. At least, not right away. No, I'll be a builder. It pays better, in any case."

"It's going to be very strange," she said, quietly.

"My building houses?"

"No, I mean a Germany without a Navy. Without a *Führer*, and probably without any Nazis. The Allies will almost certainly outlaw the Party."

"Other parties will replace it. For better or worse, who can say? But we have to hope for better, eh? In any event, my old profession will be gone, and I will have a new one."

Ingrid nodded. "When there is no Navy, no one will need a Naval officer? Is that it, Hans?"

"Yes."

She stood, walking over to the hot-plate to stir the pleasant smelling concoction bubbling in the big iron pot. "There will be a Navy again," she said. "Not right away, but it will come, and probably before too long. I don't trust the Russians. And neither will the British and Americans, once the war's over and

they see what they're really like. I've seen what the Russians
have done. They're hardly fit to be called human beings!"

Kruger nodded, thinking of Eisenberg's family, blotted out
when a Russian submarine destroyed a refugee ship. Of the
stories of rape and wanton murder whenever a Russian military unit entered German territory.

"They're throwbacks," he said. "They wage war the way it
was waged by the Huns or Mongols. Everything and everyone
conquered is no more than plunder for the victors." He sighed.
"And are we really any better?"

"More civilised, certainly."

He shook his head. "Are we?"

"I believe so, Hans. Of course we are."

"I wonder. Do you know any Jews?"

She thought a moment. "No."

"Have you ever met a Jew? Or seen one?"

"I guess so. When I was a child, perhaps. I'm not sure."

"But you haven't seen any Jews recently, have you?"

"No. What of it, Hans?"

"So where are they, Ingrid? Where have they all gone?"

She replaced the cover on the pot and returned to the bed,
pulling her legs up under her as she sat. "I don't know," she
said. "Deported?"

"Or murdered."

"Why would anyone do that?"

"Why indeed? You work for the Propaganda Ministry,
Ingrid, so you've certainly heard the speeches. Perhaps you've
even read through *Mein Kampf*. The Nazis have blamed everything bad that has ever happened to Germany on the Jews."
He frowned. "Maybe some *were* gangsters, or black market
profiteers, but so were a lot of Germans. I suspect that most
Jews were simply honest citizens, and as patriotic as anyone
else."

"Doctor Goebbels says that they're subhuman animals."

"Doctor Goebbels is also said to consider himself the greatest lover since Casanova. Do you believe that as well?"

She laughed. "He tries very hard to convince everyone of it. At least, all the women! But, no, I don't believe it—and I don't believe that any one group of people are less human than any other, either."

"My brother was a soldier, Ingrid. He wrote some very interesting letters from the Eastern Front. Very interesting. He told of German soldiers, certain SS troops, systematically murdering civilians in the conquered area. Especially Jews."

"And you think that the Jews in Germany have also been killed?"

"I don't know. I only know that they are no longer around, and that no one seems to know where they have gone. My father knew a number of Jewish officers in the Imperial Navy, and quite a few more in the Weimar forces. I know none. I am told that *Grossadmiral* Raeder managed to protect Jews in the Navy for a number of years, but the day finally came when the Party prevailed, and after that there were none left to protect. So if the Russians act like the barbarians they are, perhaps we have set them an example, eh?"

The girl shivered. "I know they will not capture me," she asserted. "I have a pistol now, and a license to carry it with me. If one of them ever tries anything I won't hesitate to kill him. Or myself, if necessary."

Kruger put an arm around her shoulders and pulled her close. "There's no need, Ingrid," he said, softly. "Just get out of Berlin while you have the chance. There's nothing left for you here. Go to Emden, if you like. I can fix it with my uncle. You'd have a place to stay, and there need be no promises. Anyway, give it some thought."

She looked around the dreary little room, the mildew-stained wallpaper, the faded photograph of the *Führer* near the door, over the tiny table, with its carefully dusted copy of *Mein Kampf* resting on a yellowed lace doily. The book had been a gift from her *Hitlerjungend* leader, in recognition of her placing at the top of her gymnasium class.

She had never bothered to read it, finding herself unable to get through the mass of semi-literate ramblings. But the book remained on display, and at one point she had even managed to get her copy autographed. It was a bad book, she thought, but it was safer to keep it.

"There's really nothing for me here," she said, after a long time. "My work is nearly finished, and when the war ends so will my job." She frowned. "If I stay here, my life will probably end with it. It will be the Russians who occupy the city. That's almost a certainty."

"All the more reason for you to leave, " Kruger said.

Ingrid sighed, shaking her head. "It's no good, Hans. The Ministry will want me here, writing fanciful stories of how our brave leaders are valiantly defending Berlin until the bitter end. Until one minute before midnight, as our *Führer* would have it. There is no way out for me."

"Then come to Bergen. You could manage that, surely? You've been busy trying to make a hero out of me, right? Tell them you need more information, and that you need to fly back with me to get it."

She looked thoughtful. "It could work," she said, at last.

"Then do it, Ingrid. Once you're actually in Bergen you'll be relatively safe. The enemy is less of a problem, and when it's all over the occupying force—if there is one—will probably be British." He grinned. "Besides, almost all the bombing *there* is confined to the base, so you won't need to worry as much."

The girl shrugged. "I'm past worrying," she said. "If you live, you live; if you die—you're dead and past caring. Besides, I'm in the cellar here. I don't even go to the shelter any more." She kissed him suddenly on the cheek. "But I *will* go to Bergen if I can, Hans. Mind you, you'll *really* have to give me a proper interview. It's one thing you won't be able to get out of this time."

Kruger laughed. "I won't even try," he said. "Just knowing you'll be safe will make up for the whole thing!"

• • •

Kapitänleutnant Rolf Wiegand stood curiously at the end of the blue-garbed line, wondering just what was supposed to happen next. Except for Ostler, who had been given local leave before the summons came, and three ratings with the same privileges, the entire crew was here. From the look of things, every boat in harbour had been stripped of her crew and all the men mustered here.

"What do you suppose this is all about?" Reuter asked, his voice hushed.

Wiegand shrugged. "Who know? Perhaps it's finally over."

"Do you think so?"

"No. Not really. But it must be something important, eh? They're not going to collect this many of us in one place just to allow the base MO to show his horror films of VD victims rotting away ten minutes after they've been laid."

Himmler groaned. "It *would* be like them, though, wouldn't it, Number One?"

Wiegand shook his head. "No, Karl. *That* they would tell us about in advance, so that we could prepare the crew."

"Terrify them, you mean?"

"Exactly."

"So what *do* you think this is all about?" Reuter asked.

"I haven't the slightest idea, Pilot."

An immaculately uniformed Chief Boatswain's Mate stepped through a door at the far side of the huge shed, snapped to attention, and bellowed "*Ach-TUNG!*" at the top of his lungs.

The gathered crews drew themselves to attention, all eyes focused on the door, wondering who would appear.

After a pause, a smartly dressed Navy captain appeared, followed by a pair of nervous young ratings, each accompanied by a Naval Policeman. As the captain mounted a low platform, a squad of Marines filed in and formed a neat rank behind him and the others.

What was this supposed to be? Wiegand wondered. Some sort of punishment parade? But why strip every boat of her crew just to hear some young idiot sentenced to permanent confinement? Which, most likely, they would escape once the war was over and justice fell into the hands of people who believed it a *good* thing if someone didn't contribute to the German war effort.

"Men of the U-boat fleet," the Captain bellowed. "Germany is now at the turning point of this great conflict! The new boats are nearly ready, and with them we will take back the sea lanes from the enemy! But until that glorious day, it is up to us—to you, to every man in the Fleet—to remain true to his oath, and to fight on fearlessly for *Führer* and Fatherland!"

A bloody pep talk! Wiegand thought. As if anyone here needs it!

"But some of you," the Captain continued, his face turning red as he shouted, "are *not* keeping your oaths! These two men here—*these faithless cowards!* These miserable traitors were your comrades until today! *Until today!* Today, when they lost all honour and decency and ran away from their duty! Deserted! Ran away from the fight like frightened animals from the hunter!"

Wiegand shuddered involuntarily. It was suddenly becoming clear just what was going on here, and he didn't like the way it was developing.

"This is *not* 1918! There will be no mutinous behavior in this command! No matter what sort of behaviour is tolerated elsewhere, in *this* command there will be absolute obedience to orders and absolute loyalty!" He glared down at the assembled crews. "*There will be no more desertions in this command! None!*"

The Captain stepped to the side of the platform. "Watch!" he screamed. "And think long and hard before anyone else in this room considers following the example of these degenerate swine!"

The Captain had been speaking for some time before Wiegand had even noticed the two lengths of heavy line suspended from the rafters of the giant shed, just in front of the platform. But once he *had* noticed them he found himself unable to look away, knowing what would happen and not wanting to watch, yet powerless to divert his eyes from the barbarity to come.

The Captain nodded to the Naval Policemen. "Do your duty, gentlemen."

The deserters were unceremoniously dragged to the front of the platform, where loops were placed around their necks. Then they were thrust over the edge of the platform and left to hang after a drop of no more than a quarter metre.

It was nearly half an hour before they were declared dead.

Finally, the Captain stepped forward again. "You see now what happens to deserters in *this* command? *There will be no more desertions!* Remember that!" He strode rapidly to the door. "No more!" he shouted. Then, "Dismissed!"

And then he was gone, leaving the assembled crews to stand and gape at the pair of dangling corpses, tongues protruding between their bared teeth, their faces black with congested blood.

•   •   •

Himmler drained his glass in one swallow and held it up for Schwartz to refill. "I can't believe they actually did that," he said. "Talked to us like we were some sort of filth, and then made us stand and watch that mockery!"

Wiegand sipped hard at a brandy. "Deserters *deserve* death," he grunted. "But no one should die like that! A quick bullet, or the guillotine, or even a *proper* hanging, I can accept. But not like that—just strung up to strangle. No hoods, their hands and feet untied. It's enough to sicken a slaughterhouse worker."

"Who the hell did he think he was talking to, anyway?" Reuter demanded. "We are the *elite*! U-boat sailors! Not bloody barrack stanchions." He swallowed some beer. "Did you notice that that captain never said just which boat those men were from?"

"So what?" Himmler asked. "Maybe he just didn't want to say."

"Him? He would have said it, just to shame the rest of the crew. I think those two were base staff. Not U-boat crew at all."

Wiegand put down his drink. "I think you may be right, Otto. I know none of our men would ever consider deserting."

"I did once," Döring commented.

"Desert?"

"Considered it. Not very hard, mind you. That was in *U-1005*, as a brand new *Fänrich*, when I was considered as being perhaps a little less useful than a dancer with a broken leg." He smiled, remembering. "We'd just had a bad patrol. Very bad. Came within a hair's breadth of being sunk. The IWO was a tyrant on his best days, and the Old Man never did a thing to discourage him. I think he may have actually been a little afraid of him. For me it was constant extra duties, very little sleep, and engines that should have been replaced months before.

"The food was horrible—moldy bread and rotten meat. And hours on end creeping through deep water, well below any safe depth, with depth charges raining down endlessly, until we thought we would all go mad. And then, to finish it off, we were bombed just outside Lorient by our *own* planes! And do you know what the Old Man said to me, once we were safely inside the pen? He said, 'Klaus, you are a useless little piece of shit, and I really don't know how we managed to survive with you always screwing things up'"

"Captains always say that sort of thing to new *Fänriche*," Reuter grunted. "Builds character."

"I was ready to kill him. Particularly since the L.I. was completely past help, and I'd had to more or less run the engineering department without him during most of the patrol."

"Well, forget it, why don't you?" Wiegand said. "You're an *Oberleutnant* now, and *you* can say horrible things to *Fänriche* if you like."

"Oh, I do, Number One," Döring laughed. "Mostly to Ostler. *He* probably would have enjoyed that spectacle tonight, the bloody little Nazi."

Himmler chuckled softly. "He'd probably *like* that description. He's a right little pig, our Commissar Ostler."

"Fortunately," Wiegand commented, "he is also junior to all of us, so he really can't give us too much of a problem."

"Oh, right, sir," Reuter offered. "But the poor bloody ratings *are* condemned to listen to his speeches." He took a long swallow of beer. "They should all receive extra pay for that."

•   •   •

Oberfänrich Gerhard Ostler lay back on the bed, his head propped up on the pillow, watching the girl. She was blond, and very fair, and he thought she might even be beautiful if she would only learn how to smile. But she was also Norwegian, and, well paid or not, her services did not seem to include actual enjoyment.

Now she was leaning against the dresser, her naked buttocks pressed against the marble insert at the centre, with her arms folded beneath her heavy breasts while she stared off into space. Ostler knew there was nothing above the bed but dirty paint, and he wondered what she was seeing there.

After a long time, she looked at him. "You are ready again?" she asked.

He looked down at himself. "Doesn't look like it, Kristen," he grinned. "But I don't suppose it'll be too much longer."

"You will be leaving soon, yes?"

He looked at his watch. "I've got a few more hours."

The girl shook her head. "No, not that. I mean, you will be leaving Norway soon?"

"Probably." He shrugged. "The war can't last much longer. Once it's over, we'll all be sent home, I should imagine." It was curious, he thought. He could talk to this girl in a way he would never consider aboard the boat. Speak his true thoughts about the futility of the war.

"I wish that this was not to happen," she said.

He looked at her curiously. A bit on the tall side, fine body, blond hair, blue eyes, attractive enough, and very skilled in bed. A true Nordic type, the Party's so-called anthropologists would say. But what she was saying now made little sense. Why in heaven's name wouldn't she want the invaders to leave her country?

"You don't want us Germans to leave, Kristin? Or me, particularly?"

"You, of course. You're a sweet, wonderful man, Gerhard."
She allowed just a hint of a smile, and Ostler almost laughed—
everyone on the boat thought he was an absolute prick. "But
also your countrymen," she continued. "Since you have come,
my whole business has been with you Germans, and unlike
many girls I have never used that contact to gain information.
I never helped the Resistance, Gerhard. I never wanted to. I
was well paid for what I did, and I was alive, and that was
enough for me." She sighed, her breasts rising enticingly. "So
long as I was comfortable, I didn't care *who* controlled this
country."

"And you're worried about the Resistance taking their
revenge once we're gone?"

"Yes. I worry."

Ostler nodded. "I don't suppose there's much to be done
about it, though."

"No—nothing." She slammed a fist onto the top of the
dresser and something fell from beneath it. A small, maroon
velvet bag.

The girl moved to conceal it with her body, but Ostler gently pushed her aside and took the bag from under the dresser,
untying it and dropping the contents onto the marble dresser
top.

"These are yours?" he asked, very quietly.

She nodded. "My father's." Her life, she realised, had just
ended. Gerhard was a sweet man, but he was also a committed
Nazi. And he clearly recognised the significance of the leather
objects in the bag.

He carefully replaced the objects in their bag. "You have to
be insane to keep these, Kristen!" he said. "You look *Aryan*.
How could you take such a foolish risk?"

"They were all I had of my father, Gerhard."

He shook his head. "Then you must hide them more carefully, if you insist on keeping them."

The girl was looking at him curiously. He should be dragging her off to the authorities, and instead he was merely telling her to be more careful.

Ostler placed the bag in a drawer. "Hide that *very* carefully," he said.

"Yes."

He put his arm around her and led her back to the bed. "I think I may know of a solution to your problem," he said. "Let me explain, why don't you."

•   •   •

Ordinary Seaman Gustav Schwartz moved silently around the wardroom, conscious of the sleeping officers behind the thick curtains that concealed their bunks. Here and there he would stop to attack a bit of dust with his rag, or to pick up a discarded magazine and replace it in the rack.

He looked up at the ceramic cat, Beethoven, who was the boat's official mascot. What do you know about this war? he thought. You just sit there and never worry. You don't even care who wins!

The cat said nothing, but remained where he had been glued to the shelf, grinning his sardonic cat grin. There was at least one thing to be said for this boat, he thought. It was a damned site more comfortable than the old ones!

•   •   •

There were bombs falling in the city, and for a moment Kruger was uncomfortably reminded of an earlier time, not so very long ago, nor all that far away, with a different girl snuggled close to him. But the girls were quite different, and the bombs were much closer.

Too close, in his opinion.

"Shouldn't we get dressed and go to a shelter?" he asked.

Ingrid shook her head, her right hand touching his cheek. "No, my darling. We're safer here." She kissed him quickly, a light peck on the end of his nose. "Besides, to reach a shelter we would have to go out into the street, and that's too dangerous."

He nodded slowly. "Then I guess we'll stay."

"If I have to die," she said, "I'd rather do it in my own bed."

"At a ripe old age, I hope?"

"I'm in no hurry, Hans. But if it must happen soon, then still in my own bed, and preferably making love."

He cupped a small, perfect breast, feeling the nipple harden against his palm. "You are very beautiful," he said.

She laughed. "So are you, my reluctant hero."

"You should see me after a patrol. You wouldn't think so then."

"I don't care. I can see you *now*, and for this moment there is no one else in the world but us. No one." She sighed, her body moving sinuously, reacting to his touch.

The building trembled slightly as a stick of bombs blasted apart a nearby street. But they did not notice, and when at last they were satiated the all-clear was being sounded, and a new day was ready to begin.

Chapter Nine

Confrontation

The weather was miserable, and *Fregattenkapitän* Hans Kruger could not have been more pleased. Above his head the radar kept up its constant vigil, extending the range of the lookouts' vision by many miles. Radar had been fitted in U-boats for several years, but *U-2317* marked the first time that the set was designed mainly for air search. The old sets, either fixed to the front of the tower, or mounted to the periscope standards with only a limited training arc, had been mainly for range finding.

But the new system was a marvel, for it permitted Kruger to cruise at high speed on the surface, with plenty of warning time to dive in the event of an attack. One or two doubters had suggested that the radar could also provide a homing beacon for enemy patrol bombers, but Kruger's experience in this boat had shown that to be a very minor worry. If it *did* provide a beacon, it also told them the enemy was coming long before he was close enough to do any damage.

U-2317 could crash dive in half a minute, while her radar would give her about eight and a half minutes warning of any aircraft in the area. Even allowing for one or two minutes of observation, to determine if the target was actually coming closer, or just passing by at a distance, there was still plenty of time to dive and slip away.

U-2317 was running south now, her diesel pounding steadily, making good 17 knots on the surface. It wasn't as fast as she could do running deep on her turbine, but it extended their range tremendously, and was at least twice as fast as was practical using the *Schnorchel*. The new L.I., Döring, had told Kruger that even larger Walter boats were being planned— ones with sufficient bunkerage to operate almost exclusively on their turbines, with diesels and batteries reserved for emergencies and silent manoeuvring.

Not that it was going to make any difference now, Kruger thought. He was under no illusions as to what the outcome of this war would be. Nor could he believe that inevitable defeat was still somewhere in the distant future. His new boat had created a great deal of havoc, destroyed many ships and valuable cargoes, but in the United States Kaiser was building new ships even faster, and in the East the Russians were continuing their advance, anxious to grab as much territory as possible before linking up with the British and Americans and completing their victory.

Already, the Red Army was said to be working its way into Berlin, so the end had to be near.

He swept his glasses around the empty horizon, not really expecting to see anything.

At least Ingrid was safe in Bergen. She had managed to fly back with him on the plane, and was now staying at a commandeered hotel near the base. With the situation in Berlin, there was no longer any question of her returning.

Just before he had left on this patrol they had decided that they would be married, provided both survived the war. A very large 'if,' he thought. His super modern boat made him nearly invulnerable at sea, but Ingrid was still on land, and a poten-

tial target for both enemy bombers and the Norwegian resistance.

As vulnerable as Hannah had been.

He smiled suddenly, considering the remarkable resiliency
of the human spirit. A bare month or two before he had been
certain that the British bomb that had destroyed Hannah's
barracks had also devastated his future. Yet now he hardly
thought of her, and when he did it was with a certain remembered fondness, and not the soul-destroying grief and fury of
the first few days.

Ingrid had filled the space left vacant by Hannah's death.
It seemed, in some ways, almost a betrayal, but he knew it was
all for the best.

"Aircraft—bearing Red two-zero!"

The shout from the voice pipe jerked Kruger back to the
present. "Range?" he barked.

"Eight-two-six," came the reply. Almost 83 kilometres,
so there was still plenty of time to react if it became necessary.

"Inform me if he turns this way."

Unconsciously, Kruger was swinging his glasses off to port.
The plane would be too far away for visual contact, especially
in the dark, but the effort was automatic.

"Aircraft bearing steady and closing," the operator called
up. "Range is now five-nine-two."

Close enough, Kruger decided. Even if they hadn't been
noticed yet, it would only be a matter of time before the plane
picked them up if it held its present course.

"Clear the bridge!" he ordered, snapping down the voice
pipe cover. "*Alarm*!!!!"

The lookouts vanished below, with Kruger leaping down
after them, dragging the hatch closed and spinning the locking
wheel.

As his feet touched the control room deck the diesel had already been shut down, replaced by the soft hum of the E-motor. "Take her down," Kruger ordered. "One hundred metres."

"Secured for diving," a rating shouted.

"Flood negative," Döring snapped. "Open main vents. Bow and stern planes, down 10 degrees."

"Fourteen metres."

"We're under," Döring announced. "Close main vents."

Kruger nodded. "Carry on, Chief. Revolutions for seven knots."

"Aye, aye, sir."

U-2317 slipped deeper into her element, while above the raging sea a Coastal Command Liberator roared low over the water in frustrated fury. Her pilot had been using the boat's radar as a homing beacon, but now it had vanished before he could get a proper fix with his own set.

"One hundred metres, sir," Döring announced.

"Very well, L.I.. I make it 23 seconds from the alarm until we were under water. Fine job."

"Thank you, sir."

Kruger glanced around the control room. Stauber, the Coxswain, was on the wheel, as he always seemed to be whenever there was any hint of trouble.

"Maintain this course and speed for 20 minutes," Kruger ordered. "Then we will put up the *Schnorchel* and see if the search receiver picks up any enemy radar. If it seems safe, we will continue on the surface."

Wiegand looked up from writing in the rough log. "We could just stay submerged and use the *Schnorchel*, sir," he offered.

Kruger shook his head. "We will make better speed on the surface. And our radar will give us ample warning of any enemy aircraft. Besides, with the *Schnorchel* we have only a radar *detector*, with a much more limited range." He walked over to the periscopes and leaned against one of the gleaming metal shafts. "Also, the weather up there is miserable. The float valve in the *Schnorchel* would be constantly closing, and I don't care for working in a vacuum."

The Executive Officer nodded. He could understand that more easily than any comparison of radar and radar detectors. No one liked it when the sea closed the intake valve in the *Schnorchel* head, forcing the engine to draw its air from inside the boat. It left you gasping for breath, while your eyes felt as if they were about to burst from their sockets.

Kruger leaned back and tried to relax. This would probably be *U-2317*'s final patrol, von Saltzmann had informed him. The chunky captain had warned him to keep a good wireless watch, as he expected the war to end almost momentarily, and there would be no sense taking any risks after that.

Regenbogen.

That was to be the signal. *Rainbow.* Upon its receipt, every U-boat was to make its way to deep water and blow herself up. Germany might loose the war, and the Reich end some 988 years before Hitler had predicted, but the enemy was not to gain from it. Just as the High Seas Fleet of the old Imperial Navy had scuttled itself while interned in Scapa Flow, so the U-boat fleet of the modern Navy would also destroy itself.

It seemed such a waste, Kruger thought. Better to turn the boats over to the British or Americans. They would probably need them, once the war was over and Stalin showed his true colours.

He saw Ostler standing near the plot table and smiled. It was curious about him, he thought. If there was one thing he would never have expected of the 'Commissar,' it was that he would suddenly come to him with a request to be married.

Even stranger, the bride proved to be a Norwegian prostitute. Tall, blond, and blue-eyed, she clearly fit Ostler's racial prejudices, but what about her morals?

It had been a nice little ceremony. The paperwork had been rushed through the base chaplain's office, with bride and groom swearing that they were of pure Aryan ancestry for at least five generations, and the base captain adding his stamp of approval as a mere formality. The Lutheran chaplain had spent most of the ceremony looking heavenward. Kruger had never been quite sure if the chaplain was expecting God to strike him dead for performing the marriage, which he obviously suspected was mostly a way to get the bride to Germany and out of reach of her vengeful countrymen, or if he expected an air raid at any moment.

Just before kissing his bride, Ostler had whispered something in her ear. He refused to say what it was, but her reaction was so genuinely happy that Kruger had wondered if it was possible the woman had actually fallen in love with his obnoxious subordinate.

"The groom looks happy," Döring commented. "Makes a change, I can tell you."

"I agree. Since I have not found a proper reason to refrain any longer, I may just go ahead and promote young Ostler. I suppose a promotion is meaningless now, but—"

"Well, in any case, sir, a wedding, or even a meaningless promotion, makes for a pleasant change from other events at the base recently."

"The executions, you mean, Klaus?"

"Yes, sir."

"I wasn't there, of course," Kruger said. "But I find such things quite shocking. Desertion is perhaps the worst thing a sailor can ever do, and it deserves death. But not in the way I heard it was done there." He smiled. "And you're right—a wedding does make a pleasant change."

Wiegand looked up at the clock. "Twenty minutes, sir."

"Thank you, Number One." Kruger walked over to the sound cubicle. "Anything around?" he asked.

"Nothing, sir," von Sänger reported. "No HE, and nothing within listening range."

"Thank you." Kruger looked aft. "L.I.! Take her up to periscope depth."

Kruger smiled, still thinking of the wedding. Ostler's request had come as quite a shock. But if it could even possibly work out for the young couple, then that was all to the good. It might save the girl, too.

Whatever the Norwegian traitor Quisling might say, Kruger had never been under any delusions as to the attitude of the majority of Norway's citizens. The sooner the Germans were gone the better, and Norway's wartime leaders had best go with them if they didn't want to end up dangling from the end of a rope.

"Fourteen metres, sir," Döring reported. "Periscope depth."

"Night periscope!" Kruger snapped down the handles as the thick-shafted night 'scope rose from its well and walked it around in a full circle. "Nothing visible," he announced. "Down periscope. Put up the *Schnorchel*, but don't open the main induction yet. We'll just use the radar detector for a few minutes first."

Döring nodded slowly. With the main induction closed they could pull the plug and dive instantly, if the need should arise. "Raise the *Schnorchel* mast," he ordered, glaring at the responsible rating.

"*Schnorchel* is raised, sir."

"No radar detected, sir."

"Very well. Five minutes like this," Kruger said. "Then we will surface and start the main engine."

•　　•　　•

"Captain in the control room!"

Kruger rolled out of his bunk and dove through the circular hatch into the control room. "What is it?" he demanded.

"Von Sänger reports heavy HE at Green nine-zero, extreme range," Wiegand said.

Kruger walked over to the cubicle and touched the sound operator on the shoulder. "What do you make of it?" he asked.

"Large ship, sir. Four shafts, with at least five escorts in company."

"Estimated speed?"

"Thirty-one knots, sir."

"Most likely a fleet carrier, sir," Wiegand suggested. "Or a new battleship. Almost certain to be a good target, in any case."

"Probably," Kruger agreed. "What's her course?"

Von Sänger considered for a moment. "She's zigzagging, but I'd put her mean course at about one-two-zero."

"Range?"

"About 30 miles, sir."

"Pilot, lay off a course to intercept."

"Course should be one-five-zero, sir," Reuter reported. "That should place us within range in about two hours at full speed."

"How much depth do we have here?"

"We're in about 400 fathoms, sir."

"L.I., take her down to 400 metres, then go to full speed on the turbines."

Döring looked at him curiously. "Do you think that's safe, sir?"

"We *have* been considerably deeper."

"Not intentionally." The engineer shrugged. "Still, you're the captain."

Slowly, the boat glided downward, her thick hull taking the strain, while in the control room the men watched the depth gauge in horrified fascination. Slowly, slowly, the needle advanced around the scale, past the red line and into the danger zone.

At last, after what seemed like hours, the boat leveled off at 400 metres.

"I still don't like it very much, sir," Döring said.

"It may give us a little extra speed, L.I.. We'll need all we can muster if we're going to catch up with our target." Kruger had studied the chart, and decided that even at full speed there was no hope of actually catching their prey. But if they could manage to get an extra knot or two out of the boat, they might at least get within torpedo range.

At Döring's order, a rating threw the switches and the turbine lit off with its usual loud 'bang,' now all the more startling at their extreme depth.

"Ahead, full."

The speed mounted rapidly, everyone watching the dial expectantly. At last the needle stopped rising, bringing a wan smile to the captain's face. It was not so good as he'd hoped. The extra depth didn't seem to help, for the log was still showing only 26.8 knots. They gained speed very suddenly at 150 metres, but going deeper didn't seem to provide any additional benefit.

●   ●   ●

"We'll not get any closer, sir," Reuter said.

"Very well. Bring her up to periscope depth."

The boat rose rapidly from deep submergence, the hull seeming to quiver as the tremendous pressure was eased. Around him, Kruger could see the men relaxing. In the Arctic they had been much deeper without suffering any damage, but that, as Döring had pointed out, had not been intentional.

Still, it had at least shown what she could take. Even Kruger had no intention of going as deep as 500 metres again, but it was nice to know that the reserve was there if needed.

"Fourteen metres, sir,"

"Reduce to three knots."

"Three knots, sir."

"Up periscope," Kruger ordered.

Quickly, as the head broke surface, he trained the 'scope through a full circle, then, seeing nothing threatening, he focused on the smudge in the distance and twisted the hand-grip, bringing the periscope's optics to full magnification.

He looked for only a few seconds, then dropped the periscope back into its well.

"Anything, sir?" Himmler asked.

"Only the most beautiful target I've ever seen in my life."

"Sir?"

There was no mistaking her, he thought. The long, almost rakish hull, the grey sides rising like a cliff from the sea, and the two thick, raked funnels.

"It's the bloody *Queen Elizabeth*, my friend," he said. "And if she's on course to England she'll be full of troops."

Himmler grinned. "Sink her and you'll be a rich man, sir."

Kruger nodded. Rich? There was a standing reward of a quarter-million dollars for the captain who sank either of the big Cunard liners, along with a Knight's Cross. Probably the war would be over before there was a chance to collect the money, he thought. And he already *had* the medal.

But it was worth a try. The *Queen Elizabeth*, along with her slightly-slower, three-stacked sister *Queen Mary*, were capable of carrying as many as 15,000 troops per crossing. Even this late in the war, such a loss could be devastating.

Perhaps even enough to make the Americans reconsider their 'unconditional surrender' policy.

The loss of a full combat division in a single day would shake the confidence of any country.

He raised the periscope again. She was presenting a beautiful target, just turning now onto a new heading in her zigzag pattern, presenting her huge flank to his cross-hairs.

"Bearing—that!"

"Zero-zero-four. Set."

"Angle on the bow—red nine-zero."

"Angle nine-zero. Set."

"Set depth four metres."

"Four metres, sir. Set."

"One—loose!"

"One is running, sir."

"Two—loose!"

"Two is running, sir."

"Three—loose!"

"Three is running, sir."

It was going to be a race, Kruger thought, as the periscope hissed into its well. The electric motors in the torpedoes were wakeless, making the 'eels' very difficult to spot, but they lacked the speed of the old alcohol-fueled steam torpedoes. And just now speed was the main thing. The old 'eels' had been capable of reaching 46 knots on their high-speed setting; the electric models, even on high speed, could do no more than 35 knots. The target was at extreme range, steaming away at a speed only slightly less than that of the pursuing torpedoes. It was going to be as much a matter of luck as anything if one of them managed to catch her before the batteries were exhausted.

But it would take only a single hit. A hit anywhere on her massive hull would force the giant liner to slow down. Once she did, it would be a relatively simple matter for *U-2317* to catch up and put a full salvo into her, even with her heavy escort of four destroyers and an anti-aircraft cruiser.

The second hand on Himmler's stopwatch crept around the dial, moving, it seemed, even more slowly with each passing moment.

"Too long," Himmler said. "They're not going to catch her up."

They had fired 'wrens,' which would follow the great ship whatever her movements. But it was taking too long. Their batteries would be nearly exhausted by now.

Bang!

"A hit!" von Sänger shouted.

Kruger signaled for the rating to raise the periscope. The distant smudge of smoke and flame was a beautiful sight, but then he watched, aghast, as the great Cunarder steamed majestically through the veil of smoke, emerging, unharmed, while in her wake the other two torpedoes exploded harmlessly.

The periscope dropped into its well. "One hit," he said. "But it was a destroyer, not the *Queen*."

"Are we going to try again, sir?"

"No." Kruger shook his head. "She's stopped zigzagging and increased speed. We'll not get within range again. We were barely within range before." Modern torpedoes, he thought. Improvements didn't always make things better.

"What about the escort we hit, sir? Won't he slow her down?"

Kruger frowned. "He'll be left behind, Karl. It's what I'd do if I were the captain of that liner. It would be incredibly stupid to risk thousands of lives a save a couple hundred."

"We'll not get a chance like that again, sir," Wiegand said, as Kruger moved away from the periscope and stood by the plot table.

"Not very likely, Number One," Kruger agreed. He sighed. An almost perfect chance and they'd missed it. If they'd only had a full load of the old-type torpedoes! Then he could have fired a fan shot, with at least one fairly sure to hit.

"I'll be in my cabin, Number One," he said. "You take over here."

Wiegand watched him go, wondering if he would have had the nerve to even attempt such an attack. The liner and her escorts would have reported the attack by now. Other warships would be on the way, ready to kill her attacker.

They were so used to having their way by now that it would just be routine. Drop a few dozen depth charges, destroy the U-boat, and steam away, job done, and a few more German sailors dead.

With *this* boat it would not be so simple, but they would still go through the motions.

He looked across at the calendar someone had hung by the control room clock. Less than 12 hours now, and April would be finished. How much beyond that, he wondered, would the war drag on?

•   •   •

Shortly after sunset, *U-2317* glided up from the depths and raised her *Schnorchel*, hurrying along just beneath the surface, her diesel throbbing smoothly, putting a good charge on the huge batteries that filled the space beneath her deck plates.

In the control room, Kruger was standing beside Reuter, peering down at the unrolled chart. It was of the Portsmouth area, where other U-boats had been forbidden to operate in recent months because of the tremendous risks involved in any action so close to the Royal Navy's historical heart.

But now it appeared that the risk was justified. *U-2317* would be able to cruise there in relative safety, utilising her advanced design and weapons. The end of the war was certainly very near now, and Kruger could still remember Hitler ranting about a fight to the end and beyond. They would go down fighting.

"How long to reach the patrol area?" Kruger asked.

"At our present speed, another 24 hours, sir," Reuter replied.

The boat was steaming at a steady nine knots. Fully submerged during the day, operating on batteries, they would have to slow considerably, but even so it was clear that they'd be in a position to do some real damage sometime the following evening.

The navigating officer looked up from his pencil-marked chart. "Not that much merchant shipping in the area, surely?"

Kruger shook his head. "We are to concentrate on warships, Otto. The war is nearly finished for Germany. We all know that. And once it ends, the bulk of the British fleet will likely be sent out to the Pacific to help the Americans. Our job is to sink as many of the heavy units as possible, before the war ends, and before they can be used against our so-called ally."

"Why?"

"Who knows?" Kruger shrugged eloquently, looking almost French as he did. "I've never really believed that our *Führer* cared very much for his Japanese partners. God knows, they've done little enough to help us in this war."

"They did supply bases and fuel for our raiders in the Pacific, sir."

"Granted. But what they *should* have done, instead of acting like fools and attacking in Malaya and at Pearl Harbour and bringing the bloody Yanks into the war, was to strike at

Russia from the east. Then it would have been *Stalin* who had
to fight a war on two fronts, and we could probably have
crushed him between us before anyone could come to his aid."

Reuter looked skeptical. His tapped his old brass dividers
on the chart, which was a copy of a recent British Admiralty
chart taken from a captured freighter, with the notations
translated into German.

"Well, sir," he said, "this is where we are. And this is
where we will be tomorrow at this time."

"In that case," Kruger said, "let's hope the enemy will be
there as well."

•　　•　　•

The flames shivered in a slight breeze, clouds of stinking
black smoke roiling up from the twin pyres of diesel-soaked
flesh. In the distance, the Russian guns had started to fire
again.

The small group watching the fires poured more diesel fuel
onto the flames, and then withdrew into the safety of the bunker as more shells began to fall around the ruined Chancellery.

In the deserted garden, the two bodies were twisting as
their muscles contracted in the intense heat. Despite the flame,
when the Russians reached the Chancellery garden a few hours
later, the bodies were still recognisable. The most powerful
man in Germany and his new bride, no longer a threat to anyone.

•　　•　　•

After the darkness of the blacked-out harbour, the small
office, high up, abaft the pilothouse of the old depot ship,
seemed almost like daylight. In fact, it was not at all well lit,
and the faces of the three men gathered there were rendered
sinister by the shadows.

"A drink before we start, Ralston?" the little admiral
asked.

Captain David Ralston nodded slowly. Taunton seemed cordial enough, and they *had* racked up another kill two days ago, so perhaps this visit wasn't the expected dressing-down for failing to kill Kruger yet.

"A small one, sir," he said.

Taunton nodded to his Chief-of-Staff, who was nearest the decanters. "Whisky for me, Jones," he said. "Captain?"

"Whisky will be fine, sir."

The drinks were passed around, and the three men sat for some moments in reflective silence. The old cabin, with its beautiful Victorian paneling and fittings, seemed the proper setting for reflection, Ralston thought. Old, and very tradi-tional, like the private office of some turn-of-the-Century shipping baron.

Then Taunton replaced his glass on the big teak desk and leaned forward. "We think we've found your friend Kruger," he said.

Ralston almost dropped his half-empty glass. "Are you sure, sir?"

"No," Taunton replied. "We're not certain. But it has all the marks of one of his tricks. Shortly after noon today, some-one fired three torpedoes at *Queen Elizabeth* as she was com-ing 'round the southern end of Ireland. We believe it might have been Kruger."

"Any damage, sir?"

"None to the *Queen*. One of the torpedoes sank one of her escorting destroyers." He looked grim. "It's what they're there for, of course, always running up one side of her and down the other, just keeping in the way in case some Jerry tries for a lucky shot. Two other torpedoes exploded within a hundred yards of her stern."

"Intelligence is inclined to think the fish were fired from extreme range," the Chief-of-Staff added. "One almost made it, but the destroyer got in the way, while the others exploded in her wake."

"What makes you think it was Kruger, sir?"

"Location, for one thing. Most U-boats have been avoiding that area lately. Particularly since Jerry was tossed out of France. It's too dangerous for them. But a boat like Kruger's could operate there with relative safety."

Ralston nodded, sipping carefully at his whisky. "Makes sense, I suppose, sir."

"Also," the Chief-of-Staff added, "a hydrophone operator in one of the surviving destroyers reported a contact at several miles range. He said it sounded very like a *damaged* destroyer, but there was nothing observed in the area."

"Could be," Ralston said. "If he was using his turbine, which he would almost have to do if he'd been chasing anything as fast as the *Queen Elizabeth*, it would probably give a sound picture very like a damaged destroyer. Only one screw, and turbine machinery. It's not something even an experience rating would associate with a submarine unless he'd been told such a creature existed."

"Quite right, Ralston," Taunton said. He looked right at home in this old-fashioned cabin, with his grey beard and moustache. Put epaulettes on his uniform, and he'd be the picture of a Victorian admiral.

"Where is he now?" Ralston asked.

"That," Taunton admitted, "we don't know. We *have* intercepted a signal directing him to operate in a particular area, but he's obviously not using the standard charts. The grid square he's been directed to would put him somewhere in the middle of Paris, based on the charts we've captured. Our best Intelligence people believe he's been sent to this area, however. They feel that his orders to sink as many warships as

possible dictate he operate in an area where the largest concentration will be found."

"Which would logically be here, sir?"

"Exactly. And the attack on the *Queen,* if it really was
Kruger, would seem to bear out the Intelligence estimate. So I
want your group to put to sea at first light tomorrow. Then
find him and destroy him."

"I will, sir. You can count on it."

The Chief-of-Staff poured more drinks, while below the
slab-sided depot ship *Apache* lay waiting for her master to
return. Eager for the final challenge.

• • •

Oberleutnant (Ing) Klaus Döring grabbed the handrails
and pulled his little cart along to the next cell. He was down in
the dimly lit main battery space, and overhead he could hear
the control room party as they went through their daily routine.

Gingerly he lifted his head, constantly aware of the minimal space allowed for routine maintenance beneath a U-boat's
interior decks, and began to unscrew the filler caps of the giant
cells directly in front of him. Electrolyte levels had to be main-
tained correctly if maximum power was to be obtained from
the batteries. Checking the cells was really a task for a rating—usually the most junior electrician—but it was one of the
few places aboard a U-boat where someone could really be
alone, and just now Döring wanted to be alone with his
thoughts.

He wondered how much longer it would be now. They had
gone up to periscope depth just after sunset and put up the
radio antenna on the chance there might be new orders. There
had been none, but the news reports were shocking. Martial
music, and a grim-voiced announcer from Berlin.

The *Führer* was dead. Killed in the battle for Berlin, according to the announcer. *Grossadmiral* Dönitz was now Germany's leader.

Döring frowned. No one seemed particularly bothered by the news. Not even Ostler, which was surprising. But it was only the captain who had seemed to recognise the real significance of Hitler's choice when he named his successor.

The *Grossadmiral* was many things: a submariner, an old Imperial Navy officer, a tactical genius, supreme commander at sea—all that. But there was also one thing that he had never been, and that was a Nazi.

"The Party is dead," Kruger had said, after hearing the news. "Hitler knew perfectly well that the enemy would never negotiate with a party man, just as they would never negotiate with him. So he picked a man with no political affiliations to follow him. A professional military officer; someone the enemy just *might* negotiate with.

It made sense, Döring thought. After what the Nazis had been up to no one really wanted much to do with them. Stalin might have negotiated with a Nazi—he was, if anything, simply a cruder version of Hitler, and more than familiar with the techniques of mass murder—but the western powers still retained some slight sense of honour and, more importantly, outrage. A butcher might talk to another butcher—and between Stalin and Hitler it was debatable who was more adept at mass slaughter—but a more civilised man probably would not.

"Hands to action stations!"

The cry echoed strangely in the cramped chamber, and after first making sure the caps were safely screwed back onto the cells and marking his chart so that he'd know where to resume his checks, Döring began working his cart back toward the access hatch just forward of the engine room.

• • •

"I make ten vessels, sir," von Sänger reported. "Course is zero-nine-zero, speed 20 knots."

"Warships, then," Kruger mused. "Even a fast convoy wouldn't normally be *that* fast." He looked at the pattern on the screen. Ten ships, the two largest in their own column at the centre of the group, then a pair of smaller vessels at either side. The remaining four vessels were in pairs, two well ahead of the main group, the other pair astern. Destroyers, probably, from the way they were sweeping back and forth across the general line of advance.

Looking for us, he thought, or for anyone foolish enough to attempt to interfere with them.

"Course to intercept?"

"One-five-three, sir," Reuter supplied. "That's calculating our own speed at 15 knots."

"How long before we're in range?"

"About an hour, sir."

"Thank you, Pilot. Steer one-five-three. Revolutions for 15 knots."

"Turbine, sir?" Döring asked, sliding into his seat at the main control panel.

"Unless you've figured out some way to get the extra speed out of the e-motor, L.I.?"

"More batteries, sir. I just can't figure out where to put them."

"Turbine, L.I.."

"Aye, aye, sir."

"Steering one-five-three, sir," Seligmann, the quartermaster, announced.

Kruger looked at him, surprised. "Where's the Coxswain?"

"Sick bay, sir. Broke his finger."

Wiegand chuckled softly. "I'm surprised he let that stop him."

"He didn't, sir," Stauber grunted, coming through the circular door into the control room. "Though it *did* delay me a bit."

"Course is one-five-three," Seligmann said, slipping out of the seat and allowing the coxswain to take the wheel.

"Fifteen knots, sir," Döring announced.

Kruger nodded. Now would come the hard part. Waiting. At this speed, running on the turbine, they made a fair amount of noise. An alert hydrophone operator on one of the destroyers was all it would take to turn things around, changing them from hunter to hunted.

There was little real danger to *U-2317*, he thought. Not when they could vanish into the depths at 25 knots, leaving the enemy without a target in minutes. But if they were detected it would mean a missed opportunity. And with Hitler dead, it was unlikely there would be many left. The end was most likely no more than a matter of days.

Regenbogen.

The end of the U-boat service. Probably forever.

"Mister Reuter?"

"Sir?"

"What's the depth hereabouts?"

Reuter studied his chart for a moment. "On our present course, no less than 500 fathoms at any point, sir."

"Good. I have a feeling that someone up there is going to hear us before long if we stay at our present depth."

"How deep, sir?" Döring asked.

"Same as before, Chief. Four hundred metres."

This time the atmosphere was less tense. They had safely been as deep before, and now it was presumed that the hull could tolerate the pressure without collapsing, as an older boat would almost certainly have done.

"Bow and stern planes, down five degrees," Döring ordered.

The deck tilted slightly, and *U-2317* began to drive downward into her element. How deep could they really go, Kruger wondered. It was a question every submariner asked, but could never answer without killing himself. A crushed hull was the only real sign that maximum depth had been reached, and then it was too late to take advantage of the knowledge.

Maximum depth, Kruger decided, is about half a metre before the pressure hull implodes. The problem was that you could never know you'd reached it until you'd gone that extra half metre.

"Four hundred metres, sir."

Uncaring, *U-2317* drove on through the depths, her screw slowed now, to compensate for her greater efficiency at extreme depth, carrying the 27 men within her toward their rendezvous with the enemy force.

Kruger was wondering if it was worth it. The war might even be over by now, and their efforts would be for nothing. They could easily be sailing to their deaths in a lost cause.

But if it was bad for them, now must be the worst time of all for the enemy. Knowing that they had it all won, yet equally knowing that they might still be killed, blown out of the water, for no good reason. A war never really ended until the signatures were all neatly affixed, and even then, when it was all settled, there was often a period of one or two days during which the fighting would continue. Right up until the final moment fixed by the treaty, when the shelling would stop, and the vanquished would lay down their arms.

And if dying for a lost cause was a waste, how much more so would it be to die for one you'd already won?

•   •   •

The three powerful Tribal Class destroyers of Killer Group 65 smashed their way through the waters of the Western Approaches in line abreast, the beams of their Asdic searching the depths for any sign of the enemy reported in the area, while overhead a flight of old Swordfish torpedo bombers, their racks crammed with depth charges, kept watch.

In *Apache*, Ralston was taking the whole thing as almost a personal insult. Like Admiral Taunton, he was nearly certain that it had been Kruger behind the almost successful attack on *Queen Elizabeth*. And he knew enough about the capabilities of Kruger's submarine and torpedoes to realise that it was no more than sheer good luck that had saved the great liner. Luck which could as easily have placed *U-2317 ahead* of the Cunarder, where a full spread of torpedoes fired from point-blank range would have blasted her to pieces, sending the 11,000 fresh American troops she was carrying directly to the bottom.

But if Kruger's boat was about, then he was determined to find and destroy him. He bore no particular malice toward Kruger. It was the *boat* that had to be killed, not her captain. Kruger himself seemed a likeable enough chap; not anyone he'd really wish to kill.

He had, after all, saved Ralston from almost certain death in the Skagerrak. Something he hadn't had to do.

That, Ralston thought, was the real trouble with this job. It was never wise to know too much about your enemy as a person. As a fellow human being. It was far better to think of him as a faceless automaton on the other side of a gun sight, and not as a man you'd met and spoken with, or even for whom you may have found a grudging respect.

It was always so much easier to kill someone you'd never met.

•   •   •

"In range in two minutes, sir," Reuter announced.

Kruger rose from his seat near the forward bulkhead and walked over to the plot table. "Go to silent motor," he ordered. "Revolutions for five knots."

At once, the high-pitched whine of the turbine was replaced by the eerie silence of the belt driven screw. There was only the soft whisper of the sea as it parted around the streamlined hull, and the gentle drip of condensation in the bilges.

"Five knots, sir," the Chief reported.

Kruger bent over the S-gear operator. "Range to target?"

"Closest target is zero-six-five, sir."

Kruger nodded. "Give me a single ping every 120 seconds, von Sänger. But be prepared to shut down active ranging and go to hydrophones if the enemy give any indication of having noticed us."

"Aye, aye, sir."

Von Sänger keyed the oscillator, looking at the screen and starting his stopwatch. A single ping every two minutes was sufficient to maintain a fair idea of surface activity. Even the fastest ship was limited to a maximum speed of about 37 knots, meaning that it could travel no more than 2/3 of a mile in that time. The position of each lighted dot changed with each pulse, reflecting any movement since the last. To a skilled operator, watching the screen was nearly as good as riding around at 10,000 feet in a reconnaissance bomber, watching the enemy ships manoeuvring below. Each new pulse gave the exact position of every enemy vessel, while his own remained always at the exact centre of the screen. By watching the returns, interpolating positions, he could build up an accurate picture of what was happening on the surface.

With the *Nibelung* there was no real need to surface, or even to go up to periscope depth. *U-2317* would be able to take advantage of her advanced design and make her attack from a safe depth, where she would hold all the advantages.

She could, but Kruger had no intention of doing so this time.

"Come onto course three-five-two," he ordered. "Bring her up to periscope depth."

"Course is three-five-two, sir," Stauber reported.

"Bow and stern planes, up 10 degrees," Döring ordered. "Zero angle."

Slowly, on an even keel, the boat began to climb up from her great depth.

"Crew to action stations."

While the men scrambled to their stations, Kruger walked over to Himmler, who was standing by his computer.

"What's your load pattern?" Kruger asked.

"The last active homer in tube four, and the six LUTs in the midships tubes, sir."

Kruger nodded. "I wish we had spares," he commented.

"I quite agree, sir."

"Fourteen metres, sir," Döring said.

The periscope hissed up from its well, Kruger stopping it just as the lens cleared the sea, swinging it around a full circle before focusing on the target.

"A pair of heavy cruisers," he said. "The escorts are new frigates."

"Just what we ordered, eh, sir?"

"Exactly." He lowered the periscope. "I want to get in closer. Make damned sure of a hit."

Himmler nodded. "Could be risky, sir. Especially this late in things."

"We'll chance it, Karl. If worse comes to worse we can always go deep and run away at high speed. And those frigates are traveling at nearly 20 knots, so they'll be making so much noise that the effectiveness of their Asdic should be severely limited."

Kruger turned to Döring. "Fifty metres again, L.I.. We are going to try to slip under the escorts. Target is a pair of lovely new heavy cruisers."

"Aye, aye, sir. Diving now."

"What will you do after the war, sir?" Himmler asked.

Kruger thought a moment. "Get married, probably," he said. "And most likely we'll all spend a bit of time in a British prison camp, too."

"Do you think they'll do that, sir? Put everyone in camps, I mean?"

"I wouldn't be at all surprised. They'll want to sort everyone out, separate the confirmed Nazis from the rest of us." He smiled. "I'm not sure *what* sort of treatment they'll have in store for me."

"You've done nothing wrong, sir, surely?"

"No. But I've never been exactly scrupulous in following the Prize Rules, either. I expect the British will consider that a serious offense."

Himmler laughed. "If they do, they'll have to condemn most of their own submarine commanders as well."

"I agree, Karl. But you have to remember that, in war, the rules apply only to the losers! The winners may do whatever they please."

"It hardly seems fair, sir," Himmler commented.

"In war is anything fair? Now, what about you? What plans do you have for after the war?"

"Go home to Munich, I suppose. With any luck I can get my Olga pregnant during the first week." He frowned. "It's been almost a year since the last time I saw her, and with the mail the way it is, it's difficult to maintain proper contact."

Wiegand, who was standing by von Sänger, looked up. "We're passing under the escorts now, sir," he said.

"Once we're past them, come back to periscope depth and reduce to dead slow, Number One."

"Aye, aye, sir."

"Not long now, sir," Himmler said.

"No. Not long."

Keep control of your nerve, the manual said. But it never said exactly how you were supposed to accomplish that trick. Just now, Kruger thought, he would prefer to be almost anywhere else. Once, long ago, this sort of thing had been almost exhilarating. But that was when he was much younger, and death was still something that could only happen to your victims.

In the boat there was silence, but for the slight hiss of compressed air as the Chief made some minor corrections to the trim.

He kept listening for the first tell-tale 'ping' of Asdic striking the hull. Now was the most vulnerable time, slipping right under the escorts, perhaps blundering into their Asdic beams. Careful engineering had insured that no enemy hydrophone operator would pick them up, but Asdic, which did not rely on the sound made by the target itself, was quite another matter.

Across the control room he could hear Wiegand's soft voice as he passed an order, the sharper sound of Döring, instructing the planesman and helmsman as they started to bring the boat up again. So it would be starting soon.

"Fourteen metres, sir."

Kruger signaled to the rating on the periscope control, pressing his eye to the ocular as the tube rose from its well, stopping it with the lens still awash. From the tiny amount of spray he concluded that they were making no more than a knot or two. Bare steerage way, but safer now, as it was less likely to give them away.

Quickly, he walked the periscope around. One of the escorting frigates was no more than 100 metres astern, steaming on, oblivious to the threat that had just passed beneath her keel.

"Frigate directly astern," he commented. "He'll have to be target number three. Number One, bring the boat around onto a reciprocal course. We'll engage the primary targets with the midships tubes."

Kruger swung the periscope back onto the nearest cruiser, reducing the magnification to minimum. Even so, she nearly filled the lens. A heavy cruiser, one of the most modern designs, with 12 powerful eight-inch guns carried in four triple turrets.

"We get a bonus with this one," Kruger said. "She's flying a vice-admiral's flag."

He dropped the periscope beneath the surface. Even exposing a few bare centimetres was dangerous this close to the enemy.

"Flood all tubes," he ordered. "We will engage with the starboard tubes first, then shift targets and use the port tubes on the second cruiser."

Himmler moved the appropriate switches, and one by one the lights came on across the panel.

"Tubes are flooded, sir."

"Open outer doors."

"Outer doors open, sir."

Up came the periscope again, the head slightly awash. Just enough to set up the shot. Not enough to send up a tell-tale plume of spray for some sharp eyed lookout on one of the escorts, or aboard the cruiser herself, to spot and bring all hell down on them.

"Bearing—that!" Kruger snapped.

"Bearing is one-eight-three," Himmler said, working it into the computer.

"Angle on the bow—Green nine-zero."

"Angle green nine-zero."

"Estimated speed, 20 knots. Range 600 metres. Set depth at 3.5 metres."

"Torpedoes are ready, sir."

"Eight—loose!"

"Eight running, sir."

"Nine—loose!"

"Nine running, sir."

"Ten—loose!"

"Ten running, sir."

"Shifting target. Bearing—that!"

"One-seven-five, sir."

"Angle on the bow—green nine-zero."

"Angle green nine-zero."

"Estimated speed, 20 knots. Range 900 metres. Set depth at 3.5 metres."

"Torpedoes are ready, sir."

Now or never, Kruger thought. Get these three on the way before the others wake everyone up and all hell breaks loose up there.

"Five—loose!"

In rapid succession, the three remaining LUTs were sent on their way while Kruger, ignoring everything but the safety of his boat, swung the periscope around to check the escorts. Even the most incompetent hydrophone operator must have heard the sound of the firing ram as the torpedoes were thrust from their tubes, and the scream of their tiny, counter-rotating screws as they sped on their way.

But the nearest frigate was still steaming on her set course, as if unconcerned with anything but reaching her destination. Was the end so near that they were growing complacent? Kruger wondered.

He swung the periscope back onto the first target just in time to see a dirty brown column of water soaring up her armoured flank as the first 'eel' struck home. Moments later another struck, just forward of the first, and Kruger was shocked to see the great ship's bow suddenly sag, folding back against itself, so that the stem was completely submerged, and the force of her onward rush sent green water sluicing up across her crumpled fo'c'sle. The third torpedo detonated a half-second later, on her starboard quarter, while the armoured giant began to slow, already showing a severe list.

Kruger rotated the periscope toward the bow and the nearest frigate swam into focus. Now she was turning. It was time to go.

"Down periscope. One hundred metres, come to new course zero-eight-two. Turbine, ahead full."

The sudden whine of the turbine mingled with the triple detonation as the second trio of LUTs smashed into the other cruiser. Behind them, a pattern of depth charges tore apart the sea, while *U-2317* slipped deeper into the safety of the depths, her turbine roaring defiance as she raced away.

Chapter Ten

Final Encounter

"I think we should just get out of here and go to Argentina," Wiegand commented. "The war can't last more than a few days, and there's no sense just waiting around for the end."

Kruger laughed. "And deny yourself the chance to die an heroic death in battle, fighting to the last breath? Now why would you want to do a thing like that?"

"Sounds like something Ostler would say, sir."

Kruger chuckled. "It does, doesn't it? At least, like what he *used* to say."

Wiegand nodded. He had noticed the change as well. Since the *Führer* had killed himself, Ostler had undergone a complete change in character. His fervent Nazism had been replaced by a rather curious altruism. With his hero dead, Ostler had suddenly become human. He had also expressed a curious regret over Gerhard Ostler's death, which made very little sense, as he was obviously still alive and showing no signs of suicidal behaviour. Time would tell, Wiegand supposed.

U-2317 was cruising slowly up the English Channel, her diesel roaring, sucking in the cool night air through her *Schnorchel*. Kruger was half reclining on his bunk, studying a small, framed photograph, which Ingrid had presented to him the evening before they sailed from Bergen. It had been taken three years earlier, when she was 17, and showed a slim, blond girl seated on a blanket by an alpine lake. She was wearing a dark coloured bathing costume that seemed to be moulded to her body, emphasising her youthful curves.

She was smiling then. Something she did less frequently now.

"I have no objection to fighting for a worthwhile cause," Wiegand continued. "But just what are we fighting for now? Really? The *Führer* is dead, and the Allies are still insisting on unconditional surrender, which we will have to concede them before much longer. So why continue to take the risks?"

Kruger placed the photograph on the narrow shelf above his bunk, shaking his head. "You heard the *Grossadmiral*'s speech, didn't you, Number One? The war *is* lost. We all know that. But there are also millions of refugees in the East who must be given a chance to escape before the Russians can get their hands on them. *That* is why we're continuing the fight. To give them that chance."

Wiegand shrugged. "Let someone else fight. If we go to Argentina we can probably sell the boat to their so-called president and live like kings on the proceeds. Then, in a couple of years, when things have quieted down, we go back home again."

"I take it you have no one waiting for you, Rolf?"

"Not any more. I *had* a girl, but she married a bloody policeman last month. So there's nothing left for me to return to."

"And what of the rest of the crew? Are all of *them* without friends or family? No, Number One, we will continue as before, and if we encounter the enemy we will attack and destroy him." He grinned. "In any case, we have only one torpedo left. Once that has been expended we'll have to return to base."

"I suppose so, sir. It's just that it all seems rather pointless now."

"Our being here ties up the enemy. That's our only reason for even existing just now. If they're busy hunting us, they can't be raising hell closer to home."

"Contact, sir!" von Sänger shouted.

Kruger was off the bunk in an instant and into the control room. "What do you have?"

"Three vessels, sir. Very fast, bearing Green two-five. Range is two-four-six and closing."

"Good work, lad. That gives us time to think what to do."

Wiegand frowned. "We *could* just get out of their way," he offered.

"We could," Kruger agreed, "but we won't. *Attack stations!*"

The IWO sighed. "I was afraid you'd say that, sir."

• • •

"Captain on the bridge!"

Ralston rolled out of his bunk, scrambling through the door of his tiny sea cabin into the pilothouse. The coxswain was on the wheel, looking solid and dependable, as always, while Midshipman Blount was, also as always, having a hard time giving the impression that he had the slightest idea of what was going on around him. In fact, Ralston had noticed, the Mid was quite competent—he simply couldn't manage to look it.

A moment later Ralston was out of the pilothouse and up the ladder to the open bridge. Lieutenant-Commander Phillips, the first lieutenant, moved to greet him.

"Asdic contact, sir," he said. "Bearing Red six-oh, range about two-zero-four."

"Asdic?"

Phillips shrugged. "Well, hydrophones, probably, at that range."

"Sounds more likely," Ralston said. "Even so, the operator must have damned good hearing. Who is he?"

"Petty Officer Betts, sir."

Ralston picked up the handset. "Betts? This is the captain. Is there anything unusual about the contact?"

There was silence on the other end of the line for a moment. Betts was an excellent operator, Ralston thought, but he always liked to think about things before he gave an answer. It was a habit which sometimes slowed things down a bit, but it also meant his answer, when it finally came, was as close to correct as possible, given the highly subjective nature of his speciality.

"I can't hear him any more, sir," Betts finally said. "At first there was faint diesel, as if he was snorkeling, but just now he went completely silent. Also, I'm getting an interesting response on the screen. Nothing I can hear, but I've noticed a slight disturbance twice now, about three minutes apart." A pause. "I think it may be the U-boat's own Asdic, maybe operating on a higher frequency than our units can properly register. Possible, anyway, sir."

"Thank you, Betts. Try to keep track of him by those disturbances until we get within Asdic range. Let me know if the bearing changes." He put down the handset. "Get Pilot up here," he snapped. "I'll want a course to intercept. And sound Action Stations."

Phillips mashed the red button just under the screen, setting the bells to ringing throughout the ship. "Signal the others, Yeo," he snapped. "Submerged U-boat at Red six-zero. Conform to my actions."

Lieutenant Walsh, the navigating officer, came bounding onto the bridge just as the Yeoman was acknowledging *Gurkha*'s response. As soon as Walsh was there, Phillips started down the ladder toward his own action station, deep in the hull in damage control.

During any action, the first lieutenant was to be kept as far from the bridge as practical. It was a standard precaution, lest the bridge take a direct hit. If the captain was killed, he would have to take over command, and he stood a far better chance of being able to do so if he was far enough away to avoid being killed by the same shell.

During an attack on a submerged submarine it was probably pointless, there being no enemy gunfire to avoid, but routine was routine, and there was no sense taking chances. It was not unknown for a damaged U-boat, forced to the surface by depth charges, to get off a round or two from her deck gun before being destroyed.

"New course should be two-eight-two, sir," Walsh said, emerging from beneath the hood over the chart table.

Ralston bent over the voice pipe. "Port fifteen."

"Fifteen of port wheel on, sir."

Slowly the gyro repeater ticked around.

"Midships," Ralston ordered. "Steady. Steer two-eight-two."

"Wheel amidships, sir. Course is two-eight-two."

Ralston leaned against the screen, staring out at the dark waters. Would it be Kruger this time? They had put down so many U-boats in the short time the group had been together, but their real target always managed to elude them. They'd think they were dropping depth charges around his ears, but at the same time he'd really be a thousand miles away, cooperating with the Luftwaffe and a heavy cruiser to destroy a vital arctic convoy.

So what would it be this time? The real thing? Or just another false alarm?

Betts' comments had been encouraging. Ralston knew that Kruger's boat was completely silent at slow speed, and also possessed some sort of advanced detection gear. So there was a chance this would actually be him.

At least they knew a bit more about his boat now. They'd captured several, almost ready for deployment, when they marched into Kiel. To all accounts it had been a bit unnerving. Had the enemy been able to hold back their land advance another six months those boats would have been at sea, along with a whole fleet of advanced diesel-electric boats and dozens of much larger Walter boats, and the whole outcome of the war might have been different.

But they had also captured certain records, and it seemed that *U-2317* was the only Type XXVI boat actually at sea. It was just as well, Ralston thought, for in the last few months she had done more damage than a whole fleet of older boats.

Was it her they were after now? Speed would be the deciding factor, he thought. If the target suddenly took off like a greyhound after a hare they would know that it had to be Kruger.

•　　•　　•

"Target has changed course," von Sänger reported.

"What's he steering?"

"Two-eight-two, sir."

"Pilot?"

Reuter bent over the chart. "Intercepting course, sir. Looks as if he's noticed us."

Kruger bent over von Sänger. "What's the range?"

"One-zero-six, sir."

Kruger walked to the night periscope. "Come up to periscope depth again, L.I.. Torpedo officer to the control room."

Döring hovered over the control station, his eye on the water column in the Papenberg. "Bow planes, up two degrees," he said.

Himmler appeared through the forward hatch, while Kruger waited patiently by the periscope. With the darkness outside he would use the thick-shafted night periscope.

"Fourteen metres, sir."

"Up periscope."

Kruger stooped to meet the 'scope as it rose from its well, his eye pressed to the ocular as the thick head broke the surface. The slender attack periscope made a smaller wake, but the difference was less important in the dark, and the big night 'scope had decidedly superior light gather capabilities.

He twisted the handgrip, bringing the periscope to full magnification. He could just make them out. Destroyers, powerful and modern. There were three of them, steaming in line abreast.

Making beautiful targets.

"Down periscope."

The few seconds had told him all that he needed to know.

"Flood tube one. Stand by to engage."

•   •   •

Walsh spoke briefly into the handset, then replaced it in its holder beneath the screen. "That was radar, sir," he said. "They've reported a contact, same range and bearing as our Asdic contact. Just a few seconds, they said. The operator thought it might be a periscope."

"Probably was," Ralston said. "Sizing us up. I expect they'll turn and run for it now. No U-boat is going to want to hang about and tangle with a killer group. Not this close to the end."

"How much longer do you suppose we have, sir?" Walsh asked.

Ralston shrugged. "Who can say? Hitler killed himself on the thirtieth. That was five days ago. It looks as if Dönitz is just fighting a delaying action now, trying to get as many of his people as possible away from Ivan before the war ends."

Walsh grinned, his teeth very white in the darkness. "Can't say I blame him, sir. I wouldn't trust the average Ruskie around a 90-year-old grandmother. Probably rape her, then make off with her bridgework so as to get a bit of profit from it!"

Ralston merely shook his head. "Those *are* our allies you're talking about, Pilot."

"They won't be when this lot's over. Let's not forget that while Jerry was swallowing up half of Poland, old Uncle Joe was right in there gobbling up the rest of it. I fully expect they'll revert to type, now we've pulled their balls out of the fire."

The telephone buzzed and Walsh snapped it up. "Bridge."

"Well, Pilot?" Ralston asked, as the navigating officer replaced the handset.

"Radar again, sir. Same brief contact. Bearing remains constant, range now zero-nine-four."

"So he's not running," Ralston mused. "This could be Kruger, Pilot. With his speed he can safely wait until the last minute to clear out, and it wouldn't surprise me a bit if he intended to make a fight of it."

"I expect we can handle him, sir."

"That's probably what *Surrey* and *Yorkshire* believed. And now one of them is sunk with most of her crew, with the other so damaged that she'll likely be scrapped."

"We're not absolutely sure if that was Kruger, are we, sir?" Walsh asked.

"*I* am." Ralston turned to the Yeoman of signals. "Yeo, alert the others to be ready to take evasive action if necessary."

He picked up the telephone. "Guns—Captain here. Radar has picked up a contact dead ahead, range zero-nine-four. Load your forward guns with semi-armour-piercing and be ready to fire the moment we get a new range."

•   •   •

"Up periscope."

The target bearing remained constant, Kruger noticed, smiling. Suddenly flame blossomed from the deck of the centre ship.

"Down periscope!" he shouted. "Take her down to 50 metres. Emergency!"

Someone was bloody well awake on that leading destroyer, he thought. The lens had barely come clear of the water when they opened fire, so either they had a damned good lookout, or their radar was even better than everyone had already come to believe.

Either way, it would be safer to continue the attack from depth.

"Fifty metres, sir."

Around them, the sea shook to the detonation of the enemy's 4.7-inch shells. But the danger was minimal. The shells were exploding at a depth of no more than about 15 metres, detonated by their impact with the sea, which at a speed of over 800 miles per hour would be like ploughing into solid concrete.

At 50 metres, *U-2317* was in no danger unless the enemy should decide to switch to full armour-piercing, which might just manage to reach their depth before exploding. Even then, it would require a direct hit to do much damage.

Ping!

"He's found us now," Wiegand commented.

"Well, he's still too far away to do much about it," Kruger laughed, walking over to the sound cubicle. "Range to target?"

"Zero-two-seven, sir."

"Bearing?"

"Zero-zero-eight, sir."

"Target bearing is zero-zero-eight," Kruger repeated. "Range zero-two-seven."

"Bearing zero-zero-eight, aye. Range zero-two-seven."

"Angle on the bow?"

"Angle is zero, sir," von Sänger reported.

"Angle on the bow is zero."

"Angle zero, aye."

"Set depth at three metres, homing to activate after 1500 metres."

"Depth is set at three metres, sir. Homing activation at 1500 metres. Torpedoes are ready, sir."

"One—loose!"

"One is running, sir."

● ● ●

"Sir! Asdic reports a torpedo in the water!"

"Bloody hell! Yeo—battle lights! Signal the group to reverse course! All ahead, emergency!"

The three destroyers swung around in tight turns, their rakish hulls leaning dangerously, while down in the engine rooms the engineers spun their wheels, ignoring the safety markings in the quest for more speed.

"Thirty-seven knots, sir," Walsh reported, a minute later. He looked concerned. "But aren't you just giving him a better target, sir? I mean, I presume from the way we're running that you believe they've fired acoustic torpedoes?"

Ralston shook his head. "Not long ago we could simply have shut down the engines and their fish would have gone off in search of something noisier—such as the submarine that fired them. But not with what they're using now. Nor will foxers work. The only chance is to outrun them."

"Can we?"

"If we've got enough of a head start, I believe so."

Walsh was on the telephone again. "Asdic says they've lost the torpedoes in our wake, sir. But Petty Officer Betts reports that just before we turned, the U-boat changed course and made off toward the south at high speed, screaming like a banshee."

"How fast?"

"He estimates in excess of 20 knots."

Ralston's knuckles were white as he gripped the screen. "Kruger!" he shouted. "The bastard's going to do it to me again!"

•   •   •

Himmler was studying his stopwatch. "It's too long," he said. "Our 'eel' will be running down soon."

Kruger shrugged. "Von Sänger reported that the enemy turned and ran away at approximately 38 knots, on the same mean course as our torpedo. Provided they don't suffer any breakdowns they should be able to get away." He grinned. "But running away will take them miles from our position, and they won't dare stop until they're certain the batteries have run down. So if we don't kill them today, at least we can be fairly sure that they won't kill us, either."

Wiegand looked up from the engineer's panel, where he had been peering over Döring's shoulder. "*Now* can we go to Argentina?" he asked.

Kruger smiled and shook his head. "No, but as we all of our tubes are now empty, we can go back to Bergen, eh?"

The Exec shrugged. "You're the captain."

•   •   •

The torpedo exploded in their wake, about 50 yards astern. Ralston, pacing the bridge, ran out onto the port wing in time to see the thrown up water subsiding into their creaming wake.

Too bloody close, he thought. And there are probably others still running.

The Chief Wireless Operator hurried up to him, a decoded signal in his hand. "Signal from headquarters, sir," he said. "The enemy command have instructed all U-boats at sea to cease fire immediately. The war's over, sir."

Ralston gestured aft. "I don't think he's received the message yet."

Epilogue

Five days later, *U-2317* lifted her slime-covered hull from the sea and started her diesel. Directly she had surfaced, a young signals rating climbed to the top of the cockpit and bound a large, black flag to the periscope, which was then extended to the limit.

It was 10th May, 1945, and Kruger had surfaced his command five miles south of the entrance to Portsmouth Harbour. Now, standing in the open cockpit in his best uniform, his decorations gleaming at breast and throat, he stared across the screen at the English port, wondering what would come next.

"Do you think we can trust them, sir?" Wiegand asked, looking up at the black surrender flag, which was supposed to guarantee their safety.

Kruger shrugged. "It's been a long war, Rolf. And they've certainly no reason to love us. But we'll have to take what comes, eh?"

"I suppose so, sir." He grinned. "But I still think we should have gone to Argentina."

"Too late for that now. Look!" Kruger gestured across the screen, where a sturdy looking Asdic trawler was steaming toward them, her crew standing watchfully by the 12-pounder gun on the fo'c'sle.

For a moment Kruger had a mad impulse to blow them out of the water. But there were no torpedoes remaining, and in a moment the impulse had passed.

Then a lamp began flashing on the trawler's bridge.

"Can't understand it, sir," the signalman said.

"I can," Kruger replied. "It's in English. *Heave to. Stand by to receive boarding party.*"

"What do we do, sir?" Wiegand asked.

"Exactly what he says, Number One." He bent over the voice pipe. "All stop."

The diesel settled down to a low rumble, while aft the great screw spun down to a halt.

A few minutes later the trawler lowered a boat, and a young lieutenant was ferried across, together with a petty officer and four ratings.

Kruger looked down from the cockpit. "Welcome aboard," he said. He meant it. With the boarding party on deck, the trawler was less likely to misinterpret some innocent action and open fire.

The young officer saluted, looking up at Kruger with a hopeful expression. "You speak English, do you, sir?"

"Yes. Come on up. The ladder's on the side of the tower."

The lieutenant climbed up the side of the tower and into the cockpit. "Thank God," he muttered. "I don't know why they sent me across. Honestly, I have no idea. Not a word of German, you see?"

Kruger shrugged. "Some navies are better educated than others, I suppose." He glanced at the wavy stripes circling the Englishman's sleeves. "Then again, perhaps your real profession didn't require foreign languages."

"It did, as a matter of fact. But French, not German. I was an importer's clerk, and nearly all of our business was with the French. Of course, I think the last time a British officer had to accept the surrender of a *French* vessel was about 1815."

Kruger grinned. "Well, if you speak French, you should get along quite nicely with my Number One. *He* also speaks

French." He nodded at Wiegand, who was watching in bewildered fascination. The IWO's command of English was almost totally literary. He could read well enough, but conversation was still beyond him.

Kruger turned back to the Englishman. "Now, Lieutenant, what would you have us do?"

"Well, uhm, I have to signal the trawler first, then you just follow her in."

"Signal lamp," Kruger said, in German. "You know how to use this, I presume?"

The Englishman took the lamp. "Yes, sir." Even in English, Kruger's question seemed to demand a formal response. And he *was* a superior officer, after all.

Pointing the lamp at the trawler, the Englishman triggered off a four-letter signal. When the trawler replied he added a one-letter acknowledgement, then handed the lamp back to the signalman.

"Just follow him in. Also, we'll want anyone not required for running your boat to be up on deck as we enter harbour. My men will be below, keeping an eye on anyone still down there, so you may as well advise them."

Kruger nodded and bent over a voice pipe, speaking rapidly in German. As he straightened, the main hatch was opened, and the crew climbed into the sunlight.

"Who's left below?" the Englishman asked.

"The Coxswain, the engineering officer, and one mechanic. Also a technician."

"And the rest of these? This is your entire crew?"

"Our normal complement is 27."

The Englishman shook his head. "I thought most U-boats carried about 60 men?"

"Older boats, yes. Not this type."

The Englishman nodded, looking around the tiny cock-pit. "You know, I've never seen a boat quite like this one. What mark is she?"

"*Typ* XXVI. And, so far as I know, there *are* no others like her. Not on active service, at any rate."

"Odd looking hull. What sort of speed can you manage?"

"About 19 knots on the surface." Kruger smiled. "That is, if you don't mind being a bit uncomfortable. She's not a very good sea boat, I'm afraid."

"What about submerged? Ten or so?"

"A bit faster than that. On batteries, perhaps 11 knots. But we also have a special sort of turbine that generates its own oxygen, and with that we've achieved a top sustained speed of 27 knots. That was at 400 metres," he added. "You go faster as you go deeper. I'm not really sure why."

"Four hundred metres, did you say?"

"Yes, and I'll save you the trouble. That's 1,312 feet."

The lieutenant looked at him curiously. "Your name wouldn't happen to be Kruger, would it?"

"Yes. *Fregattenkapitän* Hans Kruger, at your service."

"Well, then my Old Man will definitely want to see you again."

"Again? Who is he," Kruger asked, "this 'Old Man' of yours?"

"He's—well, first, I'm Geoffrey Walsh, and I don't actually belong to that clapped out trawler we're following into the harbour. I'm navigating officer in *Apache*. You'll see her, once we're in harbour. A big Tribal class destroyer. Anyway, David Ralston is my captain."

Kruger laughed. "Ah, yes. He was a—well, a guest, I suppose you could say. I'd heard that he'd escaped."

Walsh nodded. "Yes, he got away. Actually, I think you've seen my ship already. Through your periscope, on the evening of the fifth."

"You also got away, then?" Kruger asked. As if I didn't know already, he thought.

"Barely. Your last torpedo nearly took our stern off. As it is, we're going into dock tomorrow for a new port shaft. The blast *bent* the old one."

"We really hadn't heard about the cease fire, you understand?"

Walsh nodded slowly. "We assumed that. *We* found out about it while we were trying to outrun your torpedo." He grinned. "As it happened, we had every intention of going back and blowing you out of the water, cease fire or no, but by then we couldn't find you."

Kruger bent over the screen. "*Achtung!*" He bellowed.

Slowly, the crew swaying in a double line on the forecasing, *U-2317* followed the Asdic trawler into the harbour. In the distance, Kruger could make out the towering masts of Nelson's old flagship, *Victory*, somehow undamaged amidst the destruction that surrounded her.

Smiling, he bent over the voice pipe. "Ostermann," he said. "*Nun!*"

Softly at first, and then building in volume, the sound of music emerged from the hatches and bridge speaker. In the cockpit Kruger and Wiegand came to attention and saluted, while down on the casing the crew did the same.

Walsh merely stared, paralysed, wondering just how horrible it was going to look on his next fitness report to have boarded a surrendered U-boat, then brought her into Portsmouth Harbour with her Tannoy blaring out *Deutschland über Alles*.

About the Author

J.T. McDaniel is a former newspaper editor and radio personality. A native of Bedford, Ohio, he served in Viet Nam with the 101st Airborne Division and the 1st Aviation Brigade. Long interested in naval history in general, and submarines in particular, in addition to writing *With Honour in Battle* and the forthcoming *Bacalao*, he is also the creator and webmaster of www.fleetsubmarine.com. Not presently married, this book is dedicated to his children.

Printed in the United Kingdom
by Lightning Source UK Ltd.
109010UKS00001B/105

9 780971 220737